TOO MANY CLIENTS

Previous Titles by David J. Walker
in the Wild Onion, Ltd mystery series

A TICKET TO DIE FOR
A BEER AT BAWDY HOUSE
THE END OF EMERALD WOODS
ALL THE DEAD FATHERS

TOO MANY CLIENTS

A Wild Onion, Ltd Mystery

David J. Walker

This first world edition published 2010
in Great Britain and in the USA by
SEVERN HOUSE PUBLISHERS LTD of
9–15 High Street, Sutton, Surrey, England, SM1 1DF.

British Library Cataloguing in Publication Data

Walker, David J., 1939-
Too many clients.
1. Kirsten (Fictitious character: Walker)–Fiction.
2. Dugan (Fictitious character)–Fiction. 3. Wild Onion, Ltd. (Imaginary organization)–Fiction. 4. Private investigators–Illinois–Chicago–Fiction. 5. Police murders–Fiction. 6. Detective and mystery stories.
I. Title
813.5'4-dc22

ISBN-13: 978-0-7278-6930-2 (cased)

All Severn House titles are printed on acid-free paper.

Severn House Publishers support The Forest Stewardship Council [FSC], the leading international forest certification organisation. All our titles that are printed on Greenpeace-approved FSC-certified paper carry the FSC logo.

Typeset by Palimpsest Book Production Ltd.,
Falkirk, Stirlingshire, Scotland.
Printed and bound in Great Britain by
MPG Books Ltd., Bodmin, Cornwall.

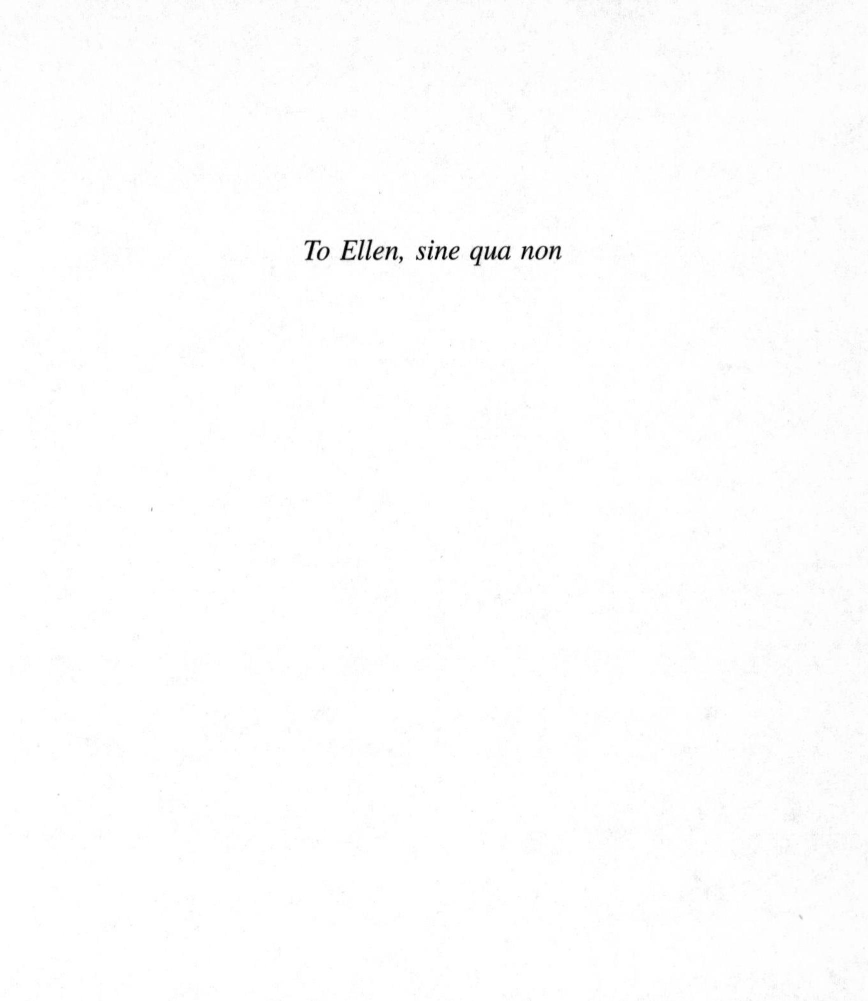

To Ellen, sine qua non

ACKNOWLEDGMENTS

This is a work of fiction. The organizations and characters are imaginary or are used fictitiously, and are not intended to represent actual organizations or persons. I *am* grateful to them, though, for showing up.

I am also grateful to very many actual persons, including: Danielle Egan-Miller, my agent, and her assistants Lauren Olson and Joanna MacKenzie, for their unflagging zeal and support; the people at Severn House, especially Amanda Stewart and James Nightingale, for believing in Kirsten and Dugan and what they had to say; Pat Reardon and Bill Rodeghier, lawyers who helped me sort out legal issues (all of them fictional, thank God) and never once chided me for not knowing these things myself; Jerry Metzger of Westrec Marinas, for his quick and generous help with some harbor-related questions; and all the Red Herrings, especially Libby Fischer Hellmann and Michael Allen Dymmoch, for their keen ears and insightful comments.

CHI-CA-GO (shi-kaw-go) n., a city in northeast Illinois, on the shore of Lake Michigan; the name is believed to be derived from the Native American *chicah goo*, literally 'stink root' or, perhaps more elegantly, 'wild onion'.

ONE

The soft rain had stopped now, and the man switched off the wipers. He lowered his window and ran his hand over his head. He was bald, and his scalp felt damp and warm. Everything felt damp and warm. He'd had a couple more drinks than he'd planned to, and was feeling it, so he drove with extra care. He didn't need a traffic stop, he thought, not tonight of all nights. And not with someone like Lauren in the car.

It wasn't like they were doing anything illegal. He'd met Lauren in an upscale bar, a favorite of his, out near O'Hare, a little before closing time. Half-Asian, he thought, with high cheekbones, brown eyes, and honey-colored skin. She had straight black hair, cut in bangs across her forehead and falling to her shoulders. She could have been a high-class hooker, of course. She had that look. But she didn't seem aggressive enough for that, and there'd been no talk of money. She wore a navy blue pants suit, expensive, with the jacket open over a shiny, silk-looking blouse. The blouse was white, and unbuttoned far enough to show just a bit of cleavage.

The bar stools were comfortable – with padded backs to lean against – and he bought her a drink and they got to talking. She said she lived near Wrigley Field and was a sales rep for a pharmaceutical firm. She'd spent all day yesterday and today, Saturday and Sunday, at a sales meeting at the O'Hare Hilton. Then they were all expected to have drinks and dinner together. 'It was awful,' she said, 'and when it was finally over everyone else . . . they're all from out of town . . . escaped to their hotel rooms. I started home in a cab, but after a few blocks I decided to stop and treat myself to a nightcap.'

'All by yourself?' he'd asked.

'I'm by myself a lot,' she said.

'That's hard to believe.' He smiled. 'I'd have thought you had lots of friends. Guys, anyway.'

'Yes . . . well . . .' She dipped the plastic stirrer in and out of her scotch and water. 'Guys . . . especially my age, you know . . . they're so . . . I don't know . . .' She picked up her glass and took a sip. 'It's not that I don't like a good time. Don't get me wrong. But I'm not . . . I'm not like most girls. I . . . well . . .' She shrugged. 'Anyway, I feel more comfortable with older men . . . like your age. Maybe it's a *father* thing, or—' She stopped and lowered her eyes. 'No offense.' She laid one hand on top of his on the bar; and with the other, finished her drink.

'None taken.' He ordered another round and stood up and took off his jacket and hung it on the back of his bar stool. He moved the stool a little closer to hers, and when he sat down again he could smell her perfume . . . mingled with her own personal scent.

There was an awkward moment of silence, but she smiled at him, looking a little embarrassed. When the bartender returned and set the drinks down she reached for hers, and as she did she leaned her breast against his upper arm. It was clearly deliberate and he felt the hardness of her nipple, and that stirred a hint of hardness in him. He kept his arm against the tip of her breast and moved it in a gentle rubbing motion. She had nothing on under the blouse.

She finally pulled away and sighed. 'Nice,' she said, and sipped at her scotch.

'Very.' He kissed her lightly on the cheek. 'Unfortunately,' he said, bringing himself back to reality, 'I have to be go—'

She put a finger to his lips to stop him, and leaned in close to his ear. 'I meant it,' she whispered, 'when I said I'm not like other girls.' She giggled a little . . . and then took his hand and gently drew it down to her lap.

The bald man considered himself a practical person, and he knew that tonight of all nights he should get some sleep. He had an important meeting of his own in the morning. But this . . . this Lauren person . . . had surprised him, to say the least. And had very much excited him – which wasn't so easy these days.

Now they were only a couple of blocks from the bald man's place.

He lived alone in the house he'd bought after his divorce. Just blocks from his ex, which had pissed her off, the bitch. It was an area of tree-lined streets and single-family homes on the far north-west side, near the forest preserve. Lots of cops and firemen and other city employees. Sunrise was a long way off and the streets were deserted, but around here the streets and alleys were always clean and well-lit. His own place was smaller than most, and overloaded with loans. He needed cash, but he had to be patient. There was money on the way, and as soon as it came in he planned to sell and pay off the loans – all but one, anyway – and get himself a condo near downtown.

There hadn't been much talk in the car, but finally Lauren said, 'It's warm for October, isn't it?' Her speech was a little slurred. 'Or is it the scosh that's making me so hot?'

He grinned. 'It's not the scotch, honey. It's—' He stopped when he glanced over and saw her fumbling with the buttons on her blouse. When she had it open all the way down she flapped the two sides in and out, fanning her bare breasts.

'Jesus,' he said. By then they were already in the alley that ran behind his house. He'd torn down his small, ancient garage and had a wide concrete slab put in and always parked in the middle. Lots of space on both sides. Safer that way. Now he pulled in and turned off the lights. 'Home sweet home,' he said. 'Let's go.'

But Lauren was leaning back in the seat, head against the headrest. She was holding her jacket and blouse wide open and thrusting her upper body forward. 'Toush me again,' she said, the slur more pronounced. 'Hurry.'

'Not here, dammit. Wait till we're inside.'

'I can't wait.' She reached down between her legs. 'Don't you wanna shee what I got?'

'I already felt what you got, back at the bar.' *Same as I got*, he thought, *only smaller.* He'd run across a few she-males on the job over the years, when he was working the street, but never up close and personal. He released his seat belt. 'We'll both see a whole lot better when we get inside.'

'Toush me.' She grabbed his arm and pulled, and he gave in and leaned toward her. Then he heard something . . . or *thought* he did . . . and froze. She giggled, pulled on him again.

'Dammit, let *go*!' He yanked his arm free, twisted around in his seat. Too late. He should've been paying more attention and now there was someone there, already close beside his open window. 'Jesus,' he said, 'what *is* this?'

Lauren must have seen, too. He heard her muffled cry, heard

her open her door and scramble out of the car. But he didn't turn, couldn't take his eyes off the pistol pointed straight at his face. *A Glock*, he thought, *like the one right under my seat.* As though that mattered. The revolver he carried high up under his arm didn't matter, either.

The sound of the shot made him jump.

He may have heard a second shot, and a third. Or they may have been echoes in his exploding brain.

TWO

'May I help you, sir?' The receptionist was silver-haired and motherly. She didn't look at all like a predator, out to rob people of their livelihoods. But Dugan knew better. That was the point, after all, of this whole office. These people got paid to take away lawyers' licenses. Lawyers like him.

He handed his business card across the chest-high barrier between him and the predator-in-disguise. 'I'm here for the deposition of John O'Hern at nine thirty.' He looked at his watch. 'I'm a few minutes early.'

The woman stared at his card, then looked up with doubt in her eyes. 'Are you here as . . . as additional counsel for Mr O'Hern?'

'Nope. I'm here to attend his dep.'

'I don't know if—' She shook her head. 'The court reporter and Mr O'Hern's attorney are already waiting in the conference room,' she said, 'and counsel for the Administrator – that's Gina Chan – will join them when Mr O'Hern arrives. But Ms Chan didn't tell me you were coming.'

'Ms Chan didn't know.' He smiled, trying to look at ease and friendly, when he felt just the opposite. 'You could let her know I'm here, though.'

'Oh . . . well, yes . . . of course.' She picked up the phone, hesitated, then said, 'You may have a seat, sir.'

Dugan turned and walked across the smooth gray carpet and sat down. The room, with its high, white ceiling and gray walls, was bright with fluorescent lighting. He'd entered by one of a pair of glass doors, set in a floor-to-ceiling glass wall. It was the only office on this floor of One Prudential Plaza, a high-rise on Randolph Street, just east of Michigan Avenue in downtown Chicago, and the words painted on the glass announced:

ILLINOIS ATTORNEY REGISTRATION
AND
DISCIPLINARY COMMISSION

Dugan read them as:

ABANDON HOPE, ALL YE WHO ENTER HERE

He sat in one of a dozen identical chairs, upholstered in the same shade of maroon and arranged in sets of two along the side walls, presumably so lawyers in trouble could confer with counsel as they waited for the axe to fall. All the other chairs were empty. It was a quiet Monday morning at the ARDC.

The receptionist put down the phone. 'Ms Chan will be with you shortly,' she said, then immediately picked up the phone again to answer an incoming call. Dugan tuned her out and sat staring through the glass wall toward the elevators. Johnny O'Hern would be coming up soon on one of them. Johnny wasn't a lawyer. He was a cop, and Dugan wondered if he'd be in uniform or plain clothes. He was a detective now, though, wasn't he? So probably no uniform.

He also wondered if maybe this was a bad idea, coming here by himself. He was too psyched up . . . way more than he thought he'd be. It had finally happened, though. The ARDC was after his license.

Not that he loved his law practice. Most mornings he woke up thinking he'd rather go somewhere else besides his office – *anywhere* else, actually. But these people were after him for something he didn't really think was so bad. In the end, they'd probably yank his ticket, but he wasn't about to let them push him around in the process.

He looked at his watch. Time was passing and, except for the constant flow of phone calls to the desk, nothing was happening. Gina Chan didn't come out. Johnny O'Hern didn't show up. Dugan didn't calm down.

Finally, at ten minutes to ten, the doors to one of the elevators slid open. Two people stepped out. But neither was Johnny. One was a short, husky Hispanic-looking man dressed like a construction worker, angry-looking and obviously pumped up to come in and scream about the terrible things his lawyer had done to him. The other was the prettiest woman Dugan had ever laid eyes on.

Her name was Kirsten, and she was Dugan's wife.

'Always nice to see you,' Dugan said, and kissed her on the cheek. He'd run out and stopped her near the elevators, while the husky man went inside and was already gesturing angrily at the ARDC's receptionist as though *she* were the crook he'd hired to handle his legal matter. 'Or *almost* always,' Dugan added. 'What the hell are you doing here?'

'Me?' She smiled ever-so-sweetly. 'I just happened to be in the building,' she said, 'and I came up to register a complaint. The thing about lawyers, you know, is they just don't—'

'Bullshit.'

'They don't communicate,' she continued, staring at him. 'I mean . . . I *live* with a lawyer, for God's sake, and does he *tell* me that he's up to his ass in trouble at the Disciplinary Commission? No, not him, dammit.' She was mad as hell, and had dropped any façade of sweetness. 'I have to find out from— Well, I can't say who from, but I—'

'I bet it was your buddy Parker Gillson. He's supposed to keep his mouth shut about ARDC investigations, and he *told* you. I should complain about *him*. Go after *his* job.'

'You wouldn't get far,' she said. 'They just made him chief investigator.'

'Oh, so that makes it legitimate for him to blab about what this damn place is investigating?'

'What makes it "legitimate" is that he's my friend . . . and he owes me. And you, dammit, are my husband. *You* owe me, too. You owe me enough to tell me when someone's coming after your license.'

'Yeah . . . well . . . I'd have told you, but—'

'Park called me on my cell twenty minutes ago. Told me to get over here. Said you'd just shown up, uninvited, and they weren't going to let—'

'Excuse me,' someone interrupted.

They turned to see a woman in a black pants suit holding

the ARDC's glass door open. She was scarcely over five feet tall, slim and pale-skinned. Her black hair was cut short and fell in curls over her forehead above large dark eyes. 'I'm Gina Chan,' she said. 'You wanted to see me?'

They went inside and the three of them stood in the middle of the reception area. The angry construction worker could be seen in a windowed conference room to their right, where a young woman sat at a table, apparently writing down what he was saying. 'Johnny O'Hern told me you're taking his dep today,' Dugan said. 'I'm here to attend it.'

'That's what the receptionist told me,' the woman said. 'Although . . . technically it's a sworn statement I'll be taking from Mr O'Hern when he arrives, not a deposition. At any rate, there's no need for you to wait, because you will *not* be allowed to attend.'

'There's a court reporter present and his lawyer's here, and you're going to sit down at a table and ask him questions – questions about *me*.' Dugan yanked his thumb back toward his own chest. 'So whatever you *call* it, I have a right to be there.'

'Actually, you're wrong.' Gina Chan didn't smile, didn't frown, didn't flinch. 'The subject matter of our investigation is confidential. When and if a formal complaint is filed, against you or anyone else, the matter will become public. Until that time, neither our policies nor the Supreme Court's rules afford you the right to participate.'

'I'm not talking about participating, just being present.' He struggled to control his voice. He knew it was stupid, but this tiny Gina Chan – competent, confident, and cute as hell – was really pissing him off. 'Dammit,' he said, 'I'm not—'

Kirsten stepped in front of Dugan and then backed up, subtly forcing him away from the woman. 'Rights are one thing, Ms Chan. But we were hoping you might not object to—'

'*Gina Chan*.' It was a female voice, coming over a paging system. 'Line three, please. Ms Chan, line three.'

Chan turned and walked to the receptionist's desk and picked up the phone. Just then a door to the right of the desk swung open and a tall, wide-shouldered black man appeared. Dugan hadn't seen the guy in awhile and he'd put on a few more pounds, but it was Parker Gillson.

Gillson came up close to Dugan and Kirsten. 'Don't argue,'

he said. 'Just move.' He herded them out through the glass doors and to the elevators. He hit the button and one of the elevator doors slid open, and he maneuvered them inside with him.

'What the hell's going on?' Dugan asked, as they started down. 'I want to attend that dep— I mean . . . sworn statement, and they can't keep me out.'

'That issue's been litigated to death,' Gillson answered. 'And the Supreme Court says they *can* keep you out. But believe me, this time they won't.'

'What?' Dugan felt suddenly confused. 'Then why are we going—'

'Just wait.' The elevator had stopped. Two men in white shirts and dark ties got on, and it was clear Gillson didn't want to talk in front of them. They continued down to the lobby and got out and he led them to a quiet corner. 'I can't stay long,' he said. 'I rode down with you and what I did was urge you to come back up with me, but you refused. Right?'

'What?' Dugan said again. 'I don't—'

'Right, I got it.' Kirsten raised her palm to shut Dugan up. 'So c'mon, Park,' she said. 'Tell us, for God's sake.'

'The sworn statement's been canceled.' Gillson kept his eyes on Kirsten, as if Dugan wasn't even there. 'If I were you, I'd tell my husband to stop being such an asshole, and to get the hell out of here and get himself a lawyer.'

'I *am* a lawyer, dammit,' Dugan said. 'I don't need—'

'He may be somewhere else by now.' Gillson still looked only at Kirsten. 'But as of not too long ago Johnny O'Hern was sitting behind the wheel of his car. Not going anywhere, though. Not after taking three bullets to the head.'

THREE

'So your friend Parker Gillson thought I was being an asshole, huh?' Dugan said.

'I got that impression,' Kirsten answered. They were out on Randolph Street and he watched her wave down a cab. He liked to watch her do anything at all, but stretching and waving her arm like that, in the outfit she was wearing that warm early-October day, was especially rewarding. 'What do *you* think?' she asked.

'That I was being an asshole.' The cab stopped and Dugan opened the door and held it for her, then followed her into the back seat. 'An arrogant, ignorant asshole.'

Kirsten leaned toward the front seat. 'Just go to Michigan Avenue and go north for awhile.' The driver nodded and she sat back and rested her hand on Dugan's knee. 'Well,' she said, 'for what it's worth? Me, too.'

'You, too?' He put his hand on top of hers. 'Well, now that you mention it, I guess you *were* being just about as bad. Poking into my affairs, barging into—'

'That's not what I meant, and you know it.' She snatched her hand away. 'Anyway, that ARDC lawyer . . . Gina Chan . . . she was just doing her job.'

'Right, and "her job" is to walk all over *me*. At least I didn't blurt out that she's a body-double for Peter Pan. I should get points for that.'

'What you should *get* is . . .' She paused, then said, 'Who's Johnny O'Hern?'

'You're the private investigator,' he said. 'Deduce it . . . or *in*duce it, or whatever.'

'OK . . . the man was asked to testify in an investigation at the ARDC, right?'

'Not just asked . . . subpoenaed.'

'And you think he was going to be asked questions about you?'

'I *know* he was.'

'How you *came* to know we'll come back to,' she said. 'Is he . . . or *was* he . . . a police officer?'

He nodded. 'You got it, Sherlock.'

'So . . . he must have been one of those cops you paid money to, to send you personal injury clients, right?'

'He never *sent* me anyone. From time to time – not recently, though – he'd come across someone who'd been injured in an automobile accident, and he'd recommend me to the person as an honest, intelligent attorney who could handle their claim competently. And if the person followed up on his recommendation I would . . . show him my appreciation.'

'So,' she said, 'Johnny O'Hern was one of those cops you paid to chase cases for you.'

'That's putting it in a rather negative light.' He shrugged. 'Anyway, it's not immoral . . . or dishonest.'

'But however you spin it, it's against the rules,' she said. 'So now the ARDC yanks your law license?'

'First they have to prove it to the Supreme Court. Only the *court* can take away the license.'

'Except, with O'Hern dead, how will they prove it?' She frowned, then added, 'Unless they find one of those other cops you've paid. And maybe they won't.'

'Either way, the commission will still come after me. I'll put up a fight, let them know they can't just walk all over me.'

'And you're sure they actually want to take away your license, right?'

'For sure. Not that it makes a lot of sense. They allow advertising, and paying someone to recommend my services isn't much different from paying someone to put my name on a billboard.' He shook his head. 'Anyway, to me, it's not that big a deal.'

'Really,' she said. 'I guess that's why you ran over there this morning, just to show them it's not a—'

'People!' the cab driver called. 'Where you want going to? We are coming to almost end of Michigan.'

'Oh,' Kirsten said, and looked out the window. 'Take us to . . . um . . . 220 East Chicago Avenue.' As the driver muttered something and hit the brakes, she turned to Dugan. 'We'll get coffee and talk this over.'

'Damn,' he said. 'You know the street address of every coffee shop you like?'

'That address is the Museum of Contemporary Art. Never been there before.' She pulled an envelope from her purse and held it up. 'I wrote out my membership check this morning. They must have a snack bar, and it probably won't be crowded. We can go over a few things.'

'Such as?'

'Such as how you can prove you were home alone last night, since I was out on a case until three a.m. And how you found out this guy O'Hern would be giving testimony against you, and when's the last time you saw him. Things like that.'

He shook his head. 'I'll gladly spend time chatting over a

cup of coffee. But if you're seriously thinking I might be a murder suspect, I'd say you're paranoid.'

The police investigators came to see Dugan at four o'clock that afternoon. Two of them: Cletus Kennison and Baxter Newhouse. They both looked to be in their mid- to late-thirties and were neatly dressed in sport coats and ties. Their cards identified their unit as 'Homicide'. He met them at the entrance to his suite, and brought them back to his office. They said they didn't like the idea of Kirsten sitting in on the conversation, but Dugan told them that's the way it had to be, that his cooperation was voluntary, and that he'd be recording the conversation anyway.

He sat down behind his desk. 'Of course, you're free to leave if you want to,' he said, thinking it's always good to get conversations such as this off on the right foot.

The officers looked at each other and shrugged, then sat down in clients' chairs across from Dugan. Meanwhile, Kirsten had cleared away enough stacked-up files to give herself space on the sofa against the wall off to the right of the desk. 'You won't even know I'm here,' she said. 'I promise.' Then she punched the button on the recorder.

The white cop, Kennison, asked the questions, while the black cop sat and looked bored and occasionally scratched his knee, or wrote something in a very small notebook.

'So,' Kennison said, 'how long and how well have you known the victim?'

Dugan leaned forward and put his palms on the desk in front of him, hoping the polished wood might absorb some of his nervousness. 'I've known John O'Hern . . . oh . . . more than seven years, less than ten. I don't know him well. We never socialized. I probably saw him face-to-face no more than a dozen times. I knew he was a police officer.'

'Do you know anyone who might have a motive to murder him?'

'I wasn't even aware he was "murdered". I just heard that he died sometime this morning from gunshot wounds to the head.'

'Please just answer my question.'

'Sure. My answer is "no".'

'If you weren't friends, and you didn't socialize, what *was* your relationship?' Kennison was clearly trying to look as though he had no clue – although Dugan figured Gina Chan had already told the cops about his possible payments to O'Hern. 'Was it . . . business?'

'Yes,' Dugan said.

'Go on.'

'Go on where?'

'What sort of business?'

'Oh.' Dugan lifted his hands from the desktop, leaving damp palm prints that evaporated as he watched. 'I'd rather not say.'

Kennison leaned forward. 'Why not? Were your business dealings . . . illegal?'

'Illegal? Not that I know of, no. But I consider them confidential.' He stared straight at Kennison. 'And that's why I'm not going to answer any questions along that line right now. Is there anything else you wish to ask?'

Kennison turned to his partner, but Newhouse just shrugged and Kennison turned back to Dugan. 'When's the last time you spoke to Mr O'Hern?'

'Do you mean "Officer" O'Hern? Or was he—'

'Just answer the questions I ask, sir. Skip the extra stuff. Think you can do that?'

'I'll try my best,' Dugan said. 'I spoke to him three days ago, Friday night.'

'Really.' Kennison was clearly surprised at the answer. 'When and where?'

'About seven o'clock. I was still in the office here. He called me.'

'At seven in the evening? Why would he think you'd still be here?'

'I don't know what he *thought*, investigator. But I was here. It's the nature of my work. I have three lawyers who work for me. Two of them, Peter Rienzo and Fred Schustein, are always gone by . . . oh . . . five thirty, anyway. Larry Candle – the third one – and myself are frequently here until seven or later. After six the switchboard's closed and I answer calls myself if I'm here. Larry doesn't. If no one answers, they go into voice mail.'

'So what did he say? What was the purpose of the—'

'Excuse me,' Newhouse interrupted. He still looked bored, but he was obviously paying attention. 'You answered the phone?'

'Yes.'

'You claim you didn't know him well. Did he identify himself, or did you recognize his voice, or what?'

'Both. He said something like, "This is Johnny O'Hern." I'd heard him on the phone before. It sounded like him.'

'So,' this from Kennison again, 'what did he say?'

'He told me he'd been subpoenaed to go to the Attorney Registration and Disciplinary Commission and give a deposition at nine thirty Monday morning . . . which would have been today, of course. That's what he called it, a "deposition", although technically, since there's no ongoing litigation, it would have been a sworn statement. Anyway, he said some of the questions were going to be about me.'

'Really. What did he mean by that? What *about* you?'

'I can only tell you what he *said*. Not what he meant.'

'So, what else did he say?'

'He said . . .' Dugan looked over at Kirsten, but she seemed to be concentrating on picking lint from the arm of the sofa. 'He said, in substance, that I could kiss my law practice goodbye, unless . . . unless I paid him a hundred thousand dollars.'

It was very quiet in the room, until Kennison finally said, 'He *said* that? On the *phone*?'

'Well, his exact words, as I recall, were: "a hundred g's".'

'Uh-huh, and what did you say to him?'

'*My* exact words, as I recall, were: "Go piss up a rope."'

FOUR

Once the investigators were gone, Kirsten left, too. She told Dugan she had some things to do for a couple of clients. She didn't tell him *he* was one of those clients. She wanted to appear as unconcerned about the O'Hern killing as he claimed to be.

Paying cops for referrals was a practice Dugan had inherited when his dad dropped dead ten years ago on a beer run at a Cubs game and Dugan had taken over his law office. It had never been a significant source of clients, and he'd gradually been phasing it out, *too* gradually. He said most of the cops had been drinking buddies of his dad, who had apparently been a genuine rebel. A big-hearted, hard-drinking free spirit. Not comfortable with anybody's rules . . . which, she thought, probably didn't make him the most responsible husband and father.

Anyway, she had the impression that Dugan felt that stopping the practice was in some weird way a betrayal, a rejection of his father. He knew it put his law license at risk, but he always downplayed that. Now, though, it had mixed him up in a murder, and that wasn't so easily downplayed.

The idea that Dugan might be considered a murder suspect was ridiculous, of course. She knew that, but she also knew it was crazy that he refused to retain an attorney to deal with the cops . . . or with the ARDC, for that matter. She loved the guy, and he was as smart as anyone she'd ever known. But damn, talk about blind spots.

She found a cab easily, but it was rush hour and the drive to Western Avenue and Belmont, on the northwest side, was a slow one. She paid off the driver and went inside the two-story brick building. On the first floor was the Nineteenth District Police Station, but she bypassed that and went upstairs, to Area Three Headquarters. Johnny O'Hern's murder had occurred in the part of the city designated by the police department as Area Three, and that's where Investigators Kennison and Newhouse worked.

She knew the building well. She'd been a cop herself. That had been her dream since she could remember, and not just to be a cop, but to be a detective and investigate homicides, like her dad before her. She'd made it, too, faster than most. Being a college grad, and female, at the right historical moment helped – and a little well-placed clout didn't hurt, either. It turned out she was good at the job, but at a psychological price, and the time finally came when she decided not to keep paying.

These days she was pretty far removed from the cop fraternity – and 'fraternity' it still was, making it a problem for females – so it was no sure thing that Baxter Newhouse would talk to her at all. But at least they knew each other. They'd both been part of a 'task force' once, working a child abduction, and she knew him to be one of the good ones. He was older than he looked, and she believed he was training

Kennison. His letting the younger detective get away with not asking whether anyone else was present when Dugan took Johnny O'Hern's phone call may well have been deliberate. It meant Kennison would have to contact Dugan again about it . . . and thereby maybe learn a lesson.

As it turned out, Kennison wasn't around and Newhouse was willing to give her some time and – to her surprise and satisfaction – more recognition and respect than she'd hoped for. 'One thing I can tell you,' he said, 'is that a guy who's worried enough to tape a simple interview oughta have enough sense to get lawyered up.'

'Tell me about it,' she said. 'He was in the state's attorney office for awhile, but . . .' She gave a what-can-you-do shrug. 'The thing is, Dugan's not capable of homicide, and he can't imagine anyone thinking he is . . . so he's not worried *enough*. The taping was my idea. Actually, when I saw it was you – a detective who knows what he's doing, and can be trusted – I almost skipped it.'

'But you *didn't* skip it. Instead, here you are, unannounced. And even if you grease me with another compliment, what do you think I'm gonna tell you?'

'No more than you can,' she said. 'But I did a quick Internet search on O'Hern. Found enough to suggest he's been under a bit of a cloud for some time.' She took Newhouse's silence as a *yes*, and went on. 'I can't believe the guy hadn't dealt with more than one personal injury lawyer, so he must have tried to milk a few others, too.'

'Maybe he was, and maybe he did, but if I *knew*, I couldn't say . . . and couldn't tell you who they might be.'

'So the field of possible suspects could be fairly wide?'

'*You* said that, not me.' Newhouse looked at his watch, then seemed to reach a conclusion. 'Look, we could play games here, but why waste the time? There are some things about O'Hern that aren't really secret, things that'll be coming out pretty soon, anyway. He had more on his plate than chasing cases for chump change. He stepped up a notch, got himself attached to a big-money guy. Trouble is, the guy woke up in bed one day with some people he and O'Hern . . . same as *you*, and anyone else with any sense . . . should've known enough to stay away from. And if someone like O'Hern . . . and I'm not saying he *did* . . . but *if* he fell under the eye of the feds, well, he might choose to "cooperate", and give up things he knows, to cut himself some slack.'

'And given his proposal to my husband,' she said, 'it seems he intended to tailor his cooperation according to how he might make a buck.'

'I'd say he needed the money,' Newhouse said. 'Because, unlike certain people we know, Johnny O'Hern had enough sense to get a lawyer . . . and they tell me that can be expensive.'

A few minutes later Kirsten was headed back down the stairs from Area Three. That lots of people had reason to keep O'Hern silent was a plus. Still, when a guy calls and announces he plans to start singing and creating problems for you, and two days later he turns up dead? It doesn't look good.

She wasn't sure losing his law license was that big a deal to Dugan. But would anyone else buy that? After all, even if he wasn't 'following his bliss', he made a damn good living with that license. And now . . . with them planning a family . . .

A baby. The clock kept ticking away and she hadn't gotten pregnant yet, which she found to be both a worry and – yes, she had to admit it – a relief. She wanted it, but still . . . it scared her. Not the money part so much, because with or without Dugan's law license, they'd always find a way. What worried her was that a baby might make her into a different person, lead her into a different life.

She snuffed out those thoughts and turned her mind to something Baxter Newhouse had said. A strange, awkward comment. It bothered her.

She pushed through the door at the foot of the stairs. Walking past the Nineteenth District desk, she nodded at the sergeant and headed through the lobby. She went out the front door and past the entrance to a separate wing of the building which held a few branch courtrooms where misdemeanor charges and felony preliminary hearings were handled.

It was still warm, at least seventy degrees, and five or six young shirt-sleeved patrolmen stood outside in the little concrete plaza, laughing and talking and smoking cigarettes. From their suddenly hushed tones as she passed, and their stares and quiet laughter, she knew exactly down what road their conversation had turned. That sort of endless macho scrutiny, and evaluation, had both embarrassed and angered her when, barely out of college, she'd first joined the force. But she'd gotten over that in a hurry. It wasn't that, but rather the pool of physical and psychological violence she'd had to swim in every day, that drove her out.

With the courtrooms closed for the day, there were no cabs waiting. As she pulled her phone from her purse, she noticed one of the young cops coming her way.

'Is there . . . uh . . . something I can help you with?' he asked.

Cops were getting younger-looking all the time. This one was tall and broad, like a football player – a *high school* football player, for God's sake. He looked bright and personable, but nervous, and more than a little unsophisticated. She had the impression he was acting on a dare. And that gave her an idea.

She let him get close, then stared at him, hard. 'Where are you *assigned*, Officer Cragan?' Taking the name from the shiny new tag pinned to his crisply pressed shirt, and putting on her best detective-sergeant-in-plain-clothes voice.

'Um . . . what was that, ma'am?' From the look on his face, and the *ma'am*, she knew she had him already.

She gestured that he should come with her, and he did. He moved stiffly, as though still not used to the gun and the stick and other equipment weighing down his belt. 'Your *assignment*, I said.' She stopped when they were out of earshot of the group. 'You *are* assigned somewhere, Cragan. Jesus, how long you been on the job?'

'I . . . uh . . . I'm a recruit, assigned to the Nineteenth District for field training; right here, days. I been out of the Academy two months is all. I mean, is there some prob—'

'Why are you still hanging around here, then? Aren't you off-duty?'

'Yes, ma'am. But I had some paper work, and my buddy's working till—'

'Where's your car?'

'What?'

'Your *car*, officer? Don't you have an automobile?'

'Oh . . . yes, ma'am. I mean . . . it's a truck, ma'am.'

'Jesus. Well, take me to it, anyway.' He glanced back toward the group, but when she snapped, 'Let's go, officer!' he turned and led her into the crowded parking lot.

It was a Chevy Blazer, not a pick-up truck, for which she was thankful, and when they reached it she explained that she and he were working a game on his friends. They would see him drive away with her and he would take her to the El at Belmont and Sheffield, fourteen blocks – just under two miles – away. 'Then if you're smart,' she said, 'you go home. And tomorrow you tell those guys whatever story you can dream up about what happened.' She reached out and patted his arm. 'I'm not helping you with that part,' she added.

'That's cool,' he said, and grinned, and she liked him and thought if he stuck with it he might grow up to be real police one day.

On the drive he obviously couldn't think of anything to say, and she didn't help him with that, either. She was busy thinking about her next stop, which was to meet the owner of a small chain of upscale Chicago restaurants, to break the news to him that he'd paid her an awful lot of money to find out that the thief lurking among his office staff was his own son, and what his son's addictions were.

As they approached the El station Cragan finally spoke up. 'So,' he said, 'I guess you're not—'

'Nope,' she said. 'Used to be, though. Now I'm on my own.' She took her billfold from her purse and slid out a business card that said:

WILD ONION, LTD
Confidential Inquiries
Security Services

She gave him the card, a twenty dollar bill, and a warm smile. 'You take care, Cragan,' she said, and got out of the Blazer and went into the El station.

FIVE

'Jesus,' Larry Candle said, 'you told the cops all *that*?' Larry dropped his round little body on to the site Kirsten had cleared on Dugan's sofa, and took a long pull from his Dos Equis. 'You shoulda shut up about O'Hern calling you, Doogs. How they gonna know?'

'Maybe they wouldn't.' Dugan popped the cap off the beer Larry had brought him from the office refrigerator. It was six-thirty. The investigators were long gone, and Kirsten was, too. She'd said she had a case of her own to get to, but Dugan suspected she thought Larry might come poking his nose in, and she wanted to be gone before he did. Larry irritated Kirsten. Actually, Larry irritated everyone. 'On the other hand,' Dugan said, 'they might find out from his phone records. Or maybe his line was tapped. Or *my* line. And, since *you* were here when the call came in, maybe they'd find out from you.'

'Yeah . . . well . . . if they asked me, and if I said I had no idea if you *ever* talked to the guy, how they gonna know that's not true?'

'From me,' Dugan said. 'They'd know it from *me*.'

'OK, partner. I got it. What you're saying is we gotta tell the truth – not that I wouldn't, of course – because it might go worse for you if we get caught lying.'

'Don't call me "partner", Larry, because we aren't . . . and we won't be. And don't use *me* as your motive for telling the truth, because . . . well, just don't. Anyway, the cops seemed to take for granted I was alone when the call came in, so—'

The phone rang, and Dugan answered. 'Law office,' he said.

'It's Investigator Kennison. I figured you'd answer, since it's after six.'

'Right. What can I do for you?'

'There's something I didn't ask you earlier. Was there anyone else with you when you took that call from O'Hern?'

'Actually, yes. Larry Candle had stopped by my office. He was here.'

'And you didn't think you should mention that when we were talking earlier?'

'You told me to "skip the extra stuff", and answer only the questions you asked.'

'Uh-huh.' Kennison gave what Dugan thought was a disgusted sigh. 'Did Mr Candle know it was O'Hern on the line?'

'Well, he heard what I heard.'

'He "heard"?'

'Sure. When the call came in I answered by hitting the speaker phone button. Larry heard everything. In fact, he's here now. You wanna talk to him?'

'Tell him we'll be there at eleven tomorrow.'

'I don't have to tell him. You're on the speaker phone.'

'Hey, Officer Jamison!' Larry called, too loudly. 'How they hangin', buddy?'

'It's *Investigator Kennison*,' the detective said, 'and my partner and I will be at your office tomorrow at—'

'I'll be tied up in court from . . . let's see . . . eight 'til noon. But after that, I might—'

'Eleven o'clock,' Kennison said. 'At your office. Or we'll come and haul you *out* of court.'

'I'll be here, Officer Kennedy,' Larry said, jabbing his middle finger up in the air toward the phone. 'Always glad to co-operate with our boys in blue.'

Dugan had a few minutes to think while Larry went to the office kitchen for more beers. Larry loved keeping the fridge stocked with premium brews . . . which Dugan paid for. 'None of that cheap shit for us, hey Doogie pal?' he'd say.

Dugan had thought long and hard about hiring Larry a few years earlier. Larry bugged people to death. That was his *modus operandi*, maybe part of his genetic structure, but the roly-poly, wisecracking little man had proved to be a surprising asset. He knew the personal injury game inside out, and he worked his butt off.

He had never told Larry about his paying police officers who referred clients. That was being phased out, anyway, as his dad's old cop-friends retired. It was rare now to get a call from one of the few remaining ones, saying he'd sent in a case and would stop by to pick up his 'package'. Dugan should have put a total stop to it long ago. He wasn't sure why he hadn't. It was something his dad had started, and it just seemed—

'Hey, Doogs! Wake up!'

'Jesus!' Dugan reached up in time to catch the flying Dos Equis bottle headed his way. 'Why do you always *do* that?' He opened the bottle carefully, so as not to spray beer all over his desk

''Cause you always catch it. When I see you slipping, I'll stop.' Larry plopped his behind on the sofa again – his legs barely reaching the floor. 'That guy that got killed,' he said, 'Johnny O'Hern. I heard of him before, you know?'

'Really.' Dugan was often surprised by Larry's wealth of knowledge. 'So then, do you have any idea what he meant on the phone, when he said they'd be asking him questions at the ARDC . . . about *me*?'

'Nope.' Larry said. 'I can tell you what he *said*. Not what he meant.'

'Fair enough.' The answer was almost exactly what Dugan had said to the detectives. 'So . . . let's pretend you're under oath somewhere, Larry, maybe on a witness stand, and the prosecutor says: "Tell me, Mr Candle . . . in what context was it that you heard about John O'Hern?" What would you say?'

'I'd say: "I heard about him in the context of it being rumored that some police officers have been known to chase cases for personal injury lawyers."'

Just what Dugan was afraid of. He stood up and struck a courtroom pose. 'And by "chasing cases", Mr Candle, tell the court . . . do you mean referring clients to attorneys in exchange for money?'

'Yes, sir.'

'And do you know of any lawyer Mr O'Hern ever . . . "chased cases" . . . for?'

'No, sir. I don't know of any.'

'Fine, Mr Candle.' Dugan gave his best cross-examiner's sneer. 'But tell us, are you aware that a lawyer's paying someone for recommending the lawyer's services violates the Illinois Rules of Professional Conduct?'

'Apart from permitted advertising, sir, I understand such conduct to be in violation of the rules.' Larry smiled. 'This particular rule,' he went on, 'seeks to prevent taking advantage of people when they're vulnerable. Why, I've heard that ambulance chasers have been known to shove retainer contracts in front of injured persons, or distraught family members, and sign them up right there in the ER . . . before some other chaser can cut ahead of them.'

'Really, Mr Candle?' Dugan had always insisted his cops just give out his name and phone number, and if the people wanted to call, fine. 'Is that so?'

'I don't know if it's *so*, Mr Prosecutor, but it's what I've *heard*.' Larry took a long pull on his beer. 'Can we cut the crap now, Doogs, about me being on the stand?'

'Sure.' Dugan sat down at his desk again. 'I was just—'

''Cause, if you want my opinion, the main reason ambulance chasing's against the rules is because it makes lawyers *look* bad. But hell, we do fine in the "appearance-of-sleaze" department without breaking any rules at all.'

'Right,' Dugan said. 'Besides, if I pay for a case and then do a great job for the client, who's hurt?'

'Right on, baby!' Larry hoisted his bottle high.

'And signing a contract doesn't chain the client to me. They can always fire me.'

'Here, here!' Larry hoisted his bottle again. 'Although we're . . . like . . . talking hypothetically, right?'

'Of course.'

'OK.' Larry frowned. 'So . . . let's say there's this guy . . . hypothetically . . . let's say he just kinda falls into the practice of paying a few chasers. Like maybe he . . . *inherits* the practice. He knows it could hurt him, but he keeps it up. He's got plenty of clients, and doesn't really *need* to, you know? So . . . I think his reason might not be financial.'

'What are you talking about?'

'I'm just saying . . . take this straight-up, honest, hypothetical guy . . . if he plays outside the rules a little?' Larry pursed his lips and nodded his round head, as though thinking this through. 'Maybe it makes the guy feel like . . . well . . . like an outlaw, a rebel. Maybe it makes him feel *free*. Sorta like the guy who did it before him.'

Dugan stared at him. 'You're talking,' he said, 'hypothetically.'

'Hypothetically,' Larry echoed. He drained the last of his Dos Equis, then looked at his watch. 'Holy shit,' he said, eyes wide. 'Gotta go pick up my daughter from soccer practice.'

SIX

Their condo was on the near north side and Dugan usually took a cab downtown. Kirsten had an office, too, not far from his, but even when she went there – which wasn't every day – she seldom left home as early as he did. Today, though, they shared a cab, and now they were on LaSalle Street, about a mile north of the Loop. It was warm out, but a gentle rain was falling and people hurried along the sidewalk under umbrellas, or huddled together under bus stop shelters.

They had ridden in silence for several blocks, but now Dugan said, 'We need to talk.'

Kirsten folded the newspaper she'd been reading. 'They're calling it an "execution-style" killing,' she said. 'But you're right. Call Mollie and tell her you'll be late getting in.'

'No way! She'll go nuts. I missed most of yesterday and she'll—'

'Dugan, she's your employee, not your boss. You pay her salary.'

'Right, because she keeps the office going. But she's an office manager, not a lawyer. I have to be there. What if Larry's sick and can't come in?'

'You know Larry hasn't missed a day since, against my advice, you hired him.'

'And it turned out I was right. He can handle anything that—' He stopped, realizing she'd out-maneuvered him. 'I give up,' he said, and flipped open his phone and called Mollie. She raised a fuss, but she knew what was going on and he figured her complaints were just to keep herself in practice.

'Good work,' Kirsten said when he closed his phone. She smiled, but she looked worried. 'I went and talked to Baxter Newhouse yesterday evening.'

'Funny,' he said, 'you told *me* you had a client who needed attention.'

'And after I talked to Newhouse I took care of that. Which is why I was so late getting home.'

'Yeah, I remember your coming to bed and waking me up. It was kinda fun.' He had no idea, though, what time it had been.

'I need to fill you in on what Newhouse told me,' she said. 'He made a remark that I'm still not sure—' There was a sudden roar from the cab's tires as they left concrete behind and started across the metal bridge over the Chicago River. She leaned forward and told the driver to go straight to her office, near Randolph and Wabash. When she sat back she said, 'Actually, that remark wasn't about you, anyway.'

'Then why—'

'We'll talk at my office.'

Dugan paid the driver and he and Kirsten made the short dash through the rain and into the building. They picked up two decafs – decaf was one of their new resolutions – at the coffee shop off the lobby and took the elevator up to her office.

On the ride up he thought of his own suite. Offices for four lawyers, secretarial stations, conference rooms, a large open area with tables where his paralegals and clerks worked – or mostly hung out and chatted, if you believed Mollie – a law library, a kitchen with tables where the staff could eat, two restrooms, and a comfortable reception area. Visitors were greeted by a receptionist, and knew they were in a first-class place. The overhead was huge.

On the other hand, Kirsten's entire suite was about half the size of his reception area. Just a tiny office beyond a tinier waiting room. No windows. No receptionist. She preferred to observe her clients on their own turf, so people seldom came there.

Dugan liked her workplace better than his.

They took their coffees in and sat across from each other at her desk. 'First,' she said, 'Newhouse thinks it's foolish of you not to hire a lawyer.'

'Right. So do you.' He sipped his decaf. 'What else?'

'You're one of a number of possible suspects. You—'

'Bullshit. I'm about as likely a murder suspect as Mollie.'

'Less likely, I'd say. But that doesn't mean the cops see it that way. Anyway, there are a number of people with possible motives for murdering Johnny O'Hern.' She went on, reciting what Newhouse had told her . . . almost verbatim, Dugan was sure. 'And when I left Area Three this cute young police recruit drove me to the El station.' She dropped her cup in the wastebasket beside her desk. 'And that's the story.'

Where she went between the El station and coming home, she didn't say. And he didn't ask. Her private eye business was her business. On the other hand . . . 'You skipped something,' he said.

'What makes you say that?'

'You thought I'd forget about that remark Newhouse made, the one you said "wasn't about" me. So . . . who *was* it about?'

'Let's wait on that. I need to—'

'What was it? And who *was* it about?'

She sighed. 'I told you Newhouse said O'Hern got hooked up with some big-money guy, who started associating with some people they both knew enough to stay away from.'

'That's what you said he said. So what?'

'What he said, more accurately, was that the money guy woke up in bed one day with some people he and O'Hern . . . same as *me*, and anyone else with any sense . . . should have known enough to stay away from.'

'Not quite the same.'

'No. He meant *me*. He meant those two were mixed up with some people *I* should have known enough to stay away from . . . in the past. He made it sound like an offhand remark. But Baxter Newhouse isn't an "offhand remark" kind of guy.'

'And you're thinking of someone in particular who's just the kind of "some people" he meant.'

'Yeah, but what I *don't* know . . . and believe me, it wouldn't have helped to ask . . . is whether he was really warning me not to go there again, or telling me that's just who I need to talk to.'

SEVEN

Whatever else Baxter Newhouse had meant to convey, he'd made it clear that in the race to be prime suspect in the Johnny O'Hern homicide Dugan had competition. And since the possible loss of a law license was, in fact, not the strongest motive for pumping three slugs into a man's head, the other contestants – people facing serious criminal prosecution – had to be way higher on the list than Dugan was.

Or so Kirsten and he told each other. She didn't want to appear any more worried than he seemed to be, and she didn't press him any more to get a lawyer. In fact, however, she *was* concerned, and the passage of two days during which the case got lots of press, but no announcement of an arrest, was no help at all.

Then, late Wednesday morning, when Dugan was at his office and she was still at home, the doorbell rang. She looked down from the third-floor window and saw two cops in plain clothes. One wore sunglasses, even though the day was overcast. She went downstairs and the one with the shades showed her a piece of paper. It was an order signed by a judge and demanding the 'immediate delivery to the Chicago Police Department of any and all firearms owned and/or possessed' by herself or Dugan. The document went on to say: 'including, but not limited to, a certain Colt Government Model 380, MKIV Series 80 Semiautomatic handgun', which was a gun registered with the state in Kirsten's name.

'To my knowledge,' she said, 'that's the only weapon either one of us owns or possesses. And I can't turn it over immediately because it's not here.'

'Where is it?'

'Your order doesn't say I have to answer questions.'

The cop lowered his glasses and stared at her. 'We'd like to come up and verify that there are no weapons in your condo unit, ma'am.'

'That would be acceptable,' she said, 'if you had a search warrant. But you don't.' The judge must have denied their request for a search warrant, and they must have wished they'd gone to a different judge. 'As soon as I have possession of that particular Colt 380 I'll turn it over to the police.' She smiled and closed the door, and headed back upstairs.

The phone was ringing and she thought she knew who it was.

She was right. 'It's me,' Dugan said. 'Your friend Baxter Newhouse just left my office. He and Kennison.'

'And they had a turnover order for "any and all firearms owned and/or possessed" by you or me.'

'How did you know?'

'Two other cops were just here on the same mission,' she said. 'My two were disappointed.'

'Yeah, well, mine left happy.'

'Of course.' She hadn't felt any need for the Colt in several months, so she'd stored it in the safe in Dugan's office. 'So you cooperated?'

'Fell all over myself,' he said. 'Including answering their questions about how long it's been here. I wonder, can they tell that a gun hasn't been fired in a long time?'

'They'll find it cleaned and oiled. I don't know if they can tell whether that was done two months or two days ago.'

'But they sure know it was available to me on the night in question.'

'Because you told them.' She paused. 'Maybe you should get a lawyer. Then the cops could present their orders to *him*, and he could advise you.'

'Or to *her*, and *she* could,' Dugan said. 'But I *am* a lawyer, and my advice to me is that I don't need another one.'

Kirsten hung up. She had to assume that the wounds to Johnny O'Hern's head were consistent with those inflicted by bullets from a .38 caliber handgun. Although there were probably thousands of such weapons in metropolitan Chicago, now it could be said that Dugan had motive, opportunity, and access to a weapon that fit the crime. He could shoot, too. She'd first met him at the Police Academy, and by the time he'd dropped the cop idea and left to go to law school, he had already proven himself a pretty good novice on the gun range.

Firearms comparison procedures might eliminate her gun, of course, if the slugs they dug out of O'Hern's head were in good enough shape, or if they had shell casings from the scene.

But no such luck, as she learned the next day, Thursday, from Parker Gillson.

Although Park worked now for the ARDC, he'd kept up the contacts he'd developed as a newsman. He'd inquired about what the cops found – or didn't find – from a freelance reporter named Bobby Becker who'd been monitoring police calls and had sped to the scene.

'Bobby's got good instincts, a sharp eye, and great police contacts,' Park said, and took a huge bite from a Polish sausage sandwich. When he'd chewed it down to manageable proportions, he talked around it. 'Trouble is, he's a tad lazy, and not much of a writer. Add in the fact that media outlets are cutting staff, and you got a guy who's barely making it.'

'Got it,' Kirsten said. 'You name his price. I'm good for it.'

'Right. Good to get the haggling out of the way.' It was a beautiful warm day and they were strolling through Millennium Park, twenty-four acres of grass, trees, and contemporary art just east of the Loop, between Michigan Avenue and Lake Shore Drive. Park chewed another bite for awhile and took a swig of his Mountain Dew. 'According to Bobby,' he said, 'the slugs were hollow points, so the cops'll get nothing there.'

'Casings?' she asked.

'He says they swept and came up empty.'

'Witnesses? That's a residential neighborhood. Even past midnight someone might've heard gunshots.'

'Might have, but not necessarily. Hot night, air conditioners going. Not that far off the expressway and some main business streets. Anyway, Bobby hasn't heard about any witnesses.'

'Maybe the shooter used a silencer. This has all the marks of a pro.'

'Or just somebody real smart,' Park said. 'Apparently no readable prints anywhere but Johnny's.'

'Shots fired through the car window, you wouldn't expect prints.'

'Bobby says no prints at all on the passenger side door, inside or out. Nowhere on that side of the interior. Like wiped clean.'

'Or no one used that side since the last time Johnny had the car washed.' She sipped some of her own lunch – what they called a *medium* Diet Coke, though the cup was so large she could barely hold it with one hand. 'They know where he was before he went home?'

'Nope. Not that Bobby's heard.'

She stirred her drink with the straw. 'Dugan didn't do it, you know.'

'I know that.' Park nodded.

'Oh? And *how* do you know?'

'You told me. To my mind that's conclusive.'

'Thanks.' She knew he meant it, too.

'But something else I got from Bobby,' Park said. 'He says the heat's on. They wanna make an arrest and wrap this case up.'

'Heat? You mean like from the press? Or the public?'

'You seen any signs of that?'

'No,' Kirsten said, 'not really.'

'So, if Bobby's right – and he usually is – it's coming from somewhere else. They wanna charge someone, soon. If they get a conviction, great. If not . . . well . . . you can't win 'em all. And case closed.'

'Trouble is,' she said, 'if they charge someone, there's always a chance they *will* get a conviction. Even with a weak case. Lots of people who didn't do the crime are sitting in jail right now.'

'*Amen* to that,' he said. 'Which is why Dugan's lucky to have you. He didn't kill anyone, and he shouldn't go to jail. Which is not to say, sweetheart, that he shouldn't have his ass kicked out of the practice for paying chasers.'

EIGHT

Late Friday morning Dugan sat on an uncomfortable wooden bench in Judge Edwin Dawes' courtroom on the fifteenth floor of the Richard J. Daley Center in the heart of the Loop. The room was jammed with lawyers, and Dugan hoped Larry Candle would show up soon. Dugan himself almost never went to court. That's why he had Larry. Although Larry had neither the patience nor the jury appeal actually to try cases, he loved to go to court for preliminary matters and argue – 'duke it out', as he put it – with lawyers and judges. The constant verbal battling, often acrimonious, drove some people nuts. Not Larry, though. Uh-uh. Larry did the driving.

'*Ratcheter versus Yellow Cab!*' the judge called. He didn't bother with a clerk.

Dugan jumped up and hurried forward. 'Your honor,' he said, pushing through the swinging gate, 'I ask that this case be passed. Mr Candle is—'

'*Talcott versus Andover!*' Judge Dawes didn't like to waste time. Dugan's case would go to the end of the morning's call.

He turned and went back to his seat and hoped Larry would be there by then. Not that Dugan couldn't easily argue the merits of the motion his firm had filed on behalf of Sam Ratcheter, who'd been beaten into a coma by a cab driver because Sam hadn't had any small bills to pay his fare. The problem was that Larry had the file with him . . . in another courtroom five floors away, and Judge Dawes was sure to ask some question Dugan couldn't answer without paging through the file. Dawes' judicial assignment was the 'Motion Call', which meant he heard nothing but pre-trial motions in civil cases, mostly personal injury matters. No witnesses, no testimony, just lawyers arguing their positions. Dawes, like most Motion Call judges was bright, decisive, and had an ego even bigger than the lawyers in front of him.

Dugan was bored. Judge Dawes had a rule against reading newspapers in his courtroom, and loved to threaten people with contempt . . . which left Dugan with nothing to do but mull over his own situation. Even after the cops had come for Kirsten's gun, he found it incomprehensible that they might seriously consider him a suspect in a homicide.

Kirsten had learned from that cop, Newhouse, that there were other people with reason to want Johnny O'Hern out of the way, including other lawyers who'd paid him for cases. To Dugan's mind, any lawyer who'd gotten an extortion demand like he had, and whose response was to blow O'Hern away, had a lot stronger attachment to his law license than Dugan did. In fact, though, there were people who made a lot of money with their licenses, and who needed every last penny to support their lavish lifestyles.

Newhouse had suggested other possibilities, too, hinting at some with underworld connections. In particular, Kirsten was convinced that Newhouse had made a veiled reference to Paolo 'Polly' Morelli, a top Outfit guy – *the* top, actually, in these parts. She'd gone to Polly a while back, seeking help with a problem. It had, in fact, been Dugan's problem, but he'd been tied up at the time – literally. The help Kirsten sought was help only Morelli could give. And he'd given it.

Maybe some mob guy – maybe even Morelli himself – was a possible suspect, but the idea that O'Hern was a mob hit wasn't at all encouraging. According to a story Dugan had read in the *Tribune* a while back, there'd been over 1,100 gangland slayings in the Chicago area since 1919. And the number of convictions for those? About thirty. So a *non*-mob perpetrator in the O'Hern case was preferable, someone the cops could get their hands on . . . and therefore keep their hands off him.

Although firearms comparison couldn't rule out Kirsten's gun as the murder weapon, the gun couldn't be ruled 'in', either, so the cops had already returned it. It wasn't even arguably a piece of evidence in a homicide case. It was just a Colt 380, legally owned by a state-licensed private detec—

'*Ratcheter versus Yellow Cab!*'

Dugan jumped up and moved forward again, surprised to look around and see just a handful of lawyers remaining in the courtroom. 'Your honor,' he said, 'could this case be passed again? Because Mr Candle still—'

'I passed it once.' The judge stared down at him. 'Counsel for Yellow Cab is here and ready,' he said, nodding toward the man who'd stepped up beside Dugan. 'Where is the apparently vital Mr Candle?'

'He's in Judge Streleski's courtroom, your honor. He had to—'

'And I take it Judge Streleski is more important than I?' The bigger the judicial ego, the more easily bruised. One more reason to stay far away from courtrooms.

'Not at all, your honor, but Judge Streleski required Mr Candle to appear before her today or suffer the dismissal of one of his cases.'

'Probably because he didn't show up in her courtroom on a previously scheduled occasion. Am I right, sir?'

'Yes, your honor. But that wasn't his fault.' As soon as the words were out he knew he'd made a mistake.

'Oh? Why not?'

He didn't want to explain. 'Mr Candle was . . . well . . .' He heard the courtroom door open and turned to see if it was Larry, but it wasn't, and he turned back. 'It's a long story, your honor.'

The judge looked past him toward the rear of the room. 'There is no standing up in my courtroom, gentlemen. Please take a seat and wait your turn.' Then, to Dugan, 'Give me the short version of your story.'

'You know what, your honor? I prefer to go forward without Mr Candle and argue the motion.' Dugan buttoned his suit coat as he gathered his thoughts. 'This motion, your honor, is—'

'Excuse me, judge,' the lawyer for Yellow Cab spoke up for the first time. He probably had twenty cases up that day and wished every one of them could be put off forever. 'To accommodate counsel, I have no problem with continuing this matter to—'

'Excuse me.' Judge Dawes' glare moved from one to the other. 'Apparently you two gentlemen have a shared misapprehension about who runs this courtroom.' He pointed a finger at Dugan. 'If I find that you were making up a phony excuse for Mr Candle, sir, you'll be subject to contempt of court. Now give me the short version of your "long story". The short, *short* version.'

'Well,' Dugan said, 'why not?' He took a deep breath. 'Mr Candle couldn't appear before Judge Streleski because two homicide detectives . . .' He turned and pointed back at Newhouse and Kennison, who had sat down when the judge told them to. '*Those* two homicide detectives, in fact,' he said, turning back to the judge, 'were questioning him at the time . . . trying to find out whether I murdered a cop.'

NINE

'I guess it's almost time for lunch,' Dugan said, looking at his watch. He and the two detectives stood alone in the hall outside the courtroom. Larry Candle was inside arguing the motion on behalf of Sam Ratcheter. He'd arrived just in time and Judge Dawes had seemed happy to be rid of Dugan and get on with his work.

'Almost,' Kennison agreed, 'but we're not here to take you to lunch.'

'Am I under arrest?' Dugan asked.

'You'll *know* when you're under arrest,' Kennison answered.

'Good.' Dugan turned to walk away, but a heavy hand on his shoulder made him turn back and ask, 'What?'

'We have a few questions,' Kennison said.

'Fine.' Dugan took a small appointment book from his suitcoat pocket, opened it, and studied a blank page. 'How about this afternoon, my office, say . . . four o'clock? Is that convenient?'

'Do you know an attorney named Harvey Starr?'

'Not well.' He slipped the notebook back in his pocket, deciding it was best not to walk away just then. 'He's a plaintiff's lawyer.'

'Just like you?'

'I like to think not.' Starr ran a high-volume personal injury shop, with hundreds – maybe a thousand – clients at any given time. He was sixtyish, a smooth-talking man known to work harder at acquiring clients than at getting good results for them. 'Why?'

'Did Starr have . . . business dealings . . . with Johnny O'Hern?' Again it was Kennison asking all the questions, while the black detective, Newhouse, just observed. 'Maybe similar to the dealings *you* had?' Kennison added.

'How would I know who Harvey Starr has "dealings" with?' Dugan didn't like where they were headed – they obviously believed Starr paid O'Hern for cases. 'Like I said, I barely know the guy.'

'But you *do* know him,' Kennison went on. 'And we're told he knows you. We're told he knows who *you* do business with.'

'How would he know what—' He stopped. 'You'd have to ask Harvey about whatever he knows.'

'Yeah, well, we intended to, y'know? We were to meet with him this morning, him and his lawyer. It didn't work out.'

'Oh?' Dugan's breath suddenly wasn't cooperating with his vocal cords.

There were a few long seconds of silence, and then Newhouse leaned forward, just slightly, and spoke for the first time. 'His lawyer showed up, but without Mr Starr,' he said. 'Fact is, Harvey Starr seems to have disappeared.'

When he got back to his suite Mollie was on her feet, ready for him. She was a gray-haired, no-nonsense, sixty-something woman who could turn on her motherly charms with clients, but who was efficient – some might say 'ruthless' – in her management of the office. Right at that moment she had a fistful of messages for him. Dugan waved her aside, though, and went straight to his office and closed the door. He tried to call Kirsten, but had no luck, and as soon as he hung up his phone, it rang. 'There's one message here that you *have* to return,' Mollie said.

'Why?'

'Because Catherine McArthur called. She got a verdict in the Perez case. It's not as much as we were hoping for.'

'Of course not. We never had a chance to get what we were hoping for.'

'Catherine says the defense is willing to settle for a little more than the verdict, to avoid post-trial motions and an appeal. But they want to know now.'

'Fine,' he said. 'Get Catherine on the phone.'

It was a case with potential damages in the millions – but way too many problems. Javier Perez had been a union pipe fitter on a construction site, an excavation for a new high-rise on the south end of the Loop. He'd been clowning around with a co-worker, some sort of phony karate fight, and had jumped backwards to avoid a wild, clumsy kick. Unfortunately, he jumped too far back, hit a barrier which gave way, and fell forty feet on to a concrete slab. There was evidence that Javier had been a happy-go-lucky guy, a terrific husband and father, and – at least as the defendant argued – consistently careless. There was also evidence – at least as the plaintiff argued – that the barrier around the pit hadn't been properly constructed. What no one disputed was that Xavier left a widow and three little kids behind. The case couldn't be settled, so Dugan sent it to Catherine McArthur for trial, with the fee to be split fifty-fifty.

His phone buzzed. Mollie had Catherine on the line. He had known all along what he'd do if things came to this.

Twenty minutes later Dugan hung up. He slipped on his suit coat and headed out of his office. He didn't want to stick around until Larry Candle got back because Larry would have pumped him for information about why the cops had shown up in court. So he went out to face Mollie, instead.

'I'll be out for a couple of hours,' he said, and ignored her look of disapproval. 'Call Eddie at the bank. Tell him we'll have to go ahead with that loan if we're going to meet the payroll. We need—'

'You couldn't settle Perez?'

'I settled it. Nine hundred thousand.'

'So the fee from that should carry us over until we get the Mahrdol money,' she said. 'Then Mahrdol will take care of everything for a long time.'

'Mahrdol won't be in for a month.'

'So the Perez fee will—'

'No,' he said. 'It won't.'

She stared at him. 'You did it again, didn't you.' She shook her head. 'No fee at all?'

'Not for us, anyway.'

'But Catherine McArthur's taking *her* half of the fee, right?'

'She cut her share . . . by ten per cent. That's fair. She should be paid.'

'What's fair is for you to be paid, too. Julia Perez is no dummy.' Mollie's face reddened. 'Dammit, she knew going in that she had to pay a one-third fee, and she knew the verdict might be low. For her to refuse to settle without you throwing in your fee is un—'

'Julia Perez has three kids . . . ten, nine, and seven. They stay with her mother while Julia works two shifts. Waiting tables in a goddamn diner, for chrissake.' He held up his hand to silence Mollie's open mouth. 'She didn't "refuse" anything. She was disappointed in the verdict, but she agreed to a nine-hundred-thousand dollar settlement after I told her I'd add my half of the fee to her amount. That's one-fifty more for her and the kids. They need it more than I do.'

'Fine.' Mollie heaved a long sigh. 'What about costs and expenses?'

'I'm eating those, too.'

'But—'

'Call Eddie at the bank and get the loan. And have him set Julia Perez up with a financial advisor.' He turned away before she could say *he* was the one who needed advice, then turned back. 'And I changed my mind. I'll be out all afternoon.'

She was already punching out a phone number, and didn't look up. Apparently she was all out of indignation.

Four hours later Dugan sat alone in a small waiting room at Doctor Sharon DeMarco's office. Doctor DeMarco was a fertility expert, and her suite was relentlessly optimistic in décor. This particular room was bright and cheerful, with two rows of four chairs each, facing each other across a low coffee table. There was a *faux* window looking out on a *faux* meadow painted on the wall to his right, and two real doors in the wall to his left. About two dozen well-worn magazines, all aimed at female readers, sat untouched on the table in front of him. At least it wasn't the room with the magazines that were there to help the wanna-be fathers produce. They were past that stage, thank God, although there was talk that it might come to that again.

Anyway, Dugan's mood clashed with the upbeat surroundings. After his *tête-à-tête* with Mollie he'd had a long, solitary lunch at a bar near home, and then walked two miles to the gym to work out. He'd have been better off back at his office arguing over the phone with insurance adjusters, because his conversation that morning with Kennison and Newhouse kept playing itself over in his mind.

He had no idea whether they believed his claim that he knew nothing at all about the disappearance of Harvey Starr – which was true. He told them he'd never had a conversation with Starr in his life beyond the occasional brief greeting on the street or in the courthouse. Never in his life, that is – and this he'd thought it best to tell them, although he hadn't wanted to – until about three o'clock the previous afternoon. That's when one of Dugan's law clerks had come back from filing motions and told him a man had stopped her in the hall at the Daley Center and asked her to tell Dugan that a lawyer named Harvey Starr would like Dugan to call him.

He told the investigators he'd made the call, and the conversation lasted only a few minutes. Starr had asked for a copy of a brief filed recently in the appellate court on behalf of a client of Dugan's, because Starr had a case which raised similar issues. 'We talked about it a little and then I told him to call Canning and Pratt, the law firm that handles most of my appeals,' Dugan said. 'And that was it. He thanked me and hung up.'

'Did he say who his client was?'

'Nope,' Dugan said. 'We didn't get that far.'

'Did he follow up? Did he call Canning and Pratt?'

'Beats me.'

'Uh-huh.' Kennison tugged on the sleeve of his sport coat, then looked up. 'So . . . this guy calls you on the afternoon before he's scheduled to meet with us and, as *you* say, asks for a copy of a brief. Did that seem . . . I don't know . . . *unusual* to you?'

'Well, lawyers do exchange research findings sometimes, to help each other out.'

'But this was a guy you say you barely knew,' Kennison said.

'That's right. So . . . yes, it was a little unusual.'

'And Harvey Starr,' this time it was Newhouse asking, 'is he well-known for doing a lot of legal research?'

'I have nothing on which to base an opinion about that,' Dugan answered. But he knew – and he was sure the two cops knew, too – that the answer was no.

So now here he was, sitting in this goddamn little room and wondering what those two detectives—

One of the doors flew open. 'Let's go,' Kirsten said. 'I'm getting claustrophobia.'

He stood up. 'Claustrophobia isn't something you *get* once in awhile,' he said. 'It's a condition you—'

'Dugan, please. I'm tired. I want to go home.' She closed the door she'd come through and opened the other one. She hurried down a short hallway – nearly running – into a larger waiting room, empty this late in the day.

He chased after her and when they were out in the building corridor, near the elevators, he grabbed her arm and slowed her down. 'Not much fun, huh?' he said.

She stopped and turned toward him. 'Dammit,' she said, 'hug me.'

So he did, and for quite a long time. 'And to think,' he said, rocking her gently from side to side, 'I spent my entire youth thinking making babies would be all fun and—' He caught himself. 'Sorry,' he said.

When she finally broke away there were tears in her eyes, but she smiled up at him. 'Thanks,' she said. 'I'm still tired, you know? But let's get something to eat, and then I want to go home.'

TEN

On Sunday they'd just started brunch at Lou Mitchell's, a landmark breakfast place near Union Station, when Kirsten suddenly looked at her watch. 'Oh my God,' she said, 'I forgot.' She stood up and threw her napkin on the table. 'Gotta run. Sorry!' She left Dugan struggling with too big a mouthful of the world's tastiest omelet, and ran outside and caught a cab. She knew he'd have objected . . . if he'd known where she was going.

The Bears were playing at home that afternoon and traffic was heavy around Soldier Field, even though the game didn't start until three. She'd planned for that, though, and with plenty of time to spare she was sitting on a stone ledge along the lakefront beside the Adler Planetarium, with a glorious view of the lake and the skyline. The autumn air was clear and clean, the ledge warmed by the sun. A very pleasant place to wait, even if waiting for a very unpleasant person.

There were lots of people around: some sitting and enjoying the warm sun and the view like she was; others strolling beneath the trees. There weren't the rows of school buses dropping off their cargoes that there'd have been on a weekday, but still there were lots of kids. A year ago she'd hardly have noticed them, but these days she had a heightened awareness of children.

She turned away and stared out at the lake. If she had to meet someone she despised – and, yes, feared – it helped that at least the wait was in one of those Chicago places she loved. Whenever someone told her they couldn't stand the winters here and were moving south, Kirsten would congratulate them . . . and breathe a secret sigh of gratitude. One less body to share these precious spaces with.

Of course, right now there was another body missing too. With ninety thousand lawyers in the state of Illinois, the fact that one of them hadn't been heard from for a day or two shouldn't have earned much media attention. But Harvey

Starr's disappearance was all over the news. Kennison and Newhouse thought it significant that a second person about to testify that Dugan paid Johnny O'Hern for cases had suddenly gone missing. Still, so far Dugan's name hadn't surfaced publicly. She wondered how long that would last, and—

'Hey! Wake up, for chrissake.' The man startled her. He was standing right behind her. 'Stand up and go over to . . . to that street . . . where the cars are parked.'

'It's called "Solidarity Drive",' she said, not turning around. 'Ever hear of Lech Walesa?'

'Just go wait beside the fucking cars.'

She knew who he must be and did as he said, and he followed her. When she reached the parked cars a black limo slid up and the rear door opened. The man behind her lifted her purse from her shoulder and she didn't object. She got into the car.

It wasn't a stretch limo, just a large, comfortable four-door Lincoln Town Car. The man closed the door behind her and got into the front passenger seat, and they were on their way. The driver maneuvered smoothly through traffic, and pulled on to Lake Shore Drive. Meanwhile, her companion in the back seat, a worthless, corrupt lizard named Polly Morelli, didn't say a word. He stared straight ahead, as though she weren't there.

He looked the same as when she'd last seen him, several years earlier. In his seventies, for sure, but still husky and solid, with his strong, square jaw and his hair combed straight back from his forehead . . . thick hair, and far too black to be natural. His skin was deeply tanned, and he looked like a man headed for the golf course, in khaki slacks and a forest green wool sweater.

They drove past Soldier Field, where the crowds were pouring in for the Bears' game. She found it ironic that this meeting was Morelli's idea, initiated by him while she'd still been unsure whether to contact him, and how to do it if she chose to. Now she sat there, looking out the window, determined not to speak first. The Lincoln sped southward, but when they passed McCormick Place, around Twenty-second Street, the driver angled sharply into the right lane and dropped well below the speed limit. That's when, finally, Morelli turned toward her. 'Your husband's a suspect in the Johnny O'Hern homicide,' he said.

'I'm fine, thank you,' she answered, 'and how are you?'

He lifted a well-manicured hand and waved it dismissively. 'What are you doing about it?' he asked.

'About the Johnny O'Hern homicide?'

'About your husband being a suspect in the murder of a police officer, and about how the public likes to see someone pay the price when a cop's killed.'

'No one's announced my husband as a suspect, and the dead police officer was as corrupt and as crooked as . . . well . . .'

'As I am?'

'Maybe not quite,' she said, and that didn't seem to bother him at all. 'Anyway, the cops think Dugan had some past business dealings with O'Hern. But lots of people did business with O'Hern. Word has it some of *your* people did. So . . . what are *you* doing about it?'

'If I had any "people", and if any of them were involved with O'Hern, maybe I'd have to do something. But I don't. And they weren't. So I don't have to.'

'OK. So then . . . what are we doing here?' *Here*, just then, was Lake Shore Drive at Forty-seventh Street. 'Which is to say,' she added, 'let's get to the point.'

'You owe me,' he said.

'Uh-uh. No way. You helped me, and I helped you. We're even.'

He shook his head. 'You wanted your husband back, and you got him. You owe me.'

She'd always known it would come to this. 'What is it you want?'

'I want to know whatever there is to know about who might have wanted Johnny O'Hern dead.'

'Why? None of your people – if you had any people – were involved, right?'

He gave her the same dismissive wave. 'There's something going on. I hear the heat's on big time to charge someone and put this case away . . . in a hurry.'

'Damn,' she said, 'you been talking to Bobby Becker?'

'Who?'

'Skip it. Anyway, why the heat?'

'I don't know. Maybe you'll find out. But what's important is that now you have a client. Besides your husband, I mean. I want a report on everything you learn.'

'I'm not shopping for a client.'

'You'll be well paid . . . if your information's good.' They were down around Fifty-fifth Street now, near the Museum of Science and Industry, and Morelli leaned toward the driver. 'Get off the Drive here, for chrissake, and go back north. I don't wanna get all the way down to Sixty-third, and be surrounded by fucking moolies.'

The idea of working for this guy turned her stomach. 'I'll think about your proposition, and get back to you.'

'I'll be in touch for your reports,' he said.

Once back on Lake Shore Drive and headed north, the limo picked up speed. Obviously, the meeting was over, and in no time they were passing McCormick Place again. To Kirsten's surprise the limo pulled right into a private parking area adjacent to Soldier Field and stopped beside a sleek silver RV the size of a bus. A group of well-tanned, mostly ageing, mostly overweight men huddled around a gigantic Weber grill that was pouring smoke into the clear fall air.

Without a word, Morelli and his bodyguard got out and joined the party, and the driver sped away with Kirsten. He stopped in front of the planetarium and gave her back her purse. She got out and didn't bother to watch him drive away, but headed back to sit beside the water.

There were even more people around now, mostly parents and children. The ones that really drew her attention were the smaller kids. Infants riding in strollers or in carriers slung over mommy's or daddy's shoulders; toddlers clinging to grandparents' hands and waddling along, swiveling their heads to take everything in; and pre-schoolers, running, falling down, picking themselves up again . . . some laughing, others crying. She seemed to be the only adult here without a child in tow.

The stone ledge was still warm from the sun, and she sat down and stared out at the sparkling lake . . . hoping her own child would be a laugher, not a crier. Hoping, though, wasn't the answer. How could she make sure her kid grew up happy? For that matter, how could she make sure her kid grew up at all? What would she have to do to make sure that happened? What would she have to *give up* doing?

The sun on the water was making her squint, and she dug into her purse for her shades . . . and her fingers hit the cool metal of the Colt 380. She stared down at that lethal weapon she too often carried and, as she did, she felt a sudden shift in her thinking. With her ears full of the cries and laughter of children, a bit of reality she'd been running from caught up with her. She felt suddenly frightened for the child she hadn't even conceived yet.

Maybe it was time to take a vacation from the fertility clinic. Just until she and Dugan could put this . . . situation . . . behind them. The threat to Dugan's law license; the murder of Johnny O'Hern with the heat turned up high and Dugan in the frying pan; the disappearance of a second person who might have testified against Dugan. All that was more than enough.

And now . . . Polly Morelli as a client?

ELEVEN

By the next morning, Monday, the temperature had dropped to the low sixties and the sky was dark and dismal. A fine day for the funeral of a dirtied-up police officer. And that funeral a fine place for Kirsten to eyeball Johnny O'Hern's family. She wanted to see them together, to form an impression before she spoke to each of them. If there really was pressure on the cops to close the O'Hern case, she couldn't sit around and hope they came up with a candidate other than Dugan.

Plus, there was Polly Morelli to keep happy. She didn't like being pushed around by low-life scumbags, even scumbags with chauffeured limousines. But she *did* owe Polly . . . although to his face she would always insist they were even. Without his help Dugan wouldn't even be alive now to be a homicide suspect. So she would give Polly the reports he demanded. She wouldn't take his dirty money, though. Which was only fair, since her reports might not always be complete.

Holy Martyrs Basilica was a huge church on the north-west edge of the city, in a suburban-like setting, with plenty of parking. There were few cars in the lot, though, and few people headed toward the church doors. Kirsten had attended maybe ten cop funerals and they'd all featured scores, some of them hundreds, of fellow officers showing solidarity with the family of a fallen comrade. None of those cops, of course, had been facing indictment when they went down.

She wasn't surprised that politicians and other notables stayed away, but she'd expected more gawkers, for the funeral of a crooked cop who'd been the victim of what the media kept suggesting – despite official denials of support for the idea – was a 'gangland-style execution'.

There were maybe a dozen uniformed cops standing around the church entrance, and three TV vans on the street. Sound and lighting guys in blue jeans and windbreakers scurried around, and reporters stood patting their hairdos and reviewing their scripts . . . and glancing up anxiously from time to time at the low-lying clouds.

Kirsten switched off her phone and went up the steps and into the vestibule. A uniformed cop, having apparently decided she wasn't about to blow the place up, let her into the church itself, where a woman funeral director in a navy blue suit solemnly handed her a program. It was a folder with a photocopied picture of O'Hern on the front, and an outline of the service inside, including the words to some hymns.

Somewhere along the line O'Hern had made sergeant, and an Irish Catholic police sergeant in Chicago might easily have brought out a bishop, if not the cardinal himself. But there'd be no hierarchy for Johnny O'Hern. He got just a priest, Father Wayne Watson, described in the program as 'Vicar General, Archdiocese of Chicago'.

Wondering what the hell a 'Vicar General' was, Kirsten went halfway up one of the side aisles, sat down in a pew, and looked around. The church was dimly lit and the air felt heavy, and smelled of fifty years of burning candles and incense. An organ played very softly, as though far off. The family hadn't entered yet, and there were maybe thirty people scattered through the huge church. Mostly older women. Maybe some of them friends, Kirsten thought, of Johnny's mother.

Ahead of her, in a pew near the front, sat a heavy-set black man whom she recognized as Superintendent of Police James Glascoe. She'd seen Glascoe on TV, saying he'd attend the funeral. He said O'Hern, although relieved of his duties, had not been charged with any crime before he was shot down, and that like any citizen under a mere cloud of suspicion he was presumed innocent, and he and his family deserved dignity and respect. Maybe it was said out of political savvy, but it sure sounded good.

When a subdued commotion arose at the rear of the church, she turned around to look. The wide doors at the end of the center aisle stood open. The casket had arrived, and police officers in dress uniform were gathered around it. Pall bearers, she thought, and maybe even a small honor guard.

The cops all stepped aside, though, and the family members started up the aisle, escorted by the woman in the navy suit. There were four of them, and from what Kirsten had learned so far, they had to be his mother, his father, a brother named Richard who was a criminal defense lawyer in Chicago, and a sister named Janice who taught at a college in Maryland. Johnny's ex-wife was a no-show, and they'd had one child, a son, who'd died in a drunk driving accident as a teenager. Although Janice's last name now was said to be Robinson, there was no sign of any spouse or children for either her or Richard.

Johnny's mother was maybe seventy, a heavy-set woman of medium height, fair-skinned and white-haired. She walked slowly and hesitantly, sobbing quietly and dabbing at her eyes with a tiny white handkerchief. Her daughter – tall, slender, and looking far younger in a simple black dress than Kirsten knew she must have been – walked smoothly beside her, eyes straight ahead, not touching her grieving mother. Behind them came Johnny's father, a dark, thin man who was a retired cop himself. He was stooped over and breathing seemed an effort for him, as though he had emphysema. He clearly had trouble walking, occasionally grabbing the ends of the pews he passed for support. Even so, as they were starting up the aisle Kirsten saw him refuse his son's offer of help. What struck Kirsten wasn't just the old man's waving the offer aside, but the clear disdain – the *meanness*, in fact – on his face when he did so. His son simply shrugged as though that attitude was nothing new, and walked beside him.

Watching the slow progress of this unhappy group, Kirsten suddenly thought of her own family. She'd loved and admired her dad, as did her brothers, and yet he'd died a tragically unhappy man. Her mom's final years had also been nothing but sadness, too much of it self-induced in Kirsten's view.

All this made her thankful again at how surprisingly satisfying her own life had become, but of course Dugan had a lot to do with that. She felt a wave of pity for her dead parents, and for Johnny O'Hern's parents, too – and suddenly wondered why everyone, herself included, took for granted that having kids was the road to happiness.

Once the family was settled into the front pew, a pleasant, middle-aged woman at a microphone up near the altar invited everyone to stand up and the organ music suddenly swelled into a solemn funeral march. Kirsten stood and watched as six solemn-faced cops processed stiffly up the aisle, a pitiful excuse for an honor guard. Behind them came the casket, riding on a wheeled cart and flanked by six pall bearer cops. Finally came Father Watson and two altar boys.

The woman at the mike told everyone when to stand and sit and kneel, which everyone did – except for O'Hern's father, who, apart from heaving his shoulders with his labored breathing, sat motionless. The woman announced the hymns, too, and lifted her arms and invited people to join in, but she was the only one who sang, while the organ pounded out the accompaniment. The priest went through the motions and droned on, obviously having been down this solemn road a thousand times. The ritual of the mass was familiar to Kirsten, too, from her childhood, and she found herself wondering if she'd ever take her own child to church. She decided probably not, which brought on a sadness which surprised her, but had more to do with nostalgia than with wishing she still believed in something she didn't.

There was no real eulogy, just a sermon consisting of a few generic words that could have been said at anybody's funeral. At communion time, about ten older women went forward to the railing, including O'Hern's mother. None of the other family members went. Then, in what seemed no time at all, the pall bearers and honor guard were lined up by the casket, ready to head back down the aisle.

Kirsten checked her watch. A forty-minute funeral. Not bad. Now she'd go straight to her car and drive to the cemetery on her own. She hated that business of getting into a slow-moving line of cars and playing follow-the-leader. She needn't have worried about that, though, because just then Father Watson announced: 'The family thanks you all for coming to share with them in their hour of grief. Please be advised that interment will be private.'

No one said anything about a post-funeral lunch.

TWELVE

Kirsten hurried out of the church before the procession got started down the aisle. The media people were still out there and she went over and mingled with them. When the church doors opened she pulled a camera from her purse and snapped some pictures of the funeral party coming out and down the steps. Then she went to her car.

She didn't care whether 'interment' was private or not. On the previous evening she'd called Holy Martyrs Basilica and easily talked the young woman who answered the phone into revealing that the burial would be at Madonna del Popolo Cemetery, just fifteen or twenty minutes away.

During the drive she decided that attending the funeral mass had been an informative first step. She'd learned that Johnny's ex-cop father was in poor health and was a mean sonovabitch she already didn't like. She'd also learned that Johnny's mother was a sad, passive-looking woman who shed tears for her son and practiced her religion, and who in her time of sorrow clung to no one . . . not her husband, not her surviving son, not even her only daughter.

She'd searched the web, and had already known that Johnny's brother, Richard, was forty-six – seven years younger than Johnny – and owned a two-flat building on the north side, near DePaul University, where he and his parents lived. She knew now that he didn't much resemble his dead brother, but looked a lot like his father . . . a father who treated him like a piece of rancid meat. And Janice, the middle child, the teacher in Maryland? The quick Internet search had turned up over a thousand Janice Robinsons. Whether this particular one was divorced, or widowed, or had a husband unwilling or unable to accompany her to her brother's funeral, was unclear. One thing, though, was certain: Janice hadn't felt moved to put her arm around her grieving mother.

Not much. Still, Kirsten was learning, bit by bit. Which bits might be helpful was another story.

Madonna del Popolo was a cemetery she had never been to, and she passed through the gate into acres and acres of rolling lawn and trees. Dark clouds still hung low in the sky, as they had all morning, and Kirsten drove along the curving roadways with her headlights on.

She had no 'thing' about dead bodies or burial grounds, and in fact she occasionally drove to a cemetery when she needed a quiet place to think, or just rest her mind. Sometimes she'd bring along a sandwich or a salad and sit in her car and make a picnic of it. No one ever bothered her. This time, though, it was all business, and she had to arrive well ahead of the O'Hern family. Otherwise she might be shut out, along with any media people that tried tagging along behind them.

She came to the burial chapel, a low brick building where what used to be the 'graveside service' could be held without subjecting the mourners to real world weather . . . or a real graveside. She drove past the chapel and circled around and found a spot where she could park, two wheels on the grass, and watch both the gate and the chapel from about fifty yards away. The other family members she could get to later, but Janice might want to beat it back to Maryland pretty quickly after her brother was in the ground.

She cut the engine and switched off the headlights, and when she did – as though on cue – the rain started to fall. Not a downpour, just enough of a drizzle to make her turn on the wipers. There was thunder, too; low, murmuring rumbles.

Time passed slowly and she was beginning to think maybe her information was bad, when a pickup truck came from behind the chapel and drove to the cemetery entrance. The driver, a man in green coveralls, got out and closed the gate. That didn't seem to bode well, but he got back in the pickup and didn't drive away. Moments later a hearse rolled up outside the gate and stopped, and behind it four cars: a black Lincoln funeral limo, a red Chevy Caprice, a brown four-door Ford sedan – which Kirsten easily recognized as a so-called 'unmarked' police car – and finally a blue-and-white Chicago patrol car. Following this short entourage was one of the TV vans she'd seen at the church.

The man in green coveralls got out of his truck and opened the gate. The hearse and the first three cars behind it came inside, and he closed the gate again. The blue-and-white stayed where it was, blocking the TV van. A cop got out and walked back and talked to the van driver, and eventually the driver turned the van around and drove away. Meanwhile, the pickup truck led the hearse and the three cars along the roadway to the chapel. Kirsten decided she'd let them go inside, then drive over and wait, and grab Janice when she came out.

Johnny's mother and brother left his father in the limo and went inside the chapel. Janice was driving the red Caprice, probably a rental, and the priest, Father Watson, had ridden with her. The two of them stayed in the car an extra minute or two, talking. They were quite a distance away, but it seemed to Kirsten that they were arguing about something. When they got out of the Caprice and went inside, she started her engine. She instinctively glanced in her rearview mirror . . . and saw a green car with an amber bubble light on the roof, coming up fast. It pulled around her, then stopped, blocking her way. It had *Cemetery Security* written on the side.

She could have argued, could have lied, could have cajoled – but what was the point? 'Cemetery's closed to the public,' the guy said, 'for the rest of the day. You'll have to leave.'

'Now?'

'Yes, ma'am,' came the answer. 'Now.'

That's when she looked across toward the burial chapel and saw Baxter Newhouse staring back at her through the open passenger window of the unmarked squad car.

She drove to the gate and the man from the pickup truck opened it for her, and closed it behind her as she left. She drove east, back toward the city, and hadn't gone far when it started to rain very hard. Yes, it was a fine day for a funeral. And yes, there was something strange going on in the O'Hern case.

She waited by a pay phone at a Shell station two blocks east of the cemetery, hoping the others would pass that way on their way back into the city. Twenty minutes later she saw the two investigators drive by in their Ford sedan, then the limo, then the hearse – this time with the priest in the passenger seat. No red Caprice, though, so Kirsten pulled out and headed back toward the cemetery.

Approaching the entrance, she saw the gate standing wide open, but she went on by, driving fast through the rain. It seemed unlikely that Janice might still be in there. She was probably on the road and headed west.

Kirsten got a break with traffic, and caught all the lights as they turned green. Still, she was a bit surprised when she actually spotted Janice ahead of her. 'Good karma,' she whispered, and fell in two cars behind the red Caprice. She followed it all the way on to I-294, south to the O'Hare ramp, down the multi-lane road toward the terminals, and on to the exit marked *Rental Car Return*.

A few minutes later she was sitting in the parked Camry, wondering where she'd gone wrong in life, watching Janice return the key to the Avis people and board a shuttle bus marked *Departure Terminals*.

THIRTEEN

On her way back into the city Kirsten checked her phone messages. There was a call from Richard O'Hern, asking her to call back. That Johnny's brother would contact her seemed odd, but that was nothing compared to the second message.

This was a man, too – that much seemed certain – but he spoke in a harsh whisper, obviously to disguise his voice. 'I want to help,' he said. 'I have to tell *someone*, and maybe you . . . Officer O'Hern's death, I . . . I heard about it. I think it might be connected to the murder of a priest, last year. Father Landrew. I can't . . . I don't know. Maybe you . . .' He sounded scared to death, and he hung up.

Landrew? The name took a moment to register, and even then she couldn't recall many details, but about a year earlier a priest named Landrew had been shot in a robbery behind his church, in a poverty-stricken neighborhood on Chicago's west side.

Neither caller ID nor the call-back feature produced a

number, so she played the anonymous message again – several times. There was something naggingly familiar about the disguised voice. Whoever he was, the man claimed knowledge – or at least a suspicion – about a homicide. So why tell *her*? Why not the police?

She called the number Richard O'Hern had left, and got his law office. His secretary said he wasn't in, and Kirsten said she'd call back. She wouldn't call back, though. She'd go right to his office. That's the number he left, so he must have planned to go there after the funeral.

First, though, she had something else to do.

'Dugan left fifteen minutes ago.' Mollie shook her head. 'Said he was spending his lunch hour at the Art Institute.' There was real worry apparent in Mollie's eyes as she looked up at Kirsten. 'It's just so . . . strange, isn't it?'

'Strange? The Art Institute?'

'Not that. But, I mean, in all the years since he took over from his father, I never heard him speak of his "lunch hour". Until now. He mentions "lunch" sometimes, of course. As in "I'll grab lunch on my way to the deposition." But the idea of taking an hour away from work, for lunch? That's unheard of.'

'Yes, well, maybe you should take a lunch hour yourself, Mollie. Get out and walk around.' Kirsten knew Mollie brought her own lunch with her every day and never went out – to eat, shop, go to the doctor, or for any other reason – from the time she arrived in the morning until she left in the evening.

'Are you kidding?' Mollie looked genuinely shocked. 'I'm already so far behind in my work that I can't—'

'I understand.' Kirsten smiled. 'I'll go find Dugan.'

As she turned and headed for the exit she tried Dugan's cell phone, but he had it turned off . . . which was about as unheard of as a lunch hour.

The Art Institute of Chicago was on Michigan Avenue, near Adams, five blocks from Dugan's office. On a warmer, sunnier day there would have been people scattered all over the broad expanse of steps up to the entrance: office workers chatting and eating their lunches, tourists taking each other's pictures by one of those two huge bronze lions. But that day the steps were cold and wet, and no one loitered on them.

You could spend a week in the Art Institute looking for someone, but Kirsten knew just where to go. She and Dugan had memberships, and they both pretty much stuck to the old favorites – Impressionists and early twentieth century American artists. Maybe her new membership in the Museum of Contemporary Art would widen her horizon a bit.

She found him – very much the downtown lawyer in his white shirt, striped tie, and blue suit – but was surprised to find him sitting down. His general approach to great art was to look at a painting or a sculpture for a few seconds, and move on to the next one. But today there he was, arms folded, sitting stiffly on a backless bench in front of Georges Seurat's *A Sunday Afternoon on the Island of La Grande Jatte*.

She could see the side of his face, but he hadn't spotted her. He was staring straight at the huge painting and she doubted he even saw it . . . or anything beyond whatever was playing inside his head. She realized then that Dugan, who prided himself on being able to handle whatever came along, was deeply worried about this bogus murder charge.

We're gonna beat this thing, Dugan. She sent the thought his way. *Whatever it takes, we're gonna beat it. Don't worry.*

She circled around and came up behind him. 'That there pi'ture ain't much,' she whispered, and touched his shoulder. She knew she'd startled him, but he hid it well. 'Just a lotta little dots, when you get up real close.'

'Please,' he said, still not moving, 'don't stiff-arm culture.' But then he turned, clearly so happy to see her that it sent a shiver through her like a sip of cold champagne.

'Hi,' she said, and sat beside him.

He kissed her on the cheek and she felt the same chill. 'How'd you find me?'

'I'm a detective,' she said. 'But I have to say, you worried the hell out of my source.' She noticed they'd caught the attention of the guard – a middle-aged black woman standing near the door – so she kept to a soft whisper, with her eyes on the painting in front of them, as though they were discussing it.

'Your source was Mollie,' he said. 'She thinks the end is near.' He stared down at his hands, massaging one of them with the other. 'And maybe she's right.'

'Damn, Dugan, you're *not* going to jail.' She elbowed him

in the side, surprised at how his attitude had nosedived. 'The cops'll come up with a legitimate suspect and—'

'Who's talking about jail? Or the cops? Screw them and their— Oops!' He'd forgotten to whisper, and he pointed at the guard. She was coming toward them, wagging a forefinger.

'Let's get out of here,' Kirsten said.

She was hungry, but she knew that by the time they got to a restaurant Dugan's macho defenses would have kicked in again, so she hustled him through a warren of exhibition rooms, and downstairs to a sort of lobby area. She pulled him to a bench and they sat down again.

'OK,' she said, 'where were we?'

'We were sitting in front of Seurat's *A Sunday After—*'

'Don't *do* that, Dugan.' She stared at him. 'I need to know what's going on in your head. And don't tell me you aren't worried about something.'

'I'm not worried. I'm . . . concerned. About the end of my law practice.'

'But you've said all along that that wasn't a big deal.'

'It wasn't, not as long as it was just speculative . . . or in the future sometime. This morning, though, I got served with a subpoena from . . . from that Peter Pan person.'

'Gina Chan? At the ARDC?'

'Right.'

'Jesus, Dugan, you don't even *like* practicing law.'

'What's "like" have to do with anything? I mean . . . part of it is . . . what are my employees gonna do? Fred and Peter, and Larry Candle. And Mollie, and the rest of the staff . . . secretaries, clerks, paralegals. They all depend on me for their livelihood.'

'Um . . . excuse me, Hercules,' she shook her head, 'but I've got a surprise for you. The world . . . the one you think is resting on your shoulders? It's going to keep on going, with you or without you.'

'It's Atlas you're thinking of, not Hercules. But anyway, I can't just leave them all out in the cold.'

'Mollie and Fred and Peter should all retire. They're only still working so they don't have to sit down and figure out what the hell else to do. You'd be doing them a favor. The clerks and paralegals come and go, anyway. And Larry?

Unfortunately, he'll survive . . . whether the rest of the world likes it or not.'

'Yeah . . . well . . .' He was fumbling around and she knew he was beginning to acknowledge that he'd been puffing up his own importance. 'Anyway,' he finally said, 'that's what's bothering me.'

'OK, but you said that was *part* of it. So what's the other part?'

'I . . . that was just a manner of speaking.'

'Bullshit. What else is bugging you?'

'It's . . . well . . . it's the baby,' he said.

'What?' She was stunned. 'I thought we were both on the same—'

'No . . . wait . . .' He must have seen the shock on her face. 'I don't mean I don't *want* a baby. What I mean is, without my license how am I gonna support him? Or her? Or whatever? Do you have any idea how much college will—'

'I get it.' Relief swept through her. 'So the big strong ox has to pull the wagon uphill . . . and suffer and hate his life . . . until he drops in his tracks. And all so the little wifey can play at her pretend job, while he gives the kiddies a better life than he had.'

He stared at her. 'You're making fun of me, goddammit.'

'What . . . me?' She stood up. 'Let's go get some lunch.'

FOURTEEN

At about two o'clock Dugan stood on the sidewalk outside the restaurant and watched Kirsten walk away. He still didn't know what lay ahead for him, but just being with her lifted his spirits. Finally, when she was around the corner and lost from view, he turned and walked to his building and up to his suite . . . and found two detectives waiting.

Kennison sat with his arms spread wide and draped over the chairs on either side of him, looking full of himself, like a man back in the dugout after hitting a homer. Newhouse, though, was standing, arms crossed, looking pissed off but resigned . . . like a manager whose slugger had just ignored his bunt signal.

Dugan led them back to his office, and when they were all sitting down he said, 'I suppose it's not Larry Candle you're here to see.'

'Nope,' Kennison said.

'Well, you know me. Always the cooperative witness.'

'First,' Newhouse said, 'I have to tell you this: You have the right to remain silent, but if—'

'Cooperative,' Dugan interrupted. 'And exercising his rights, starting now.'

'Whatever,' Kennison said.

Both officers stood and Kennison reached to his belt behind his back and came out with handcuffs. Newhouse, though, stepped in front of him. 'Since you're being cooperative,' he said to Dugan, 'we won't need the cuffs.'

'I appreciate that, Investigator. Thank you.'

He stood up and stretched his arms out to his sides and spread his legs, while Newhouse searched him. On the way out, Dugan told Mollie he probably wouldn't be back that afternoon.

FIFTEEN

Kirsten walked north on LaSalle Street, passing City Hall and the State of Illinois Building. She'd spent a good part of lunch trying to convince Dugan that she wasn't the only one who deserved to do work she felt good about.

She had quit the police department to escape a world where cruelty and violence were part of the air you breathed. She tried a job with a security agency, but finally found her niche as an independent private investigator. And Dugan? When his dad died he'd gladly left the state's attorney's office to take over his dad's law practice. The income was great, but he was shut up in his office fifty or sixty hours a week.

The important thing, Kirsten had argued, was to live the life he wanted. She insisted he shouldn't worry about finances. Between them they would always manage. She'd been adamant about that.

Now, though, she walked and thought of the baby soon to

be on its way . . . once she managed to get pregnant. Kids were terribly expensive, and the expenses went on for years and years, and . . . well . . . they *would* manage, dammit. She had to be as adamant with herself as she'd been with Dugan.

She passed under the El tracks at Lake Street and came to Wacker Drive, which runs east and west at that point, alongside the Chicago River. At LaSalle and Wacker she went inside, up to the fourteenth floor, and down the hall to a door with the names of about a dozen lawyers. They were all listed separately, which meant they were sole practitioners who shared the rent and other expenses for a suite of offices. One of them was Richard J. O'Hern, and the others were probably all criminal defense attorneys like he was.

She entered a small room where two people waited. One was a distraught-looking heavy-set woman and the other a husky, sullen teenager who might have been her son or her grandson, listening to music on an iPod that probably would have cost the woman's weekly pay check if she'd bought it – which she probably hadn't. Kirsten walked to the receptionist's window and said she was there to see Richard O'Hern.

'I'm sorry, ma'am,' the young woman said, 'but Mr O'Hern has had a death in his family and isn't seeing anyone today.'

Kirsten insisted, though, and in the end she proved the receptionist wrong.

Richard came out and led her back to a large office that smelled of overheated coffee. Law books lined the shelves along one wall, and file folders were stacked in piles on a long table against another. A smaller table held a coffee-maker and two small speakers hooked up to a Sony Walkman, the sort of thing the sullen kid in the waiting room probably dumped when he stole his iPod. She sat in one of the client's chairs and Richard handed her a mug of dark, bitter coffee. He refilled his own, too, and then sat down behind a mahogany desk that was covered with papers. A computer – turned off – rested behind him on a matching credenza, along with lots more file folders.

Despite the clutter, the room seemed well-organized, if not exactly comfortable. There were some framed law licenses and certificates on the wall, but no other pictures or photographs.

She decided to get condolences out of the way first. 'I'm sorry for your loss,' was all she could muster.

'Johnny's death wasn't a true loss to anyone I know of, other than my mother,' he answered, 'and she lives in another world.'

'Oh, I'm sorry. Is it Alzhei—'

'It's a fantasy world, one I've been a witness to all my life. A world in which Johnny was a good boy and a good son, and grew into a fine man and a fine police officer.'

'I take it you don't share that view.'

In lieu of an answer he sipped some of his coffee, then looked at her. 'What is it you want to learn from me?'

That startled her. 'You called *me*, Mr O'Hern.'

'I saw you at the cemetery. Why else would you be there but to learn something . . . and from whom but me? My mother and father sure wouldn't be much help. And as far as I know my sister hasn't been in Chicago, or in touch with anyone in the family, for thirty years.'

'Did Investigator Newhouse tell you anything about me?'

'Yes, he said you were looking into Johnny's murder. The white cop, Kennison, told me I didn't have to talk to you.' Richard gave a slight smile. 'I told him criminal law is my profession. I *know* who I don't have to talk to.'

'But here we are.'

'Newhouse was different. He was careful what he said, but it's clear he respects you. He said you were interested because of your husband's . . . well . . . possible involvement.'

'So you'll answer a few questions?'

He lifted his mug, then set it down again. 'When Johnny found out he was under federal investigation he retained counsel. Naturally he stiffed the guy on his fees and the guy quit. So Johnny came to me.'

'To represent him?'

'Yes, but I couldn't represent my own brother, so I referred him to Chris Baker, whose office is two doors down.' He pointed. 'Still, since Johnny consulted me with a view to retaining me, what he told me would be privileged. You understand that, right?' When she nodded he went on. 'The privilege was his, not mine, and as far as I know he didn't waive it.'

'Yes, but—'

'But he's dead. And whatever the legal arguments are, one

way or the other, I'm assuming he'd waive the privilege if he could, so I told the cops what little I learned from him, and what little else I know. I'll tell you, too.'

She was surprised at his easy willingness to help her, but she dug into her purse for a pen and said, 'Let's get—'

'Hold on,' he said. 'Don't you want to know *why* I'd help the wife of a suspect in my own brother's homicide?'

She looked up. 'I don't know that Dugan's technically a "suspect", but yes, the question had occurred to me.'

'It's because I want to hire you to investigate my brother's murder.'

'What?' She almost dropped her pen. 'Why?'

'I want to know what happened.'

'Right, but . . . anyway . . . I already have a client.'

'I know, your husband, but I'm not convinced. Anyone with half a brain knows that killing a cop – even a cop like Johnny – turns on a lot of heat. I think the fear of losing a law license is a pretty slim motive.'

'The cops don't seem to think so.'

'Maybe not, but even if they charge him I don't think they'll get a conviction.'

'So who do *you* think did it?'

'I don't know. That's why I'm hiring you.'

'Like I said, I already have a client.' She already had two clients, actually, but didn't say so.

'Now you'll have another. There's no conflict of interest. We both want all the facts uncovered.'

'Of course you do,' she said, though beginning to wonder just how true that was. 'The thing is, you obviously didn't even *like* your brother, so why the expense of hiring a private investigator?'

'Johnny was seven years older than I. He stayed away from home as much as possible and, growing up, I barely knew him. What I did know – both as a kid and later on – I didn't like. The guy was a bully, a mean bastard, all his life. He took everything he could, however he could, from anyone he could – including his own family.' He swiveled his chair to face the window, which looked out across the river at the buildings on the north bank, then turned back to her. 'But this particular mean bastard was my brother. I paid the lawyer I got to represent him . . . and I'll pay you.'

'It's actually an interesting idea,' she said. It wasn't the fee that attracted her, but the information he might provide. 'All right, then,' she said, 'three thousand a week, each week in advance. Plus expenses.'

He flinched, but to her surprise he said, 'I'll have a check to you tomorrow. I'll want frequent progress reports.'

'I understand,' she said, although she didn't . . . not at all. 'My reports, though, won't be in writing. I don't have the staff for that.' He nodded and she said, 'So . . . let the investigation begin.' She paused. 'What do you know about a priest named Landrew?'

'What?' He stared at her like she was crazy.

'Just asking,' she said. 'Do you know anything about him?'

'The name sounds familiar, but I don't—'

'Let's try an easier question: Who do you think had a motive to murder your brother?'

Richard drank some more coffee, then set down his mug and frowned at it. 'I'm sure he had more enemies than I'll ever—' His phone buzzed and he grabbed it and said, 'I'm out,' and hung up again. Then to Kirsten he said, 'There's a bar on the first floor of this building. I want a drink.'

SIXTEEN

They sat in a booth in a comfortable bar called Hatfield's. At that time of the day the place was nearly empty and they were served right away. Kirsten took a sip from a surprisingly good Pinot Grigio. 'So,' she said, 'tell me who wanted Johnny dead.'

'That list could take all afternoon, but I'll stick to people with an actual motive for murder.' Richard took a hefty swig from his scotch and soda and waved to the waitress. He already wanted another. 'Some of this comes from what Johnny told me, but a lot of it comes from what I put together from news reports and talk on the street.'

He told her how a few years earlier Johnny had found himself with money to invest. Someone put him in touch with a man named Barry Zelander, who developed strip malls in the city, and who had lots of connections, some of them political, some mob-related. The two of them went into business together. They did quite well for a time, with Zelander bribing city officials when necessary, and with Johnny acting as 'enforcer' when the need arose, such as when some immigrant didn't want to sell out his little business that was in the way of one of their projects, or when some mope didn't pay what he owed Zelander. Things fell apart when Zelander came under federal investigation, and the net snagged Johnny as well. There were questions first about his complicity in the bribery schemes, and eventually about the money he invested with Zelander, such as where he got it, and whether he paid taxes on it.

The waitress arrived with a second scotch for Richard, and when she was gone Kirsten spoke up. 'I take it your brother was the easier of the two for the feds to break down.'

'From all appearances,' he said, 'Zelander's stonewalling them. He has a powerful lawyer, a lot of money – and I mean *a lot* – and some high level friends. But still, he's in much better shape with Johnny out of the way.'

'But I understand they have other witnesses lined up,' she said, 'including people he bribed. I hear some of them were wired.'

'Maybe, but recordings aren't always clear, witnesses don't always hold up . . . and anyway, Johnny may have had stuff on Zelander that nobody else did. I don't have any details, but he obviously knew of the strong-arm methods the two of them used against property owners, and he may have been aware of some mob involvement – investment, probably – in some of their deals.'

'So the Outfit guys may be better off with Johnny out of the way, too,' Kirsten said, 'but you mentioned "a few" paths I might go down.'

'Yeah, well, the kind of money Johnny had to invest with Zelander didn't come in his pay check. He was a cop on the west side for years, much of that in the narcotics division. And Johnny? I'd be surprised if he wasn't on the take.' Richard drank more of his scotch. He was taking it in large doses now. 'Hell, he may have been partnered up with some of those dope-dealing gang-bangers.'

'And you think some of *them* might have wanted him shut up, too?'

'They might. But those mopes would be too dumb to find him, and most of them are probably dead already. But there'd be other cops in on it with him. He couldn't have dealt with those assholes on his own.' Richard drained his second scotch and soda. 'With your husband, Johnny talks and his law license goes out the window. But a cop? Johnny talks and the guy gets put in a cage with the animals.' He waved to the waitress. 'Make it a double,' he called, 'and forget the soda.' His face was becoming flushed, to go with his loosening tongue.

The waitress nodded to Richard and looked inquiringly at Kirsten, who shook her head and lifted her glass, showing she was still on her first Pinot. 'So,' she said, 'one, there's this guy Barry Zelander; two, some unknown Outfit people; and three, some unknown cops. Who's your first choice?'

'I don't know. That's why I hired you.'

The waitress set Richard's third drink on the table and he reached for it. 'OK,' Kirsten said, 'tell me about your family.'

The glass stopped halfway to his mouth. 'What are you talking about?'

'I need to know about Johnny, what made him what he was.' She paused. 'It's a sort of . . . I don't know . . . a compass I use in a case with too many suspects, to help point me in the right direction.' What she didn't say was that family members were always among the first potential suspects to be ruled out . . . or ruled in.

'The cops didn't ask about the family.'

'No, but I did.' She smiled at him. 'For example, I'd have thought you couldn't care less who killed a brother who took all he could, however he could . . . even from his family. But you *do* care, so there had to be something to make you care. That could be helpful, you know?'

'I don't see how.'

'I don't either, not yet,' she said. 'But humor me. What made Johnny tick? Let's start with your father. How'd he treat Johnny? He doesn't seem to like *you* much.'

'He's treated me like shit all my life, but he treated Johnny even worse. Turned the kid into the kinda man *he* was – only more so. Johnny was a bastard, y'know? But what no one ever thinks of is that Johnny never had a chance to be anything else.' Richard took a slug of scotch. 'You wanna know my first real clear memory of my father and Johnny? It was just before Christmas when I was . . . four, maybe five years old . . . which would make Johnny maybe eleven.' Richard sat back and blew out his breath.

Taking a tiny sip of her wine, Kirsten kept her eyes on him. And didn't say anything.

'Our home was never what you'd call cheerful,' he said, 'but that day was a pretty good one. Johnny and my sister and I were helping my mother decorate the tree. It was supposed to be a nice surprise for my father, but when he got home he was . . . well . . . I know now he was drunk. All I knew then, though, was that he was talking loud, said he didn't care about any goddamn Christmas tree. My mother said supper wasn't ready and he went into a rage. I guess it wasn't the first time, but it's the first one I have a real memory of.

'He yelled and cursed, and then went over and picked up the Christmas tree, stand and all, and swung it around the living room, knocking over a lamp, sending ornaments smashing against the walls. My sister was screaming and Johnny was telling him to stop, but . . . Anyway, I just shrank back and watched. My mother ran into the kitchen and my father, still carrying the Christmas tree, started after her. I guess Johnny thought he was gonna hit her with the tree. He was still a little kid then, but he ran over and started pounding my father on the back with his fists.

'My father dropped the tree and turned around and grabbed Johnny and dragged him into the kitchen. Janice and I watched from the door. My father was asking my mother if a boy who hits his own father should be taught a lesson. Johnny kept screaming, "Don't let him hurt me, mom. I was trying to help you." She . . . she didn't answer him. Just went ahead starting supper. I know she was scared . . . but she didn't try to help Johnny. My father took him to the basement and we heard him whipping Johnny with a belt. Then he came upstairs and yelled that Johnny could spend the night down there, and locked the basement door.

'I guess we had supper . . . I really don't remember . . . but I know that after my father fell asleep my mother went and let Johnny out. He was in just his underwear and he had terrible red welts and bruises on the backs of his legs. I remember my mother crying and warning us not to tell anyone, saying Johnny shouldn't have done what he did. She said we owed everything to our father, and being a policeman was a hard job. Johnny just stared at her, didn't say anything. She tried to hug him, but he pulled away and left the room.' Richard shook his head. 'He sure never stood up for her again. From that day on, though, she treated him special, trying to make up I guess, but it didn't do any good. He treated her like dirt.'

Richard picked up his glass, saw that it was empty, and set it down again and stared at it.

'Did your father beat *everybody* in the family?'

'What?' He looked up. 'Oh . . . no. He maybe slapped me a couple times, that's all. I had asthma, y'know? I grew out of it, but . . . anyway, I stayed out of his way. Like I say, though, he was always worse with Johnny, lots of physical stuff, at least till Johnny got big enough to hit him back. I don't think he ever actually hit my mother, or my sister. But verbal abuse? Sonovabitch wrote the book.' He drank whatever few drops were left in the bottom of his glass, and waved to the waitress for another. 'Any more questions?'

'Yes,' she said, 'but I think they'll have to wait. You don't look so good.'

'I'm fine.' He stood up. 'I'll be right back.'

He headed for the men's room and while he was gone the waitress brought his fourth drink – scotch, no soda – and Kirsten added a little water to it while she waited.

He came back and sat down, and picked up his glass. 'It's a long time since I've had more than one or two drinks. This'll be my last.'

'OK, but let me ask just this: why was Johnny's funeral at that particular church? Did he live way out there? Did he attend there, or something?'

'Are you kidding? Johnny's been in church probably once since he got out of eighth grade . . . for his wedding. Which is once more than I've been. I got married and divorced by the same judge. But anyway, my mother couldn't stand her beloved Johnny not having a Catholic funeral. She went to the parish where we live – I own a two-flat, with her and my father on the first floor and me on the second – and the priest told her no way. Can you believe it? She goes to mass every goddamn day, and they won't bury her son because he didn't live in the parish and he had a bad reputation.'

'Seems sort of cold.'

'I mean . . . she's not a big giver, either. My dad gets his police pension . . . but he keeps her on a tight allowance. Bastard doesn't pay me any rent, either. So there's my mother, moping around and weeping about how her son deserves a Catholic funeral. I mean, he never showed her a goddamn thing but his back. Anyway, my sister can't take my mother's moaning, so she goes and finds a priest that'll do it. My *sister*, for chrissake. We haven't heard a word from her in twenty-five years, since she graduated high school and went off to college on a scholarship the nuns got her. And then suddenly she shows up. I mean, I didn't *like* Johnny much, but Janice *hated* him. I guess she read about the murder somewhere.'

'How did she find a church for the funeral if she doesn't even live around here?'

'Hell, I guess she called the cardinal's office and gave them a hard time until they passed her along to this priest – this Father Watson, who's a high level bureaucrat at the archdiocese – and he said he'd do the funeral himself, at the church where he lives.' He took a drink of his watered-down scotch. 'Guy's a real inspirational speaker, huh? But at least he *did* it.'

'He rode with your sister to the cemetery. Do they know each other somehow?'

'I don't know how they *would*. No, she just said she called Thursday morning and kept demanding to talk to the cardinal, and they finally gave her to this guy Watson. As for the ride to the cemetery, I think he just didn't feel comfortable spending that much time in the limo with my parents. I know I didn't.'

'When they got there it looked to me like your sister and he were arguing.'

'Yeah? Well, my mother was moaning about the guy not saying one damn personal thing about Johnny during the whole funeral. Janice said she gave him hell about that.'

'He *was* a little formal,' Kirsten said. 'But Janice . . . what college did she go to?'

'It's called Mount Saint Joseph College, in Maryland, some little town north of Baltimore. She's still there, on the faculty.'

'Really. Teaching what?'

'Literature, I think. We didn't really talk a lot while she was here. She stayed in a hotel and I didn't see her all that much. Of course, I don't know her at all, and—' He stopped short, then made a gulping sound, then a belch. 'Oh shit,' he said, and got up and stumbled toward the men's room.

Kirsten paid for the drinks and gave the waitress an extra twenty. 'Don't serve him another drink,' she said. 'And follow him out, would you? And make sure he finds a cab. He just had a death in his family.'

Then she went outside to wave down a cab for herself.

SEVENTEEN

Dugan climbed into the back seat of the unmarked squad car and Newhouse slid in beside him. Kennison got behind the wheel. 'Shoulda cuffed the sonovabitch,' he growled.

Newhouse ignored him and turned to Dugan. 'You sure you want to play it this way? Fifth amendment bullshit?'

'Wouldn't you?' Dugan asked. He leaned back in his seat, and after a long moment of silence he said, 'I take it there's been some new development in the case.'

'What sort of development would that be?' Newhouse asked, twisting around to look out the back window, seemingly more interested in something behind them than in Dugan's musings.

'How would I know?' Dugan answered, and knew at once that he shouldn't have said a goddamn thing. Newhouse wouldn't forget it, might even put it in his report. *The defendant was aware, ladies and gentlemen of the jury, without having been told, that there had been a significant new development in the case.*

Dugan thought he'd better get a lawyer.

The sign outside the building said Area Three Headquarters, and they marched him up the stairs to the second floor, and into the sort of small room the cops call an 'interview room'. They left him there, alone, with the door closed.

It was meant to be nerve-wracking, but Dugan had never had any claustrophobic feelings, and his past experience gave him an advantage over most arrestees – at least the first-timers. He couldn't be certain, because these places looked much alike all over the city, but he'd probably been in this very room before. He'd certainly been in Area Three many times.

During his time in the State's Attorney's office – not long, once he discovered how many of his co-prosecutors were way more interested in conviction rates than justice – he'd done his share of 'Felony Review' duty, which meant being available around the clock to review arrests. He'd talk to the cops, read their reports, sometimes interview witnesses or arrestees, and then make a decision as to whether the evidence warranted felony charges. Knowing what he knew so far, he certainly wouldn't have given the go-ahead for a charge against him, but then, no one had told him what it was they had . . . or what they thought they had.

No one had asked if he wanted to make a phone call, either. He didn't. Not yet. He had a couple of ideas about lawyers he might call to represent him, but that could wait a little longer. Mollie, who already knew he wouldn't be back that day, didn't need to know any more at this point. And Kirsten? They'd made no dinner plans, and both of them frequently worked late, so she wouldn't miss him, at least not for awhile. He'd rather not call her until he knew more about what was going on – like whether, once they tried to question him some more, they'd release him . . . or charge him with homicide.

The thing to do now was to sit and wait calmly for them to come back and ask their questions. When they did, his responses would all be the same: silence. No matter what they asked, even the easy questions. Except, maybe, whether he needed to use the bathroom.

EIGHTEEN

Kirsten left Hatfield's, planning to go to the two-flat where Richard and his parents lived, and to interview the O'Herns. In the cab, though, she felt a strange frenetic sense that she was falling behind, that she had to move faster. Which meant, she decided, that she ought to slow down . . . and think. She'd let the O'Herns recover from their son's funeral.

She told the driver to take her to the Lakeview Y, and after a workout and a shower she felt better, calmer. When she got to the condo Dugan wasn't there. Staying late at the office, she thought, making up for his unprecedented 'lunch hour'.

She sat down with a glass of tonic water and some crackers and listened – over and over again – to the anonymous message on her voice mail. Finally she rinsed out her glass, changed her clothes, retrieved her Camry, and drove back up to Holy Martyrs Basilica.

A young woman, a teenaged girl, really, was the evening receptionist at the rectory. Kirsten asked to see Father Watson and the girl said, 'Sure. What's your name, please?'

'Just tell him I need to talk to him. It's about . . . about the man who was murdered. He'll know.'

The girl stared at her. 'Oh . . . I'm sorry . . . you must be the one who called Tuesday. I'll get him. You can wait in here.' She led Kirsten to a little office and closed the door as she left.

The floor was carpeted, the walnut desk was highly polished, and the chairs looked comfortable. Still, the room reminded Kirsten of a police station interview room. That's because the only window, a large picture window, didn't look outside, but back into the reception area she'd just passed through. It was clear glass, though, not the sort of one-way mirror that would let cops observe without being seen. She decided the window was there to avoid allegations of misconduct taking place inside the office.

She turned a chair so she could see through the window and sat down. She watched the receptionist pick up a phone and talk into it, then replace it. Ten minutes passed, while the girl sat and read a school textbook lying open on the desk before her. Finally, at eight thirty, she stood up. She slipped on her jacket, obviously getting ready to leave, when Father Watson came into sight. He stopped and spoke with the girl and, though Kirsten couldn't hear him, he seemed to be reassuring her about something.

Kirsten judged the priest to be mid-fortyish. He was of medium height, with a kindly, pleasant face, and thinning black hair. He smiled as he talked to the girl, but he seemed ill-at-ease. He had a tan that spoke of time spent on the beach or the golf course – or maybe the tanning salon. Did priests go to those places?

The receptionist left and Father Watson came into the office. He stood just inside the door, not closing it. 'Sorry to take so long,' he said, with a quick, nervous smile, 'but I . . . uh . . . I had no idea anyone was coming.' Twisting a ring on his right hand, he added, 'People don't . . . you know . . . generally come in without an appointment.'

'Really. Well, I *often* do that.' She stared straight at him, hoping to raise his discomfort level even higher. She was certain he knew who she was and why she was there. She didn't dislike him. On the contrary, he'd taken a big step, despite his fears, and she was ready to admire him for that. She did not, however, plan to let him off the hook. 'So,' she said, 'let's talk.'

'I don't think that's . . .' He didn't finish. 'I'm on my way over to choir practice. It's probably almost over and I can't just skip it, because the choir's one of the few responsibilities I have here in the parish.'

'Your main job's at archdiocesan headquarters, right? The chancery office?'

'We call it the "Pastoral Care Center" now,' he said. 'I'm the vicar general, and I really don't—'

'Look, I'm *not* going away.'

'Well . . . all I *do* for the choir is encourage them, so . . . I suppose you could come with me to the church and we could talk there.'

'Great,' she said. 'Let's go.'

A well-lighted walk led from the rectory to the church, and as they got closer Kirsten could hear the organ playing, but couldn't hear any singing. Using a side door, they passed through a tiny vestibule, went up a short stairway, and then entered the church itself. They came out right up in the front, in a marble-floored area close to the altar, five or six steps higher than the main body of the church.

From there, looking out over row after row of pews, and in the dim illumination from just a few floodlights in what must have been a four-story high ceiling, the church seemed even larger than it had that morning. She guessed that it sat over five hundred people. In the rear, above the main entrance doors, was the choir loft. That area was brightly lit. The organist sat facing the organ, with her back to the church. Maybe a dozen choir members, men and women, stood to one side, facing her.

The priest's heels clicked on the marble floor as he led Kirsten across to the steps and then down to the red carpeted main floor. When they reached the head of the center aisle, he stopped and stared up at the choir loft. Meanwhile, the organist played a few notes, sang the words herself, then had the others sing the same phrase. Over and over.

Kirsten was thinking it wasn't a very catchy tune, when suddenly the priest called out very loudly, 'It sounds *wonderful*, Francine. Very nice. *All* of you. *Very* nice.' His voice echoed in the empty church.

They all called back, 'Thank you, Father,' in unison, reminding Kirsten of fifth grade. Then the director – Francine, certainly – said, 'Come join us, Father. We could use another baritone.'

'I'm afraid not,' he called. 'There's someone here,' gesturing toward Kirsten, 'who's come to talk. Just ignore us.'

The choir went back to learning its new hymn and the priest stood looking up at the loft, clearly unsure what to do. He'd taken Kirsten out of a private office into this huge, cavernous space, with over a dozen witnesses. She thought she knew why.

'Well,' he finally said, turning toward her, 'shall we sit down, Miss . . . uh . . . Miss . . .'

'Like you don't know my name?'

'Well, you wouldn't tell the receptionist.' He paused, then added, 'You . . . you frightened her a little.'

'Uh-huh,' Kirsten said, and sat down in the front pew.

He joined her, leaving several feet of space between the two of them, and they twisted on the polished wood to face each other. 'So,' he said, 'what can I do for you?'

She shook her head. 'You don't do pretense well,' she said. 'And isn't it a bit late for hiding now?'

He tilted his head to the right. 'Excuse me?'

'Once you took that first step, and called me, it was a bit late to try to avoid me.'

He sighed, and his shoulders slumped. But he looked relieved, too, as if he could finally put down a burden he'd been carrying.

'Two murders,' she said. 'A police officer and a priest. A year apart. And they're connected?'

Several long seconds passed, filled only with the choir's repetitive practice, and then the priest held his hands out in front of him, palms down, well-tanned fingers spread wide. He clenched them into fists, then opened them again, several times . . . as if doing exercises. 'I ought to have given it more thought,' he said. 'How did you know the call came from me?'

'I'd listened to you talk for forty-five minutes at the funeral. And I played that message a dozen times. You can disguise the voice, but not . . . well . . . the "inflection", let's call it.'

'Making that call was a mistake.'

'It's seldom a mistake to want the truth out in the open.'

'Maybe not,' he said, 'but . . . you can't get the truth from me.' He must have seen the look on her face, because he added, 'What I mean is I don't know very much, and the little I *do* know I can't talk about. People could be hurt. Not just me, but the whole . . . I mean, lots of people.'

'Still, you called. And you left that message.'

He didn't answer and she noticed that the organ and the choir were into a different piece. It was one they were obviously familiar with – a Bach chorale, she thought – and they did it quite well.

'I made a mistake,' he repeated.

'No, you did the right thing. And anyway, there's no going back. So what's the connection between Johnny O'Hern's murder and the murder of Father Landrew?'

'I said I think there *might* be a connection. I don't know for sure. Dear God, I don't know *what* I know for sure.' He rested one arm on the back of the pew and leaned toward her. 'OK, here's why I called you. At the cemetery today I overheard one of the police detectives telling Richard O'Hern, the dead policeman's brother, who you were. He said you were investigating his brother's death. I had this sudden idea that maybe I could help, by steering you in a certain direction.' He stopped. 'I suppose I'm not making much sense.'

'You'll get there, though. Keep going.' She smiled encouragingly. As a cop she'd learned that it took time for frightened people to spill things they'd held in for a long time. 'I'm a fast learner.'

'And will this remain just between you and me?'

'I don't know that I can promise that,' she said. The choir finished the Bach piece, and the members were so pleased they applauded themselves. 'You're the one who wanted to come to a place where lots of people would see us talking.'

'But I just . . . I didn't want to talk in the rectory.'

'Why?'

'I just didn't.'

'OK, so if I have this right, you wanted me to know that the deaths of Johnny O'Hern and Father Landrew might be connected, because that might somehow help me get to the truth about the killings.'

'That's what I was thinking. Hoping, anyway. For one thing, the police say the case is still open. They think Father Landrew was killed by a drug addict, and I don't want them accusing an innocent man.'

'I understand,' she said, but *didn't* say that a year-old homicide like that was still an open case the way a thousand other homicides were, and the chances of the cops charging anyone now were pretty remote. 'So . . . why do you think they're connected?'

'I can't tell you that.' He was clearly frightened.

'You know, you don't have to be afraid of O'Hern any more. He's dead.'

'I'm not afraid of *him*.'

'Then who?'

'I can't tell you that, either. I'm sorry. I shouldn't have called you.'

This priest was getting on her nerves. She took a deep breath, which is when she noticed that the choir loft was silent. She looked back and saw that most of the people were gone, and the remaining few seemed to be putting books away. She turned to the priest. 'So, whoever you're afraid of,' she said, 'did they kill both men?'

'I really don't know,' he said and, from the look on his face, that much was true.

'OK.' She recalled Richard's comment about his brother being an enforcer for Barry Zelander. 'The person you're scared of, is it someone in the real estate business?'

'What? What does real estate have to do with it?'

'I have no idea. You called *me*. You're the one who's supposed to know something.' He just shook his head. 'OK,' she said, 'let's try a different topic. Johnny O'Hern's sister, Janice? Do you know her?'

His eyes narrowed. '*Know* her? She came to the funeral.'

'No. I mean did you know her *before* that? I ask because I'm told she got you to do the funeral when the family couldn't find a priest.'

'Yes. She asked, and I said I'd give the man a Catholic funeral.'

'Right,' Kirsten shook her head. 'But my question was: Did you know her?'

'She came in from out of town. How could I know her?'

'Dammit, Father, you're starting to *piss* me *off*, and—'

'*Excuse* me.' A woman's voice, and Kirsten spun around to see the choir director, standing two feet away. 'Is everything all right, Father?'

'Oh, everything's fine, Francine,' he said. 'We're just having a discussion about . . . about one of those issues on which the church has to stand firm.'

Francine shook her head, clearly sympathizing with him, then gave him a set of keys – probably to the church – and left.

'I take back what I said a little while ago,' Kirsten said, 'sometimes you do pretense *quite* well.'

NINETEEN

Dugan spent the evening sitting around alone doing nothing but dozing off from time to time, either in the 'interview' room or in a cell in the lockup. Once he realized the cops weren't going to let him walk, he called several lawyers, and couldn't reach any of them.

By the time he called Kirsten it was nine fifteen and she was in her car. She was mad as hell that he'd waited so long, and said she should let him sit there all night because he was a 'bullheaded ass'. He said that was a mixed metaphor, and she hung up.

Within half an hour, though, she had somehow steamrolled her way through Area Three and gotten in to see him. 'No lawyer yet?' she asked.

'I tried a few, but . . .' He paused. 'I'll call Larry Candle. He'll do until I can—'

'No way!' Kirsten said. 'You need a *real* lawyer.'

'I told you before, you underestimate Larry.'

'Even if I do – which I don't – you need someone independent, someone who won't just listen to what *you* want. What about Renata Carroway? Try calling *her*. Or . . . better yet, I'll call her myself.'

He hadn't thought of Renata Carroway, but he liked the idea. Renata wasn't one of those big-name criminal defense attorneys whose clients were always high-profile people with deep pockets. But she'd been slugging it out in the trenches a long time, and Dugan knew from his days as a prosecutor that she was considered one of the best. Even cops liked her . . . or at least respected her. As for Kirsten, she said the last thing she'd heard about Renata was that she'd represented a local private eye – a somewhat eccentric colleague named Foley whom Kirsten admired – in a recent run-in with the legal system.

'Not a great outcome, as I recall,' Dugan said. 'The guy went to jail.'

'But that wasn't Renata Carroway's fault,' Kirsten said. 'It's because Foley's even more stubborn than you are.'

By one o'clock Tuesday morning Dugan and Kirsten were home. Kirsten had gotten through to Renata Carroway and talked her into coming all the way up to Area Three from her home in Hyde Park, on the south side. Renata hadn't been thrilled about it, but she came. She spoke to him for about five seconds, long enough to verify that he wanted her to represent him, then did her thing and didn't give up until she'd gotten him released. Of course, he'd missed most of that. Except for the best part . . . walking out.

Renata had left by then, and had told Kirsten when and where Dugan should meet with her. He didn't like being left out of the scheduling, but since Renata spent half the night getting him out of the slammer, he figured he'd follow orders.

At nine the next morning Kirsten was still asleep when Dugan left home. With the rain and the traffic it took forty-five minutes to go the eight or ten miles to the criminal courts building at Twenty-sixth and California.

Everyone called it 'Twenty-sixth and Cal', and it was actually two buildings: a squat, stolid, seven-story structure of gray stone, fronted with Romanesque columns to show the world it was a courthouse; and a steel and glass high-rise that housed the hundreds of offices needed to run the largest unified criminal justice system in the country. Connecting the two was a wide, glass-fronted one-story lobby that served as the entrance for both buildings.

Dugan went through security – a procedure expedited by his lawyer's ID, but still a time-consuming pain in the ass – and headed for the elevators on the courthouse side. He was to meet Renata outside Courtroom 407. He was in time, he thought, to go into the courtroom and watch her at work.

At the fourth floor he stepped off the elevator into a wide hallway. The odd-numbered courtrooms were to his left, and looking that way he saw a crowd, including a large number of law officers. They all seemed on high alert, many of them exchanging what were technically known in the criminal justice trade as 'eye-fucks' with a bunch of gangbangers. Conversations were kept to hushed tones, obviously under threat of expulsion, and an uneasy truce prevailed. All this going on mostly around the entrance to Room 407.

A deputy blocked the door to the courtroom, so Dugan stepped away from the crowd and leaned back against a wall. He'd once moved in this milieu on a daily basis, but he knew he'd lost track of the ever-evolving culture of the street criminals he used to prosecute. These guys wore the usual baggy clothes, pants halfway down their butts, untied sneakers, complicated cornrows and pigtails. He saw no gang insignia, but he knew these were hard-core members of a major organization.

Some looked as old as thirty-five, some as young as fifteen; but all were men, none of them boys. It was a crowd marked by hard, sullen expressions, and all-too-frequently by terribly crooked teeth and deeply scarred faces. Their crotch-grabbing posturing and kiss-my-ass cockiness were designed to intimidate. All Dugan felt, though, was sadness, watching these young-old men who entertained no hopes, no dreams, nothing at all that might extend beyond the next half-hour or so.

Business in the other courtrooms was proceeding as usual. People of all racial and ethnic groups arrived and departed, all keeping their distance, but otherwise showing little concern about the thuggish crowd around 407. They'd been here before. They knew that when you came to criminal court you were bound to run up against . . . well . . . criminals.

The door to 407 opened and Renata Carroway came out. Other than parting to let her pass through, the gangbangers paid her no attention, and she paid them none. An intense-looking young man – fresh out of law school, Dugan guessed – walked beside her, lugging a huge briefcase. When Renata spotted Dugan, she spoke to the young man. He nodded and headed toward the elevators, and she came toward Dugan carrying her own, much thinner, briefcase.

She was scarcely five feet tall, stocky, and wore an expensive-looking suit that pretty well hid whatever feminine curves she had. She looked anywhere from forty to sixty years old, and he got the sense she didn't focus much on appearances. She had an attractive face, though, with dark hair framing smooth tan skin, and she peered up at him – in an era when surgery could correct most myopia – through thick lenses set in round, dark frames. Dugan couldn't keep the word 'owl' out of his mind.

They greeted each other with a handshake and headed for the elevators. 'Thanks for coming out last night,' he said. 'I know it was inconvenient.'

'It's what I do,' she said. 'And the alternative was having your wife take after me with a baseball bat.'

'Yeah,' he said, 'she can be persuasive. So, what do you think?'

'About the case against you? I think it sucks. The report will say: "Released. Investigation pending", but that Felony Review guy couldn't wait to cut you loose last night.' She paused. 'On the other hand, I think for some reason the cops wanna nail your ass to this murder and close the case.'

Outside the courthouse the rain had stopped. 'I have to be in Markham at one fifteen,' Renata said. 'No way I'm gonna drive downtown to my office, and then have to leave again right away.'

Dugan knew the drill. Local defense attorneys spent a major part of their time at Twenty-sixth and Cal, but there were a dozen other 'branch courts' around the city and suburban Cook County – such as Markham, twenty-five traffic-clogged miles away – not to mention courts in neighboring counties. So the lawyer's life was a frantic dash from one court to another, driving an hour to appear for one ten-minute hearing, and then rushing off in a different direction for another.

'There's a little Mexican place up here,' she said. For a small person she set a fast pace, and Dugan had to hustle to keep up as they crossed Twenty-sixth and headed north. 'We can talk over an early lunch.'

'A late breakfast for me,' he said. 'I barely made it out of bed and over here.'

'I had to get my daughters up and out to school,' she said. 'Don't you have kids?'

'No.'

'Damn, what wouldn't I give for those days again? With kids, you never get enough sleep. There's always *something*.'

'That's what I hear,' he said. 'But still, we're hoping and trying.'

'Oh . . . well . . . it's worth it. Children make your life *so* much richer. I wouldn't trade our two girls for the world.' She pointed ahead. 'That's the place.'

The restaurant apparently had no name other than *TACOS*, which is what the hand-painted sign over the door said. Inside it was pretty dark, a condition Dugan always found suspect – especially in a place that clearly wasn't trying to do *romantic*. Still, there were maybe twenty people crammed into the small space, and that was encouraging. Most looked like lawyers, and they seemed healthy enough, although mostly overweight. *Too much Mexican food*, he thought.

Spotting an empty corner table, Renata went over and laid her coat on it, and then they went to the counter. They ordered Diet Cokes and tacos – two beef for Dugan, one chicken for Renata – on corn tortillas.

'I have a question,' Dugan said, turning and leaning back against the counter while they waited. 'Why did you say—'

'Wait till we're sitting down.' She waved her hand toward the tables. 'Half these people are state's attorneys, and they have big ears.'

After they'd carried their food to the table and were starting to eat, Renata said, 'You're wondering why I said the cops seem anxious to stick *you* with this homicide and close their file. It's just a feeling I have. I'm sure you know that once they close a case with an arrest – even if the defendant is later found not guilty at trial – they seldom open it again unless some pretty startling new evidence appears. They figure, "Hey, we caught the bad guy. And if he gets off, you can blame the goddamn, weak-kneed, criminal-coddling justice system, not us."'

'That actually wasn't what I was—'

'So I don't think it's *you*, really. I get the sense they'd like to close out their case with a quick arrest, and you happen to be handy. The mayor's up for election, and maybe his hand-picked police superintendent has a push on to close more files. So . . . does that answer your question?'

'Actually, my question was why with one breath parents say their kids are driving them nuts, and then right away say kids are the greatest thing that ever happened to them.'

She stared at him, then shook her head. 'Like I say, they'd love to charge you.' She swirled the ice around in her Coke. 'And it sounds as if you might be helping them. Did you actually give a statement to those two investigators? In the squad car?'

'Not really. I said something like, "I take it there's been some new development in the case." I was thinking there must have been, since they picked me up.'

'Jesus.' Renata shook her head. 'I thought you were a *lawyer*.'

'It's different when it's your own case. Won't happen again.'

'Actually, though, there *has* been a new development.' She looked at her watch. 'What about this Harvey Starr guy? Did he call you, and did you actually *talk* to him?'

'I talked to him. He called about some appellate case he was working on. That was just before he went missing.'

'Uh-huh, well, he's not *missing* any more.'

'Oh God, is he—'

'He's fine,' she said. 'Appeared yesterday, with a lawyer, and told the cops why he went into hiding.'

'Damn. Why do I think this isn't good?'

'He says he called you out of courtesy, told you he was subpoenaed to testify at the ARDC, that he'd have to admit he paid police officers to send him cases, and that if he was asked he'd have to say he knew *you* did, too.'

'He's lying. He never said any of that. Not to me.'

'Right. Thing is, he says you told him he better keep his mouth shut. Told him he *saw* what happens to people who don't.'

TWENTY

Kirsten heard Dugan leave home. She saw that it was raining outside, and promptly went back to sleep. When she got up an hour later the rain was easing up, and by the time she'd finished breakfast it had moved on and the sky was clearing.

She'd left Holy Martyrs Basilica the previous night focused more on what Father Watson *didn't* say, than what he did. They'd parted on friendly enough terms. He clearly felt he was in over his head, and was afraid someone would be hurt. 'Not just me,' he'd said, 'but the whole . . .' He'd caught himself, talked about 'lots of people' being hurt, but she was sure he'd meant 'the whole *church*'. After all, he was a priest, an archdiocesan official, and he'd naturally be concerned about his church.

Whatever connection he suspected between Johnny O'Hern's murder and the priest's murder a year ago, it seemed clear it involved people who might be able to listen in on a conversation in a quiet rectory office, but not in a huge, cavernous space, with lots of ambient noise – such as a Bach chorale.

Then there was Johnny's sister, Janice Robinson. According to Richard, Janice said she called the archdiocese on Thursday to demand a Catholic funeral, and was handed off to Father Watson. But the receptionist at the rectory said a woman had called Father Watson about the murdered man two days earlier, on Tuesday. Had that woman been Janice? When Kirsten asked him if he'd known Janice before the funeral, the verbal gymnastics he went through were a virtual admission.

He'd seemed truly concerned that an innocent person not go down for Father Landrew's murder, and it had taken some courage for him to call her. He was no fool, and was a decent enough person for a bureaucrat – a church bureaucrat, at that – but he wasn't ready to talk yet. So in the end she'd settled for his promise to pray over whether to tell her more.

And if he did pray? Would God lean down and whisper the right answer in his ear? Kirsten had her doubts about that. But by his prayer he just might convince himself to stand tall and follow through on his own best instincts. She hoped so, anyway.

Meanwhile, talking to Johnny O'Hern's parents was next on her agenda.

Before she left home, though, she checked her office voice mail. Another message. A man, no name given, but this time definitely not Father Watson. All he said was: 'Noon today. Lincoln Park Driving Range.'

It was turning into a bright, crisp day, and Kirsten took a cab east on Diversey to Lincoln Park. The driving range, about a half-mile north of the zoo, was a tiny, little-known pocket in a twelve-hundred-acre park on the city's north side lakefront. She didn't play golf and was amazed to find so many people there on a weekday, standing in one spot practicing their swings. *Boring*, she thought, as she watched the ceaseless stroke of club into ball, club into ball.

She was early and she stood and listened to the rapid, almost hypnotic, *whack*, *whack*, *whack*, *whack*. Then she noticed, from farther away, what sounded like a bunch of noisy kids on a school picnic, and from beyond that the traffic on Lake Shore Drive. Then, at noon on the head, the same ugly thug who'd escorted her to Polly Morelli's limo at the planetarium came along and led her to the far end of the driving range.

When they got there she found a surprise: a miniature golf course. That's where the kid noise came from. There must have been fifty or so nine- or ten-year-olds, all of them screaming and laughing at once. A sign at the entrance said *Closed Today For Special Event*, and another said *Harriet Tubman Academy*.

'Wait here,' the thug said, and walked away.

Kirsten moved closer to the fence and stared at the boisterous group, surprised that they had an outing this early in the school year. Kids – all African-American as far as she could tell – lined up putts to send golf balls over foot bridges, under waterfalls, up ramps, and through tunnels, while others watched and whooped in gleeful derision at every missed shot. More kids were lining up at a long table where three men were serving hot dogs and drinks, and near the table stood two white women, both wearing pretty expensive outfits for teachers at a picnic. One held a clipboard and seemed to be supervising the men passing out lunches. Meanwhile a huge dimpled golf ball, about four or five feet in diameter and topped with a wild plaid golfer's cap, walked around on two legs, posing for pictures with laughing children. The whole scene was as cheerful as it was chaotic, and it made Kirsten smile.

She nearly choked, though, when one of the men passing out hot dogs turned her way. It was Polly Morelli.

He saw her, too, and at once walked over to the woman with the clipboard. They had a discussion – in fact, what looked like an argument – and then Polly and his limo driver came out the entrance, leaving just one man to dole out the hot dogs. Coming her way, Polly had what seemed to be a real grin on his face, something Kirsten had never seen – never even imagined.

Turning aside and waving for her to follow, he walked to a bench about twenty yards away and sat down. She joined him, while his driver hung back and lit up a smoke.

'So whaddaya think?' Polly asked.

'About what?'

'About the goddamn miniature golf, for chrissake. You ever hear of Harriet Tubman?'

'Yeah, she was an ex-slave who started the Underground Rail—'

'I'm talking about the *school* . . . Harriet Tubman Academy. It's on the west side. Used to be a Catholic school, but they closed it and someone reopened it as a private school. They run it on a shoestring and my wife . . .' He pointed. 'That's her running the lunch line. She heard about the school and she took it on as her charity. Gives her something to do, y'know? Something useful.'

'Sure,' Kirsten said. 'Useful. That's good for every wife.'

'Absolutely.' Polly didn't seem to catch her sarcasm. 'Anyway, every year she organizes a big fundraiser for the school. Black tie and shit. But then she has events like this one, just for the kids. *My* money, of course. I mean, four bills for Dimples alone.'

'Dimples?'

'The walking golf ball,' he said. 'But it's kinda fun.' He shook his head at some especially loud screeching from the kids. 'Man, these moo . . . I mean . . . these black kids. They make a lotta noise, don't they? I think their lungs are different from regular people, or their voice boxes or something.'

'Different from "regular" people? What does *that* mean?'

'Don't gimme that shit. You know what I mean.'

'Right,' she said. 'I know.'

'Forget about it.' Polly waved his hand dismissively. 'I hear they picked up your husband, and then let him go again. What was that about?'

Once again Polly had information on what the cops were doing, if not what they were thinking. 'You seem to hear everything,' she said, 'which is why I still don't understand why you need me.'

'I'm paying you to do a job. I don't *need* you. So why'd they pick him up?'

'His lawyer talked to the cops about it. I didn't.' She paused, wondering how far to go, then decided she might learn something from Polly. 'I know,' she said, 'that they asked him questions about a personal injury lawyer named Harvey Starr.'

She'd hoped for some reaction, but all she got was, 'So what have you found out for me so far?'

'I found out Johnny O'Hern was mixed up with a real estate developer named Barry Zelander. He may have done a little strong-arm "negotiating" for Zelander. He also invested in some of Zelander's deals, some think with money Johnny and some fellow cops extracted from drug dealers.'

'Jesus, a busy boy.'

'Seems so. Anyway,' she went on, 'Zelander's business model includes bribing public officials, and he fell under the eye of the feds. His associates, too. Investors and such.'

'Like Johnny.'

'Johnny, not so much any more. But other investors? I hear some investors are persons with ties to . . . well . . . let's call it "organized crime".'

Again, Polly's expression revealed nothing. 'Where'd you hear that?' he asked.

'You're paying me for information, not to divulge my sources.'

He frowned, but didn't press the point. 'So . . . you got any names for these "investors", the ones with "ties to organized crime"?'

'Actually, I thought I'd ask *you* that.'

'Why ask *me*?'

'Right. What was I thinking? Anyway, if Johnny was ready to sing to the feds, a cop investigating his murder would take a look at anyone who didn't want that to happen.'

'Which would be Zelander himself, first of all.'

'Maybe, but let's say you have what looks a lot like a professional hit, and for possible suspects you have: "A", a real estate developer, even a shady one; and "B", a guy who's reputed to be a member of an organized crime syndicate. Who'd be *your* pick?'

'You forgot "C", a cop who shakes down drug dealers; and "D", a personal injury lawyer who pays cops to bring him cases.'

'OK, throw them in, too. Still, who'd be *your* pick for the hit?'

'I save my picks for the ponies,' he said. 'Anyway, whatever a "professional hit" looks like, this didn't have to be one. Coulda been someone hated O'Hern for personal reasons, hated him bad enough to put three bullets in his face.'

'Yes . . . well . . . maybe.' Kirsten leaned down for a twig and threw it toward a fat pigeon who had waddled over looking for a handout. The pigeon pecked at the twig, then leaned back and gave her a dirty look. 'One piece I don't have – and believe me, the cops are not in a sharing mood – is where Johnny had been that night. If he was coming home when he got shot, where from? Or if he was on his way out, where to? And why? I don't know if the cops know. I don't know if anyone knows.'

'*Someone* knows,' Polly said, 'but it doesn't have to be the guy who killed him. He could have gone to Johnny's house and waited for him to get home.'

'Right, but this thing happened maybe two, three o'clock in the morning. How long would a person wait around a house if he doesn't know when – or even *if* – the target's gonna get home? Maybe it was someone who *followed* him home. Or came home *with* him.' She raised her hands, palms up, and shrugged. 'Anyway, I'd like to know where Johnny was that night. Think you could help me on that? Like find out who his friends were?'

Morelli gave her a disgusted look, then asked, 'What else you got?'

'Not much. I got some background from Johnny's brother Richard. I tried to talk to the rest of his family, but I got thrown out of the cemetery. I'll try again.'

'And what else?'

'And nothing else. I'm just getting started, y'know? And my husband got hauled in and I had to get him out. I've been busy.'

'I'm not paying you to work on family problems.'

'Yeah, well, any time you wanna downsize me . . . feel free.'

He stood up. 'So that's it?'

'That's it,' she said. 'So far.'

Polly nodded, then turned and walked back toward the miniature golf course.

'Say hello to Dimples!' she called, but he didn't look back.

She wondered if he knew she hadn't been entirely open with him. She wondered if he knew anything about a priest named Larry Landrew . . . or one named Wayne Watson. Or about Johnny's sister, Janice.

Mostly, she wondered whether she'd been any help to him so far. She sure hoped not.

TWENTY-ONE

After lunch Dugan walked with Renata back to the courthouse parking garage. 'That was quite a crowd outside the courtroom,' he said.

'Uh-huh.'

'They were there because of your case, right?'

'Right.'

'Who were they? Friends of your client?'

She glanced up at him, but didn't break stride. 'My client's name is Lancelot Holmes. Those were members of a rival gang who had a comrade cut down in a drive-by. Five of them will testify that Lancelot was the shooter.'

'*Was* he the shooter?' Not a question to ask a defense attorney, but he wondered how she'd handle it.

'I wasn't there,' she said.

'Are you . . . worried . . . about the rival gang? Like they might take their anger out on Lancelot's lawyer?'

'Why would they? They know I'm doing my job. They do theirs . . . I do mine. Different roles in the same ongoing saga.'

'I had a role too, once,' Dugan said. 'I was a prosecutor. I hated it. But I don't know if I could represent the sort of social misfits you do, either.'

They'd reached the parking garage and she stopped and looked up at him, her eyes magnified by her lenses. 'The people of the State of Illinois spend an awful lot of money to lock these "misfits" up. Someone oughta make sure they can prove they picked the *right* misfit . . . and make them follow the rules.'

'Well, sure, but—'

'That's what I'm doing for Lancelot Holmes,' she said. 'And it's what I'll do for you. What's the difference?' When he didn't come up with a quick answer, she went on. 'The only difference is that I'm a little more confident that you didn't kill anybody. I think the lead investigator on the case . . . Newhouse? . . . he's not so sure you did it, either.'

'Well, then, why—'

'Because he's not in charge. Anyway, if those idiots actually charge you with homicide, they'll have to beat *me* to get a "guilty". Meanwhile, don't you say a goddamn thing to anyone about the case. Leave the talking . . . and the thinking . . . to me. Believe me, I'm on your side.' She turned to go.

'Hey, Renata,' he said, and she turned back. 'I bet you say that to *all* your misfits.'

She smiled then, which was a first. 'Yes,' she said, 'I do.'

Dugan spent the cab ride to his office wondering what to do. He had Renata to handle the legal side. And he had Kirsten, too. She hadn't said so, but he knew she was already working on finding Johnny O'Hern's killer. It wouldn't be the first time she'd saved Dugan's ass, and of course he'd do the same for her. And *had*. But it seemed time now for him to take an active role on his own behalf.

When the cab stopped in front of his building, he paid the driver and got out, but didn't go inside. He needed to think.

It was a warm afternoon, and the Loop streets were bustling. He walked to the corner and as he waited for the light to change, two things struck him. One, he already had his cell phone in his hand, poised to call Mollie at the office. Two, he was headed east – for Millennium Park, or the Art Institute, or even all the way to the lakefront – to find a place to think. Neither was the result of conscious decision.

When the light changed he didn't cross the street, but turned around and went the other way. And he didn't call Mollie. He switched off his phone.

A few minutes later, with no plan in mind other than to shake up his thought patterns, Dugan was westbound on Madison Street. He ran into construction clogging up pedestrian traffic – there was *always* construction in the Loop – so he hustled across the street. That side was clogged, too. He did another about-face and went back to LaSalle, then south a block, then west again on Monroe. He reached Wacker Drive, which ran north and south at that point and which – although it was outside the 'Loop' formed by the El tracks – many considered the real boundary of downtown. The light turned red, but he hurried across, and happened to glance back when he reached the other side.

Right then he decided to abandon his aimlessness.

Another half-block brought him to the Chicago River, and just across the bridge he made a right turn on to a pedestrian walkway along the west side of the river. The walkway was wide, forming a sort of riverside plaza, complete with a few trees and benches. He headed back toward Madison Street, but about halfway there he turned and went to the railing above the river. He leaned on the cool cast-iron top of the railing and gazed down at the water, some twenty feet below.

He would wait there, allowing the two men behind him to pass on by, and prove that he was wrong . . . and that they weren't following him.

He'd first noticed them back at that construction site, when he'd crossed Madison in the middle of the block and made a U-turn, and two men had made a sudden similar reversal in direction, although without crossing the street. He'd thought little of that until, having dashed across Wacker against the light, he'd glanced back and seen the same two men waiting on the other side.

And now they were still with him. Two tough, hard-looking men. One maybe five-nine, in a dark blue windbreaker. The other about six feet, a few inches shorter than Dugan, and wearing a tan corduroy sport coat. They'd stopped walking, and the shorter one crouched down to retie his shoe while the other guy busied himself lighting a cigarette. They could have been cops, or they could have been thugs. Or they could have been pipefitters looking for work at downtown construction sites, not at all aware of him.

Dugan rested his forearms on the railing and stared down at three seagulls bobbing along the surface of the river. They were moving forward, paddling like ducks, one in the lead and the other two following. Much like his own situation, he thought. He recalled Kirsten saying it took watchfulness and skill to spot a good 'tail'. But hell, he'd done it without even trying. Which could mean, of course, that these guys weren't very good. Or that they didn't care.

He was certain they'd been following him. But why? Not to kidnap him, surely. He'd been kidnapped once before. That was, in fact, the difficulty Kirsten had enlisted Polly Morelli to help her get him out of. He'd been snatched by just one person that time. And a woman, at that. But quite a large woman, thank you, with quite a large gun . . . and quite a large psychosis. And it had been night and he'd been alone in a dark place – not to mention half in the bag. Now, though? On a busy downtown plaza in the middle of the day? Even if they had a car trailing along to throw him into, they'd have to drag him half a block along the plaza to get to it.

He waited long enough to let his heartbeat slow, then stood upright and turned his back to the railing. He leaned against it and looked around casually. The plaza was full of people. Most were on the move; but a few were sitting on benches, eating their lunches or reading. His two friends had moved close to the railing, too, maybe twenty yards back toward Monroe.

They were both staring back at him.

His cell phone was in his pocket, but he couldn't call 911. Nothing threatening was happening. He could call Kirsten, but . . . what the hell for? Advice? Because two guys had walked the same direction he did downtown?

There was a sudden squawking scream from the river below, and he turned in time to see the three seagulls take to the air, with the one in the lead easily pulling away from the two following.

Flying, however, wasn't in Dugan's repertoire, so he did the only other thing he could think of. He left the railing and walked quickly, straight at his two stalkers.

TWENTY-TWO

Kirsten left Polly Morelli at Lincoln Park and went home. She picked up her Camry, filled the gas tank at a station near DePaul University, and drove west on Fullerton.

She found the two-flat Richard O'Hern shared with his parents nestled on a northbound, one-way street in what was fast becoming a pretty expensive neighborhood. But if he'd bought it just six or seven years ago, he picked it up for a song . . . plus, of course, the cost of rehabbing it. It was a stone building, probably eighty or ninety years old, with a small, well-maintained front lawn behind a wrought-iron fence.

She parked down the street, where the sign said she shouldn't park without a residential permit, and walked back. The fence had a gate, with a key pad and an intercom system. She pressed the button and waited, then pushed again. Finally a woman's voice came over the intercom: 'Yes?'

Kirsten identified herself and the lock was released and she pushed through the gate. As she headed up the short walk to the steps the woman was already opening the front door. She was stout and white-haired, and Kirsten recognized her from the funeral. 'I'm so sorry to bother you, Mrs O'Hern,' she said, 'but could I have a few moments of your time?'

'I . . . well . . . yes. I guess so. Please come in.'

Inside was a small foyer with a stairway leading up and, to the left of that, the door to the first-floor apartment. The woman used her key and they went inside and down a hall and into a parlor. The odor of stale cigarette smoke hung like a sickness in the air. The furniture had to be at least thirty years old, with an ancient phone on the table beside the sofa and a very out-of-place-looking flat screen TV perched on a coffee table against the opposite wall. The TV was tuned to a shopping channel, with the sound muted.

'Oh,' Mrs O'Hern said, 'would you like . . . a cup of tea?'

'No thanks. Let's just sit and talk.' When they were seated at opposite ends of the sofa, Kirsten said, 'I apologize for not having called first.'

'That's OK. My son . . . Richard . . . said you'd be calling. He said you're looking into . . . into John's . . .' She lowered her head and stared down at her hands in her lap.

'First, Mrs O'Hern, let me say how sorry I am for your loss.'

'Thank you, I . . .' She stopped, then said, 'Please, call me Betty. Everyone does. Except my husband. He calls me "Betty Clare". He just always has and . . . well . . . anyway, Richard said I should try to help you, but I really don't know how.'

'I need to know what I can about your son, Mrs . . . I mean . . . Betty. He was a police officer, of course, but I'm wondering about his friends, his social life. Things like that.'

'Oh . . . well, I don't know anything about all that. I'm sure he had lots of friends, but I wouldn't know who they were. John was very busy, you know. He was a good son, and a fine police officer. The department was his whole—'

A door slammed and Kirsten knew it had to be the back door of the apartment.

'*Betty Clare?*' It was a man's voice, harsh and angry-sounding. 'Where are you?' There was a slight pause, and then, 'Where the hell *are* you?'

Betty sighed and got to her feet. Her heavy body sagged and she looked very tired.

'I'd like to talk to your husband too, if I can,' Kirsten said. 'But I . . . I guess he can be a difficult man at times, huh?'

'Difficult? Why do you—' She seemed irritated – but embarrassed, too – by Kirsten's comment. 'My husband's not well. He suffered from alcoholism. That's an illness, you know.'

'I know,' Kirsten said.

'But he overcame it. He hasn't had a drink since his stroke. That's two years now, and he gets around quite well. I just wish he could stop smoking, because—'

'*Betty Clare!* God *damn* it.'

'Oh.' Betty jumped, then gave an embarrassed smile. 'I'll be back in a minute.'

Kirsten had the room to herself. She stood up and wandered around. Johnny O'Hern may well have been killed because he was about to rat out someone to the feds, but she was trying hard not to presuppose anything. Starting from zero, what she hoped for was a little insight into who Johnny was, how he'd gone from being 'John', 'a good son', to being a man someone would want to pump bullets into.

The furniture was worn-looking, but the room was neat and clean. Spotless, in fact. Three side-by-side windows looked out on to the street in front of the apartment. Another window had a view of the side of the brick wall next door and was open a few inches. The air that drifted in through gauze curtains did little to clear the cigarette odor that Kirsten knew would cling to her own clothing long after she was out of here.

To the right of the open window was a fireplace. Small and shallow and painted white, it was obviously never used. Over the mantle hung a large picture of two parrots – in bright shades of green and red and yellow – perched among palm leaves. It was a painting on black velvet, the sort bought from men who used to sit by rows of similar paintings in plastic lawn chairs near busy intersections at the edges of the city. Below the parrots, in the center of the mantle, stood a foot-tall ceramic statue of the Virgin Mary, a rosy-cheeked woman in ankle-length blue and white robes. With her hands clasped over her bosom and her eyes raised upwards, she was smiling, apparently unconcerned by the snake pinned under her bare feet, its angry mouth wide open.

There were four photographs on the mantle, two on each side of the statue. From left to right they were: a wedding photo of Patrick and Betty O'Hern on the front steps of a church; a pudgy, blond boy who had to be Johnny, although Kirsten had never seen him except in a newspaper picture; a thin, dark-haired boy, obviously Richard; and a cute little dark-haired girl, obviously Janice. The children in the photos all looked about eight years old, both boys in white shirts and dark ties and Janice in a white dress. The Betty in the wedding photo was blonde and pretty, hardly resembling today's tired, overweight, frustrated-looking version. Her groom, on the other hand, looked much as he did today, thin and tense, maybe anxious to get to the reception and that first cold beer with—

'I'm back,' Betty announced. 'Sorry to keep you.' She came in with a white plastic basket full of clothes. 'I asked my husband if he'd come and talk to you, but he . . . he's feeling a little tired just now. He has to be careful, you know.'

'Oh, that's all right,' Kirsten said, and they both sat again. Betty put the basket on the floor and took out a towel and started folding it, and the odor of fabric softener joined that of stale smoke. 'I was enjoying your family photos. The children . . . I bet those are all first communion pictures, right?'

'That's right.' Betty seemed genuinely pleased. She put the folded towel on the sofa between them and reached for another. 'Are you Catholic, then?'

'Ah . . . well . . . not really. But I *was* once, and my first communion dress looked a lot like Janice's.' She paused, then added, 'It was so nice that Janice could get here for the funeral. I take it you don't see her often.'

'Never. And good riddance. She didn't like it here. She used to make up lies, mostly about John. She even—' Betty paused in mid-fold and stared at her. 'I thought you wanted information that might help you find out who murdered my son.'

'I do.'

'Well, then, if you want my opinion, I think John was murdered by some crook he was after, probably someone in the Mafia. I don't know how many times John told me he'd been given some special police assignment. "Working undercover", he called it. He never actually said so out loud, but I know he meant something involving the Mafia. They're animals, you know, those people. They found out, and they shot him.'

'The police,' Kirsten said, 'don't seem to see it that way.'

'Of course they don't *say* so.' Betty was matching socks now, balling them into pairs.

'The police think my husband might have killed your son, to keep him from telling the authorities something he knew.'

'I heard that. One of the detectives said John and your husband were involved in something illegal.'

'And doesn't that make you suspicious? Of *me*, I mean.'

'Not really. I know my son, and he wasn't mixed up in anything crooked . . . not with your husband or with anyone else.' She was near the bottom of the basket now, folding faded blue boxer shorts. 'I want someone to get to the real truth. That's why I agreed to talk to you. But John's friends? Or what he did when he wasn't working? That had nothing to do with his death. My John was killed because he was such a good police officer. He found out something about someone and they—'

'Betty Clare? Get *in* here!' The venom in Patrick O'Hern's voice made Kirsten shudder. 'Tell that damn rent-a-cop she's got no business bothering us at a time like this. I need your help.'

'I'm coming,' Betty called back. She leaned toward Kirsten and said in a hushed tone, 'I really can't talk now. He's *so* helpless.' She hurried to stack the folded laundry in neat piles back inside the basket, and stood up. 'You know how these *men* are.' She stood up and smiled, as though she and Kirsten shared a feminine insight.

Kirsten stood and smiled back, and followed Betty out of the parlor into the hallway. Betty headed toward the rear of the apartment, and Kirsten let herself out the front door.

So Betty O'Hern's husband was a typically 'helpless' male, and her son had been 'such a good police officer'. Fables told – and clearly now even believed – by a woman who'd long ago given up on reality.

TWENTY-THREE

Dugan fiddled with his cell phone and then clipped it to his belt, as he walked straight at the two men who'd been following him. He was sure he'd caught them off-guard, but they didn't seem at all nervous about it. They exchanged a few words, then stood with their backs against the railing above the river, about five feet apart, and watched him approach.

The shorter man was even bulkier than Dugan had realized – a walking beer keg with short, thick arms. His eyes widened in surprise when Dugan walked right up between the two of them, as though unaware of the advantage that gave them.

He leaned forward and rested his forearms on the railing and looked down at the river. The seagulls were long gone, but to his left a sailboat was approaching, headed south, its tall mast lowered as it passed under the Madison Street bridge. Finally he said, 'I'm just wondering . . . do seagulls have webbed feet?'

'What the fuck?' the Beer Keg said. 'What're you—'

'Shut up,' the taller man said. He was slim, hard-looking, maybe forty years old; and the calm, quiet tone of voice made it clear he was used to having people do what he said.

'I mean, there were some seagulls down there, paddling on the river like ducks,' Dugan said. 'I never thought about their feet before.'

'You got more important things to think about, Ace.' The man in charge lit himself another cigarette. 'And not just think about. *Worry* about.'

'Worry?' Dugan lifted his arms from the railing. He turned and looked at the man. Dugan was a couple of inches taller than he, and probably outweighed him by forty pounds. 'Hell, the worst you could do with all these people around is throw me into the river. And if there's one thing I'm good at, it's swimming. I was a Park District lifeguard. I mean, we *trained.* They made us jump into the lake off Navy Pier . . . with our shoes on, and all our clothes . . . and then—'

'I have a message for your *wife*.' The man's tone stopped Dugan cold, made it hard for him to draw a breath. 'She's a pretty woman. Great tits. Great ass. The whole package.'

'Who are you?' Dugan managed, when he could get his breath.

'I deliver messages. And today's message is . . . well . . . put it this way: It's interesting what a strong, sharp blade can do to a pretty face.'

'Uh-huh,' Dugan said. He wanted to grab this man, smash his face against the iron railing. Instead, he spread his hands wide and said, 'Thing is, I'm not the one to pass that along.'

'Oh?' The man dragged on his cigarette, and shook his head as though disgusted. 'You're saying you don't get my message?'

'No.' Dugan shrugged. 'I'm saying she doesn't take orders from me.'

'Fuck what you're saying. Just give her the message.'

The man took a short drag and dropped his burning cigarette to the pavement.

'Jesus,' Dugan said, 'that's *littering*.' He dropped into a crouch and reached toward the smoking butt, then shifted his weight and wrapped both arms around the man's legs at the knees. As he stood up he lifted the man, arms flailing, high off the ground . . . and heaved him over the railing.

'Help! Man overboard!' Before the guy hit the water Dugan was shouting. 'He's drowning!'

The Beer Keg, wide-eyed, looked first at Dugan and then down at the water, obviously unsure what to do. But people were already gathering and the Beer Keg turned and walked away. No one in the crowd seemed to have seen what happened. The man in the water was calling for help and thrashing his arms around.

'Anybody have a cell phone?' Dugan yelled, switching his own cell off.

Several people said yes, they had phones, and they were already calling 911.

Dugan slipped a few yards to the side and looked around. The Beer Keg was nearly to Monroe Street. Dugan walked the other way, toward Madison, taking his phone from his belt. But he heard sirens drawing near, so he folded the phone away again and picked up his pace.

TWENTY-FOUR

Kirsten wanted to interview Patrick O'Hern, but a confrontation wouldn't help, so she went back to her car, cursed and plucked the parking ticket from the windshield, and drove to a Wendy's. She sat by the window with a pretty decent salad and paged through the *Tribune*.

She turned to the Metro section and was shocked to see a familiar face: Father Wayne Watson. The caption said: *Local Cleric To Head Spokane Diocese*. A bright, articulate priest with enough ambition to climb the ecclesiastical ladder as high as he already had? No surprise he was bishop material. But was this sudden boost just a coincidence? He was to be 'ordained' a bishop in two weeks, and 'installed' – like a washing machine, she thought – as head of the Spokane diocese a few days later.

She called the archdiocese, asked to speak to him, and was told he was unavailable. 'I'm a reporter with the *Spokane Herald*,' she said . . . and was put through.

'It's Kirsten,' she said.

'They told me it was a reporter.'

'I know. I lied. But then . . . so did your receptionist. When can we meet?'

'That won't be possible,' he said. 'I'm awfully busy. Something's come up.'

'I *know*. They're shipping you off to Spokane. Funny you didn't mention that when we talked. You said you'd think and pray, and I told you I'd be in touch again.'

'I didn't even . . . anyway . . . no one's "shipping" me anywhere.'

'Listen to me.' She took a deep breath, and hoped the call wasn't being recorded. 'I'm not a crazy, and I understand your desire not to cause problems for people. But you started this. *You* called *me*. Now, if you don't meet with me I will follow you wherever you go . . . from Chicago, to Spokane, to *Rome* for all I care. You don't know me well, but I *will* do that.' She was on a roll. 'Believe me, you don't want—'

'Wait,' he said, giving her a chance to take a breath. 'I suppose we could meet.'

'Right. Today, then. Where?'

'I . . . it has to be somewhere . . . out of the way.'

'OK, just name . . . wait . . . is there someone *following* you?'

'I don't . . .' He paused and she stayed silent. 'My parents' graves,' he said. 'Do you know where Calvary Cemetery is?'

'That's the one on the lakefront, right? The Evanston border?'

'Yes,' he answered. 'I'll have to borrow a car. I can meet you at . . . say . . . four? The south-west corner of the cemetery.'

At a quarter to four Kirsten parked nearby and entered the cemetery on foot, carrying a bouquet of flowers she got cheap because they were wilting, and walked along the roadway toward the south fence. The sky was bright blue, but a chill wind was driving lots of thin white clouds overhead toward the lake. The only cars in sight were those passing by on Sheridan Road, a couple of hundred yards to the east, and the only person was a man raking leaves beside the burial chapel. Near the corner of the cemetery she picked a headstone at random and walked straight to it. According to the inscription, it was the grave of Sebastian Podula, who'd been born in 1906, died in 1960, and was 'Beloved By All'.

She stood motionless, head bowed. The temperature was dropping, and with the wind out of the west and gusting the way it was, she was glad she'd worn wool pants and her knee-length leather coat. Finally she heard a car come through the gate. It stopped some fifteen yards away, and when she heard the car door open she looked over and saw Father Watson getting out of a dark green Mitsubishi SUV. Turning back to Sebastian Podula's headstone, she waited what she thought was a decent amount of time for a priest to say hello to his parents, then stooped and laid her flowers on Sebastian's grave. She stood again and dabbed at her eyes with a tissue from her handbag – feeling a bit silly, but who knew who was watching? – then walked over to the priest.

He was wearing his roman collar, and a black topcoat over a black suit. He didn't look at her or say anything as she stood beside him and stared down at the two markers set in the ground in front of them. Finally she said, 'They both died in the same month?'

He nodded, but still didn't look at her. 'My dad died of lung cancer, and my mom . . . well . . . they'd been married fifty-seven years. I guess she just decided it was no use sticking around any longer.'

'I'm so sorry. Was it . . . suicide?'

'Oh God, no. She pretty much lost interest in eating, and then one morning she . . . well . . . she just didn't wake up. They . . . they enjoyed their time together so much.'

'I guess that's what counts.'

'And now they're enjoying eternity together. That's what *really* counts.'

'Uh-huh. If you say so.' Wrapping her coat tighter, she looked around and still saw no one but the man raking leaves. 'I suppose we could just stand here and freeze to death. Or . . . we could go sit in the car.'

'Sit in the car?' He seemed startled. 'No, that's not a good idea.'

'Right, not a good idea,' she said. 'I might accuse you of grabbing my . . . my leg or something.'

He stared at her, clearly shocked. 'Why would you *say* such a thing?'

'Let's at least sit down, out of the wind.' She headed for a concrete bench on the other side of the roadway. It was a curved bench, placed up against the trunk of a huge tree that would serve as a windbreak. He followed her, and when they were seated she turned to face him and said, 'I would "*say* such a thing" because I'm starting to think protecting your career is what's most important to you. You're afraid if you screw up, maybe they won't make you a bishop, and you won't have people bowing down and saying, "Thank you, Your Eminence." Or . . . whatever they say to bishops.'

'You have no right to talk that way.'

'You might have evidence that will help solve a murder.'

'I don't have *evidence* of anything,' he said. 'I thought I should tell someone about a . . . a suspicion. So I told *you*, thinking maybe you could . . .' He stopped and stared into the distance. 'I shouldn't have bothered you.'

'It's not a question of *bothering* anyone. You have reason to think Johnny O'Hern's murder is connected to that priest's murder. Someone said something, or did something. And guess what. I know who that *someone* was.' She stared at him until he couldn't help turning toward her, and she said, 'It was Johnny's sister, Janice Robinson.'

He tried to cover it, but his mouth dropped open and his eyes widened. 'What makes you so . . . so sure of that?'

'I wasn't.' She shrugged. 'But I am now. And I'm wondering, why does a woman who's had no contact with her family for years, suddenly show up for her brother's funeral?' She paused. 'What did she say to you in the car?'

'How did . . . why do you say that?'

'At the cemetery I saw you and Janice in the car, arguing . . . or at least in deep discussion. Then that night, in church, you said you called me because "something had just come up". I'm thinking it must have been something Janice said, something connecting O'Hern's killing with Father Landrew's.'

'*Maybe* connecting them,' he said.

'So tell me what—' Kirsten broke off because the priest was already shaking his head. 'Let's try it this way. I'll tell you some things I think are true,' she said. 'But let me say this: I'm *very* good at what I do, and I *will* find out whether I'm right. With or without your help.'

'You know,' he said, 'I'm not just trying to be difficult.'

'First,' she went on, 'Janice lied when she told her family she *happened* to get put through to you when she called the archdiocese. She called you directly, right?'

'I . . . yes.'

Kirsten smiled. Ambitious he might be, and scared, too. But he refused to lie, and she admired that. 'Next,' she said, 'I've been checking and I know Janice graduated high school and left for Mount Saint Joseph College, in Maryland, on a full scholarship. She never came back, and she's had no contact with her family since then. I also know she's on the faculty there now, listed as an associate professor of English, but she's had no classes in the catalog for at least four years. When you try to call her there do you know what they tell you?'

'I never had any reason to try.'

'They say she's on sabbatical and they can't give out any further information. A four-year sabbatical. Seems a bit odd, doesn't it?'

'Yes.'

'So I'm thinking . . . could this teaching job in Maryland be a cover? That opens up all kinds of interesting possibilities.'

'It's getting late,' he said, looking at his watch.

'Right. Anyway, as far as her family knows Janice has never been back to Chicago, and yet she has this . . . this *relationship* with you.' Seeing the look on his face she quickly added, 'I'm not saying a romantic relationship. But she's able to go to you, and to get what she wants.' She paused, then asked, 'How'm I doing so far?'

The look on his face showed how right she was, but he quickly dropped his gaze and said, 'I don't think I can answer that.'

'Oh, you can answer, all right. You just choose not to.'

'Sometimes innocent people get caught up in things, and they could get hurt. Even if you promise to try to avoid that,' he added, shaking his head slowly, 'I don't know that I'd believe you.'

'Really,' Kirsten said. 'I guess that's because you're a priest, and in your world you're not used to people keeping the promises they make.'

He jerked his head up and stared hard at her, anger burning in his eyes. 'That's a . . . that wasn't fair.'

'No,' she said, 'it wasn't. But it got your attention. You talk about people getting "caught up in things". In my experience people don't often just get "caught". They *choose* to do this, or do that . . . even if later they wish they hadn't.' Watson stood up. 'So now,' Kirsten said, 'I guess you're choosing to run away.'

He took a step and turned back to face her. He was beyond the protection of the tree now, and he leaned into the chill wind and pulled his coat around him. 'I'm not running away,' he said. 'I'm cold. Let's go sit in the car.'

TWENTY-FIVE

It was only slightly warmer inside the car, and Father Watson started the engine. 'The temperature must have dropped twenty degrees,' he said. He turned the heater fan to high. 'That wind is—'

'Whose car is this?' Kirsten asked.

'What?'

'You said you had to borrow a car. So . . . whose car *is* it?'

'A friend of mine, a priest. I already sold my car. I told him I had an unexpected appointment and he said I could use his. Why?'

'Because anyone who can bug the house you live in, can probably bug the car you drive, as well.'

He stared at her. 'I never said the rectory was bugged.'

'But you sure *acted* like it. Anyway, tell me about Johnny O'Hern, and this priest, Father Landrew, and I'll do my best to keep you out of it.'

'And if I refuse?'

'Like I said before, I'll go forward without you. And I'll have no reason to hide the fact that it was a phone call from *you* that got me started.'

He sighed. 'I guess I have no choice.'

'There you go with that "no choice" stuff again.'

He reached out and turned the heater fan down. 'OK,' he said, and twisted in his seat to face her. 'Janice Robinson . . . I don't really *know* her, but I think she works for the government. The CIA.'

'You *think* she works for the CIA?'

'Yes. I mean . . . I should start at the beginning. Starting sometime in the nineties, the archdiocese sponsored a medical clinic in Guyana, serving poor people.'

'Guyana,' Kirsten said, 'that's . . . on the north edge of South America, am I right?'

'Yes, on the Atlantic coast, or the Caribbean. Next to Venezuela. Anyway, the clinic, called "Fair Hope Clinic", was in a remote area, not that far from where Jonestown was. You know, where they had that mass suicide?'

'"Mass murder", I'd call it,' she said. 'So this clinic was pretty close to the Venezuelan border?'

'Yes. It was staffed by nearly all volunteers, and I don't think it was that expensive to operate. But still, around the middle of last year the cardinal decided we couldn't keep supporting it. Then an anonymous benefactor appeared, someone willing to fund the clinic.'

'And the anonymous benefactor,' Kirsten said, 'was the CIA.'

Watson looked startled. 'How did you—'

'You're the one who brought up the CIA, and I'm sure they'd love access to a facility in what they must consider a critical area, what with Venezuela sitting on all that petroleum and thumbing its nose at the US.'

'Yes, well, there was certainly no hint of that at the time. But long after the fact I was informed that for a time the CIA had been using a building on the Fair Hope property.'

'For a *time*? You mean not any more?'

'If what was told to me was true, and if they *were* using it, they haven't been there for about a year. The archdiocese doesn't even operate the clinic any more. About six months ago we turned it over to the Guyanese health ministry. And now it's not even operating.'

'Uh-huh.' Kirsten nodded. 'And O'Hern's sister . . . Janice . . . she was supposedly one of the CIA people there?'

'I got the impression she wasn't just *there*; she was in charge. She . . . she was pointed out to me, but that was months ago, and I had no idea at the time who she was.'

'So who pointed her out? Who told you all this? And why?'

'That part I really need to keep secret. I'm required by . . . you know . . . by my priesthood. But it seemed . . . I mean it wasn't likely to be false information.'

'Right. So all you can say is that the Catholic Church was secretly helping the CIA, which was probably down there plotting to overthrow a foreign government, right?' Kirsten couldn't resist pushing it. 'Maybe assassinate a few elected officials?'

'You don't . . . there's no evidence of . . .' He paused. 'Anyway, it wasn't "the Catholic Church". I couldn't find anyone on the staff at the archdiocese – including the cardinal – who knew anything about it.'

'You *asked*?'

'Yes. I mean, only indirectly. But really, no one knew much at all about anything going on down there, and—'

'It's getting dark,' Kirsten said. She pointed through the windshield. 'And I think that caretaker is coming to throw us out.'

Father Watson drove out through the cemetery gate and Kirsten pointed to where she'd left the Camry. 'Park behind that car,' she said.

'I don't know. It's late, and—'

'You *gotta* be kidding.'

He parked.

'OK,' Kirsten said, 'so someone told you Janice Robinson was a CIA agent.'

'Well, let's say I was led to believe that. Except I didn't know her name then.'

'Uh-huh. So tell me . . . whoever or whatever she is . . . tell me what she said that connected Johnny O'Hern's death with Father Landrew's. But first, didn't Landrew used to write a column for the *Sun-Times*?'

'Yes. He was the pastor of a church on the west side, in a very poor neighborhood. He was quite . . . "liberal", I guess you'd say. Larry could be irritating, you know. Critical of both government and church leadership. Still, a very dedicated man. Involved in interracial programs and a member of the

Archdiocesan Peace and Justice Commission. That's a group that—'

'I get that,' she said. 'Tell me the connection between the murders.'

'Well, about a year ago, when Larry . . . Father Landrew . . . was killed, it seemed like just a random murder. A robbery.'

'I remember,' Kirsten said. 'Another priest was with him when it happened, right?'

'Yes, Father Clarke. Paul Clarke.'

'And didn't the police say he . . . well . . . he wasn't co-operating or something?'

'I don't know about that. I know Paul was terribly traumatized. Seemed to be suffering from survivor's guilt. But I'm sure he talked to the police, more than once. As far as I know, they were satisfied.'

'Where is he now, this Father Clarke?'

'I don't know. Nobody knows. He took a leave of absence after . . . after Father Landrew's death, and now he's just . . . gone.'

'And the police aren't looking for him?'

'No. I'm sure they'd have contacted the archdiocese if they were. Like I said before, the police told me they think Father Landrew was killed by an addict.'

'And you? You know differently?' Kirsten asked.

'No, I don't *know* differently. It's just that . . . before he was killed Father Landrew spent a week volunteering at Fair Hope Clinic. I know that for sure, and I'm pretty sure it would have been during the time the CIA was there, if they *were* there. If he saw them . . . and I don't *know* whether he did . . . he'd have been outraged, and Larry wasn't the type to keep quiet about things like that.'

'Which makes you think his death maybe wasn't just a robbery.'

'I know it sounds crazy, but . . .' He looked a little embarrassed.

'Lots of things sound crazy. Just go on.'

'OK.' He took a deep breath. 'A week ago, when I heard about a police officer being murdered, it didn't mean much to me. But then a woman called and said her name was Janice Robinson and she wanted to talk to me. She said the dead police officer was her brother. We made an appointment and when I saw her I was so shocked I could hardly speak. It was the woman who I'd been told was with the CIA. I managed to offer my condolences about her brother, and I'll never forget her answer. "Johnny O'Hern," she said, "was a mean, despicable person. No one with any sense cares that he's dead."'

'Jesus,' Kirsten said. 'I mean . . . go ahead.'

'She said her *mother* was sad, though, and very upset with her pastor. He wouldn't give her brother a Catholic burial. The pastor said he wasn't a parish member and had abandoned the church years ago, and that he had a "public history of violence". Over the years he'd been involved in two fatal police shootings. Both times he was exonerated, but both were questionable. He was also under investigation for criminal behavior, and for involvement with organized crime. The pastor said canon law forbade him to bury someone like that.'

'That's not really *true*, is it?' Kirsten thought of some of the funerals she'd attended.

'What canon law says is that "public sinners" should be denied Catholic burial unless they've shown repentance before death. I told Janice some priests interpret that pretty strictly, and she became very angry. "That's *so* hypocritical," she said. "What's a 'history of violence' got to do with burying someone? Don't we *need* violent people? Don't we *train* people to kill, and send them off to kill others? And when they're brought home in body bags you priests are there, to drape flags over their caskets. We may not like the idea, but sometimes violent people . . . men like my brother . . . are useful." Then, just as suddenly, she calmed down, said she wasn't there to discuss violence, just to get her brother a funeral.'

'Basically, then, Janice said "jump", and you jumped.'

Anger flared up in the priest's eyes, but he beat it back. 'I would never deny *anyone* a Catholic funeral if their family wanted it. And besides, a public fight over a priest denying a mother's son a funeral was something the church didn't need, and I could easily avoid it.'

'Anyone question you on that? The pastor who wouldn't do it? Or the cardinal or someone?'

'No. The only questions were ones that came from inside me. I couldn't get Larry Landrew's death out of my mind. Was it possible the CIA would kill a priest? And Janice . . . and what she'd said about violence and killing people, and about her brother, and I wondered if he'd been involved, if he'd been "useful" to the CIA.'

'You thought *he* might have killed Father Landrew?'

'My mind was running wild. I was scared, too, but I rode with Janice to the cemetery, thinking this was my chance to . . . well . . . at least to bring it up. See what her reaction was. Hoping I'd learn it was all nonsense. Finally, as we pulled into the cemetery, I said . . . like I was just making conversation . . . I said I'd heard her brother was a detective in the same neighborhood where one of our priests was killed. I said the case was never solved, and I wondered if he'd worked on it.'

'And?'

'She kept driving, like she didn't hear me. So I said the priest was quite well known, and was killed just after he came back from volunteering at a clinic the archdiocese sponsored in Guyana. "Did you ever hear about that?" I asked.'

'And did she answer?'

'By then she was parking the car. She turned off the engine and finally looked over at me. "Apparently you're talking about things that happened a long time ago," she said. "And sometimes when things are in the past, we'd be better off to let them *stay* in the past." Then she opened the door and got out. I sat there for a few seconds, not able to move. I knew it wasn't my imagination. When she said "*we'd* be better off", I knew she meant *me*. Afterwards I . . . it was like I wanted to scream or something . . . to *tell* somebody. So I called *you*.' Watson lowered the car window about an inch and cold air rushed in. 'I guess I shouldn't have.'

Ten minutes later Kirsten was back in her Camry. She wondered who'd first whispered 'CIA' into Father Wayne Watson's ear, but that was a secret she knew he'd never reveal. He wouldn't even say when, or under what circumstances. But otherwise, he insisted, he'd told her everything. And she believed he had.

But buying into his suspicions? That was something else.

Not every conspiracy sighting, she knew, was a product of paranoia or an overactive imagination. Maybe the CIA *was* working out of that clinic; maybe Janice Robinson *was* involved. But tying that to the murder of a priest in Chicago? And tying that murder to Johnny O'Hern's murder, a year later?

She wondered whether this apparently sensible priest, having been given a glimpse through the conspiracy window, was seeing connections where none existed.

TWENTY-SIX

Dugan hadn't had a chance to tell Kirsten about his encounter with the two thugs by the river because she hadn't come home until past midnight and she was still asleep when he left that morning. Later he'd reached her and insisted they had to talk, so she'd picked him up at his office at four. Now they were on River Road, out near O'Hare.

The wipers weren't keeping up with the rain streaming down the Camry's windshield, and he couldn't see a damn thing. He watched Kirsten lean forward and peer out over the steering wheel, and wished she'd slow down a little.

'So you didn't wait for the cops?' she asked.

'After I'd just thrown a guy in the river?'

'I wish I'd been there,' she said. 'Anyway, you speed dialed our number on your cell phone. What'd you catch on the answering machine?'

'I got far off, unintelligible voices and some screaming sea-gulls. But still, you gotta admit, it was a great idea.' He shifted his bulk around in the passenger seat, still wishing she'd slow down, and wishing even more that she'd get a bigger car.

'So nobody made a police report?' she asked.

'Not me. And apparently not the gorilla in the water, either. It says in the *Tribune* that witnesses saw two people in a sailboat pull him out. He took off before the cops got to him.'

'So,' she said, 'the remarks they made about me. Were they . . . derogatory?'

'Actually, more complimentary than derogatory. But I really don't want to repeat them. The threats, though . . . maybe you *should* back off. I can't believe the cops won't come up with a better suspect than me.'

'They haven't so far.'

'I know, but you're taking it too seriously.' In fact, his

own attempts not to take it seriously were becoming more difficult. 'It's total bull—'

'Hold on,' she said. 'We're here.' She hit the brakes and yanked on the wheel, and they made a hard right toward a two-story tall bubbling martini glass, made of flashing blue and green neon lights and superimposed over the words: *FLIGHT PLAN II*, and below that: *Cocktails and Fine Dining*.

The storm made it dark enough to be past sundown, but it was only four thirty and there were plenty of empty parking spaces. Kirsten, though, drove right up under the awning at the front entrance and stopped beside a sign that said: *Valet Parking*. As they got out of the car a kid in a red windbreaker came out the door to get her keys, but she kept them. 'Safety inspectors,' she said. 'Won't be long.'

The guy started to object, but Dugan handed him a twenty and they went inside.

The lighting was indirect and the décor comfortable and expensive-looking. A slender young woman in tight black trousers and a man's white shirt stood beside the hostess desk, talking on the phone. She had high cheekbones and a nice tan and her blonde hair was pulled back. When she saw them she hung up and came their way, and in Dugan's eyes her masculine outfit accented her quite feminine figure. Tilting her head, she gave a cute flirtatious smile and said the bar was to their left and the dining room to their right. 'But we don't start serving dinner till six.'

'Thanks, but that's perfectly OK,' Dugan said, and smiled back at her. 'We just came in for a drink. It's raining like crazy out there and we thought this place looked like a cozy—'

'This way, darling.' Kirsten took his arm.

'*Darling?*' he asked, as she steered him through the doorway into the bar. 'I hate it when you call me that.'

'I know. I only do it when you're drooling.'

'Damn,' he said. 'How can someone as intelligent and sexy as you be jealous?'

'I'm not jealous. I'm working. I need to talk to this guy Teddy before it gets busy in here.'

They sat on swivel stools with backs upholstered in brown faux leather. Just one other person sat at the bar, a man at the far end, a salesman-looking type, nursing a beer and writing in a notebook lying open on the polished wood. The bartender was a happy-looking guy. Jamaican, Dugan guessed, complete with dreadlocks; his freshly pressed white shirt in sharp contrast to his ebony skin. He must have picked the easy-going, old-time reggae music that was floating softly through the air. Kirsten ordered a ginger ale – practicing for when she was pregnant – and Dugan a Guinness.

'Who told you about this place, and Teddy, anyway?' Dugan asked. Still not charged with a crime he and his lawyer had no right to see any police reports. 'Was it that homicide detective, Newhouse?'

'No way I could tap that source again.'

'Parker Gillson?'

'I really can't say. I promised.'

'So it was Gillson. He probably knows a guy who knows a guy, who knows a cop . . . or lots of cops. Am I right?'

When Kirsten didn't answer, Dugan spun around on his stool and surveyed the room. What little light there was came mostly from tiny electrified candles in the middle of each of the dozen or so round tables. Only one occupied table. Four women who looked to be in their fifties, with bags and parcels piled on the floor around them. Obviously erasing the rigors of a hard day at the mall. Beyond the tables was a wall lined with plush-looking booths, all of them empty except the one where a young couple sat thigh to thigh and whispered and nudged at each other.

The Jamaican came back with their drinks and Kirsten asked him, 'Are you Teddy?'

'Oh no, miss,' he said. 'Teddy much better looking and . . .' He stopped, and a wide grin spread across his face as he looked past them toward the entrance to the bar. 'Here come Teddy now.'

They turned. Coming toward them, flashing that same flirtatious smile, was the blonde who'd greeted them at the hostess desk. Dugan leaned close to Kirsten and said, 'Remember. Not jealous. Working.'

'It's about the night that police officer was killed,' Kirsten said, handing Teddy her business card.

Teddy took a quick look at the card. 'I already told the police everything I know,' she said. But then, glancing around the nearly empty room, she added, 'But hey, I can spare a few minutes.' She didn't seem upset about being approached by a private investigator. She seemed intrigued, maybe even flattered. She slid the card into her hip pocket.

Pants that tight, Dugan thought, *it's surprising she got it in.*

'Be right back,' Teddy said. She went behind the bar and said something to the Jamaican, then filled a tall, thin glass half-full with ice, and added a squirt of soda from the bar gun. When she came back she nodded toward the booths. 'We can sit over there.'

They grabbed their drinks and followed her toward the booth closest to the entrance. On the way Kirsten whispered, 'I'll do the talking.'

'Right, boss,' he said, 'and I'll keep an eye on her.' Then, seeing the glare that got him, he added, 'In case . . . you know . . . she tries anything.' They slid into the bench seat across the table from Teddy.

'I don't really know very much,' Teddy said, and took a sip from her drink. 'Like I told the police.'

'You never know what might help,' Kirsten said. 'How'd they happen to contact you, anyway?'

'The police?' Teddy's dark brown eyes widened in surprise. 'They didn't contact me.'

'No?' Kirsten asked. 'What happened?'

'The guy . . . Officer O'Hern . . . I mean, I didn't know his name before . . . but he was in here pretty often. When I heard about a murder, and then saw his picture in the paper, I called, and the detectives came out. I don't know what I can add now that you couldn't get from them.'

Like the cops might tell a private eye what a witness said, Dugan thought. *Doesn't this woman watch TV?*

'Why don't you run through it again, OK?' Kirsten didn't take out a pen, and spoke as though this was all no big deal. 'And then I might have a few more things to ask you.'

Teddy told how she'd been working solo that night when O'Hern came in, sometime after midnight. How he arrived alone, but was joined later by a woman she'd never seen before. 'I'd say she was part-Asian, y'know. Attractive, kinda sophisticated-looking.'

'Did she come in after he did?' Kirsten asked.

'Actually, I never saw her come in, but she was there for at least an hour before him, maybe more. After he came in she went and joined him. He bought her a drink, and they talked, and a little later they left together.'

'When was that?'

'I know it had to be before two o'clock, 'cause that's closing time.' Teddy shrugged. 'And that's it. That's all I know.'

'Did it look like she was *waiting* for him? Like they had an appointment?'

'Police asked that, too.' Teddy paused, as though thinking it over. 'I wasn't paying real close attention, y'know? But I don't think so, 'cause then she'd have just got up to meet him when he came in. But he was there five or ten minutes before she went and sat down next to him. I don't think they knew each other.'

'OK,' Kirsten said. 'And are you sure they left *together*? Or could they have just both left at the same time?'

'Oh no, honey.' Teddy smiled, and her dark eyes lit up. 'Definitely together. Like they planned to *be* together . . . for a while, anyway.'

'So,' Kirsten said, 'she was a hooker?'

'I don't . . . I'll say one thing, she *did* know how to make a drink last a long time. Which the girls in the life have to do. But my job's pouring drinks, not thinking about . . . you know . . . what people do. And like I say, I was alone and we were busy. There was this group in town for a dog show at the Allstate Arena, and they all—'

'Uh-huh. But the woman . . . did she approach any other men? Or talk to anyone else? Besides O'Hern?'

Teddy frowned. 'Y'know, I never really . . . well . . . yes, people were coming and going, and she talked to a few. Just casual, like people do. Like she chatted awhile with this one woman who came in with a guy and sat next to her. They had pictures of their dog or something, but then they left. And I think she was talking to this other guy for a bit. Sandy-haired guy, kinda chunky. They talked, and she *could've* been trying to start something up with him. But then he left, too.'

'Anyone else?'

'I dunno, probably a few others, but nobody I really remember.' Teddy sipped at her drink. She glanced over at the bar and Dugan looked, too. The stools were starting to fill up.

'And you haven't seen her again since then, huh?' Kirsten asked.

'No. That's the only time.'

'Did she use plastic or cash?'

'Oh . . . cash. The police asked that, too.'

'And you said she looked "part-Asian". Can you narrow that down a little? You mean *east*-Asian? Like Japanese? Thai?'

'Oh, jeez,' Teddy said, 'I don't know. I mean, the eyes, the straight black hair, the skin. But pretty tall, about your height.'

'Uh-huh. Anything else?'

'Well . . . slim, but a nice figure. Expensive clothes, too; like a business suit, with pants.' She looked over toward the bar again. 'Really, that's about all I can say.'

'That's fine,' Kirsten said. 'We appreciate your help. And if you see that woman again, or if you recall anything else, I hope you'll call me.' She looked at Dugan. 'I think we should thank Teddy and let her get back to work.'

'Oh. OK, yeah.' He pulled out two twenties and slid them across the table.

'Well . . . *thank* you.' Teddy took the bills and stood up. As she walked toward the bar Dugan could see the outline of the business card in her hip pocket.

'Let's go,' Kirsten said, and he realized she was already standing. He hadn't even finished his Guinness.

They were just out the door and headed for the Camry when the valet in the red windbreaker appeared. 'So,' he said, 'how'd it go?'

'What?' Dugan asked. 'Oh, you mean the safety inspection?'

'Yeah, how'd it go?'

'A-minus,' Kirsten said. 'Only one violation we gotta write up.'

'What's that?'

She opened the car door. 'You can't let people park here. It's a fire lane.'

TWENTY-SEVEN

Dugan had told Mollie not to call or text him short of a national emergency, and now he wanted to get back and catch up on the day's messages and paperwork. He had Kirsten drop him at the CTA Blue Line station on River Road, not far from Flight Plan II. The Blue Line runs from O'Hare to downtown, and during rush hour was faster than driving. He was at his building, signed in with the security guard, and riding up on the elevator by six thirty.

These were difficult days. He had to keep reassuring himself that the idea of a murder charge against him was ludicrous, and he had to hold up his end as he and Kirsten kept pretending to each other that there was nothing to worry about. The effort was wearing him down.

In fact, Dugan was flat-out tired . . . and he was *never* tired.

He let himself into the office suite and was relieved to be surrounded by the after-hours quiet. A law student sat alone in the clerks' room, drafting a motion to compel a defendant bread company – whose driver was texting while backing up to a loading dock, and ran over Dugan's client – to produce its personnel records. The only other sign of life was light from the open door to Larry Candle's office.

He didn't have to pass by Larry's door, and he moved quietly so Larry wouldn't know he was back. He didn't need another interrogation about how the O'Hern murder investigation was going. He reached his own office, went inside, and closed the door without a sound. He was hanging his suit coat over the back of his chair when the door swung open again.

'Hey, Doogs,' Larry said. 'How they hangin'? You look like you could use a cold one.'

'I'll take a pass tonight,' Dugan said, but by then Larry was already gone, headed for the office refrigerator.

Dugan sank into his desk chair and stared down at the stack of notes Mollie had left him. *Damn*, he thought, *how can so many—*

'Hey, Doogs!' Larry said. 'Look up!'

Dugan did not look up, and kept his voice low and calm. 'If you throw a bottle at me, you're out on the street . . . for good.'

There was silence then, during which Larry opened one bottle of Dos Equis and set it on the desk top. He perched his butt on one of the client's chairs, opened his own beer, and took a long pull. 'Jesus,' he finally said, 'for a second there, I thought you meant it.'

Dugan looked up. 'I *did* mean it, Larry.'

'Yeah, well, sure.' Larry grinned. 'But you're over it now, right?'

'No, I don't think I—'

''Cause like I told you before, man, I only throw when I think you're up to it. And when you're not? Well . . . damn . . . I'm not irresponsible, y'know. I mean, not *completely*.'

'Is there something on your mind, Larry?'

'Hey, that's more like it, partner.' Larry wiggled like a puppy. 'Glad you asked.'

'Don't call me that. You're not my partner.'

Larry waved his hand in the air. 'Figure of speech, Doogs, that's all.' He took another gulp of beer. 'But anyway, thing is . . . there *is*.'

Dugan shook his head and tried not to smile. He could *not* stay mad at Larry. Kirsten could. Hell, the whole *world* could. *The lawyer for the little guy*. That had been Larry's slogan when he had his own firm. He had his faults, but he was so irrepressibly cheerful . . . even while he was driving you nuts . . . that it sort of rubbed off. '"There *is*" what?'

'Something on my mind.'

'Bullshit. You came in here to pump me for information.'

'Nope, not this time. I got something to tell you. Two things, really.' He paused. 'One is, I settled the Belwether case today. *Beaucoup* bucks, man. *Beaucoup* bucks.' Larry shrugged. 'I mean, at least *beaucoup* for a slip and fall in a bar at ten in the morning, and only soft tissue injuries.'

'Damn, that *is* good news,' Dugan said, and meant it. 'Leonard Belwether's been a problem since he stepped in the door. I was about ready to pay him myself, to go find another lawyer.'

'Who'd take that pain in the ass as a client? Only you, the

last of the good guys.' Larry drained his beer. 'Anyway, that's part one. Part two's more important. At least I think it is.'

'OK, so?'

'Remember that creep you told me you threw in the river the other day?'

'That's not somebody I'm likely to forget.'

'Haven't found him yet, have you?'

'Nope. We can't even find the people on the boat who fished him out. They put him on hard ground and went on their way.'

'Yeah, well . . .' Larry pointed his thumb at his own chest. 'Larry Candle, the private eye for the little guy, at your service. I know who pulled him outta the water.'

TWENTY-EIGHT

'Larry Candle? How the hell did *he* find out who it was?' Kirsten asked. 'And why did you tell him you threw the guy in the river in the first place? I wouldn't tell Larry I threw a peanut at a pigeon.'

'You don't work with him every day like I do. He grows on you.'

'Right,' she said. 'Like a wart.'

Dugan stood up, not the easiest thing to do since he'd been seated on a too-small, too-shaky aluminum lawn chair and had a bottle in one hand and his own empty glass in the other. He bowed slightly. 'Would *madame* permit me to refill her *flute à champagne*?'

'We shouldn't celebrate until we're sure the boat people can ID the guy,' she said. 'Plus, you can't call these plastic cups "flutes".'

'Yeah, well, you can't call this non-alcoholic bubbly stuff "champagne", either. But even apart from the sailboat stuff, Larry got rid of my most obnoxious client today. That's worth celebrating in itself.'

'I suppose,' she said, and held out her cup.

The air was clear and cool, and Dugan was feeling less tired now, even though it was near midnight. They were out on the roof of their condo building. Not a deck; just a flat, tar-and-gravel rooftop. To reach it they had to climb a ladder, supplies in hand, and raise a heavy trap door. They had the top-floor unit in a three-flat building, and had the only access to the roof.

He refilled both cups, then lifted his into the air. 'Here's to Larry . . . super-detective, wart, take your pick. But as to how he found out about the boat, he swore me to secrecy.'

'I bet he said you could tell *me*, though.'

'He did,' Dugan said. 'He likes you.'

'That's a scary thought. But anyway . . . tell me.'

'He figured a sailboat on that part of the river at this time of year was probably headed for dry dock. There's only a couple of boat storage places out on the south branch of the river and one's owned by a former client of Larry's.' Dugan sipped some fake champagne and listened to the sounds of the city – muffled traffic and distant sirens, music spilling out of the night spots just walking distance away. 'That's a great story, by the way. Larry's client was sued by a guy whose yacht was in his storage place and got trashed when someone broke in and had a wild party on it. Larry proved that the host of the party was the teenaged daughter of the boat owner. Seems the girl—'

'OK,' Kirsten broke in, 'let's get back to Larry. I suppose he called his former client to see who brought boats in that day.'

'He didn't just call. He took a cab out there. And it turns out a man and a woman came in with a sailboat that afternoon.'

'So how do we know that's the boat that picked up your swimmer?'

'We can't be sure, but that was the only sailboat the guy took in that day, and Larry had him call the only other storage place out that way, and that one had no sailboats at all.'

'And this man and woman, *if* they're the ones who fished the guy out, why would they just take off? Why not stick around and play hero for awhile?'

'Maybe the guy paid them to be quiet. But it's more likely because, according to Larry's storage guy, the two of them are married . . . but not to each other.'

'Uh-huh.' Kirsten set her cup on the rooftop beside her, and pulled her jacket tighter. 'He get addresses to go with the names?'

'Just the woman's. She owns the boat. Or her business does.'

'It's not likely the goon told her who he was, but I'll go see her tomorrow.' She didn't sound enthusiastic. 'We should head downstairs,' she said, and got to her feet. 'It's getting cold up here. Besides, did you forget?' She took his hand and pulled him to his feet. 'We have to go make a baby.'

Dugan saw how tired she looked, and a new wave of fatigue suddenly washed over him, too. He knew he ought to be honest with her, admit that all he wanted to do was go to sleep. But he didn't. Instead, he folded his chair, thinking how odd it was that the next item on their agenda was a *requirement*.

TWENTY-NINE

'Dea Hannson, Portrait Photographer' had a rather elegant website, with solo guitar music in the background. Kirsten clicked and scrolled her way through a sampling of Dea's 'casual, yet sophisticated, child and family portraits' which, in fact, showed good humor, and lots of creativity. Many were set outdoors, including several on a sailboat.

She had the address and phone number Larry Candle had gotten, so she called the number and a pleasant voice said: 'You've reached Dea Hannson. Please leave a message and I'll return your call as soon as possible.' Kirsten left no message.

The autumn air was clear, bright, and cool, and the cab ride was a short one, so by ten fifteen she was walking up the steps of a century-old, well-kept brownstone in the 1000 block of North Clark Street. Two small brass signs were set in the wall beside the front door, one above the other. The top one said: *randall bradford, consultant*. The other said: *dea hannson, photographer*.

She pressed the button, heard a deep, two-tone gong sound inside, and waited. It was probably only fifteen seconds, but she pressed again. And waited again.

The man who finally opened the door was Kirsten's height, with thick brown hair that was turning gray and was carefully tousled. His clothes – casual jeans, flannel shirt – as well as his arrogant, sullen pout were straight out of Abercrombie and Fitch. He had to be old enough, though, to be an Abercrombie model's father.

He stared at her, not saying anything. As though not *deigning* to say anything.

She stared back. 'My guess,' she said, 'is you're not Dea Hannson.'

'Huh?' He frowned, seemed to be thrown off his game.

'A joke,' she said. 'I'm here to see Ms Hannson.'

'Dea's not in.'

'That's OK. I can wait.'

'I don't think so,' he said. He had his arrogance back. No wonder Dea liked to go sailing with some other guy.

'When will she be here?'

'Who wants to know?' Not being protective. Being a smart-ass.

She could do smartass with the best of them, but this wasn't the time, so she handed him one of her cards . . . one of those with just her name and cell number, nothing else. 'Dea doesn't know me,' she said, 'but please tell her I'd like to talk to her.'

He stared at the card. 'About what?'

'A couple of days ago a friend of mine was in a jam and Dea helped out.'

His eyes narrowed. 'Helped out?' It was clear he didn't know what she was talking about. 'Helped out *how*?'

'Well . . .' Kirsten cocked her head and frowned. 'I guess I could tell *you*. You're Mr Bradford, right? Dea's husband?' Two safe enough guesses, she thought.

'I am.'

'It's just that my friend didn't have time to thank Dea properly, and . . .' She paused. 'You know what? I better talk to Dea.' She smiled again. 'Dea doesn't even *know* my friend.' She had to make this creep curious, get him to remember her, make him actually give Dea the damn card. 'Thing is,' she said, 'my friend may want some photos taken. Family portraits. And it's . . . you know . . . a pretty wealthy family.'

She was barely down the sidewalk and out at the curb, looking for a cab, when her cell phone rang. She hoped it was Dea Hannson. But it wasn't. It was Polly Morelli.

'I haven't heard from you,' he said.

'You will, when I have something to report.'

'You working on it?'

'Only when you're not taking up my time.'

'Good. But I needa hear something.' Jesus, the guy was like a kid: *Are we there yet?* 'Tell me what you're doing now.'

'Someone sent muscle to shut me down. That could be helpful. Once I find out who the muscle was, I'll find out who the someone is who doesn't want the killer ID'd.'

'And then you'll tell me,' he said. 'Get on it, and have a nice day.'

She folded her phone and kept walking. By the time she spotted an empty cab she was halfway downtown, so she walked the other half, too. She was on Michigan Avenue, near Randolph, when she called the ARDC and was put through to Parker Gillson.

'You got a few minutes sometime soon?' she asked.

'Meet you for lunch,' he said, 'at . . . say . . . eleven forty-five?' Park *loved* lunch. In fact, Park never met a meal he didn't love.

'How about coffee? In . . . say . . . five minutes.'

'Damn, Kirsten, don't you—'

'I'll bring the coffee and meet you in that little plaza behind your building. You'll be back before they miss you.'

'I'll be there.'

She didn't like to take advantage of Park. But after all, she *had* saved his life. Or that's the way he always put it. She knew what she'd done was give him a chance to save his own life. She was the one who'd hunted him down when he'd alienated everyone he knew and nobody else gave a damn any more. She'd dragged him out of a pool of his own vomit and piss and God-knows-what, and got him to a hospital. And after that to rehab. And after that . . . well, after that's when he saved his own life.

She picked up two coffees, both black. He preferred lots of cream and sugar, but the very thought made her queasy. And it wasn't good for him. And she was buying.

'And no doughnut to go with it, either,' she said, as they settled on to a cold stone bench. The building blocked out the sun, keeping the temperature down in the little plaza . . . and keeping other people away.

'Straight coffee and no pastry.' Park shifted his bulk around on the bench. 'And a possible case of hemorrhoids to boot.'

'Hemorrhoids aren't caused by cold surfaces. But . . . not to change the subject . . . do you know anyone at the CIA? Or anyone who knows anyone at the CIA?' Park knew people who knew people. Once that had been his business. Now it was something of a hobby. Or . . . more than a hobby. A compulsion.

'If I did, and I told you, then I'd have to kill you,' he said. 'Why?'

She gave him a fast rundown of Father Wayne Watson's fears and theories. She knew the tale would go no farther than Park. 'So,' she said, 'what do you think?'

'I think anything's possible, but that one's a bit of a stretch. More important, though, even if it's true, how you gonna prove it? Even if I knew someone, which I don't. Better find another suspect, if you wanna get Dugan off the hook.'

'OK then, how about one of Polly Morelli's lieutenants? Someone who had Johnny O'Hern killed because Johnny was about to talk about shady stuff going on between the lieutenant and Barry Zelander. How's that?'

'More plausible. Who you got in mind?'

'No one in particular. Not yet. But someone sent a couple of thugs to try to convince Dugan to scare me off. If I come up with a sketch artist's picture of one of them, or both, I'm thinking you might know someone who . . . well . . . who knows people in the life, and who could fit the pictures to real persons.'

'So let's see . . .' Park sipped some coffee and frowned, obviously missing the additives. 'You give me a couple of drawings that will probably both look pretty much like every generic male person in the world, and I run the drawings by Joey Know-it-all, who says, "Sure, this one's Billy Thug, and that's his cousin Rudy. They work for Jimmy Lieutenant, one of Polly Morelli's crew members." Is that it?'

'I know a better-than-average artist, and for one of the two guys I may have a second person, besides Dugan, someone with a trained eye, to add input to the drawing.'

'Uh-huh.'

Kirsten shrugged. 'Sounds like you think my plan's a little shaky.'

'Oh?' He looked at his watch and stood up. 'How'd you ever get that idea?'

THIRTY

Conventional wisdom wasn't on Kirsten's side. What surgeon operates on his own child? What lawyer represents her own sister? What PI has her own accused husband for a client? But her main concern wasn't having the wrong client. It was having too many clients.

First she had Dugan and, wisely or not, she wouldn't trust his freedom and survival to anyone but herself. Next she had Polly Morelli, whom she owed, and who in any event wasn't easy to walk away from. Finally, she had Richard O'Hern, who hired her maybe because he didn't like the approach the cops were taking – like he said – or maybe because he killed Johnny himself and he wanted to avoid suspicion, and stay up-to-date on whatever she turned up. But either way, having access to Richard had its advantages.

'I need to take a look through Johnny's house,' she said.

'What good will that do?' Richard asked.

They were in the hall outside a fourth-floor courtroom in the Daley Center, in the heart of the Loop, where Richard was defending an attractive, forty-something suburban mom in a drunk driving case. The lunch recess was almost over.

'Maybe no good at all,' Kirsten said, 'but it's something I have to do.' A few yards down the hallway Richard's frightened-looking client was standing with her husband and two obviously bewildered teenaged daughters. 'The house isn't sealed off, is it?'

'No, it was never part of the crime scene itself. But the cops have already been through it from top to bottom, looking for anything that might be connected to his death.'

'They find anything?'

'Not that I know of.'

'You have a key?'

'No, but—' He stopped. His client was coming their way and he raised his index finger toward her in a *just-one-moment* gesture. 'I don't have a key, but my mother does. She goes in and cleans the place for Johnny . . . or she did . . . even washes his clothes.'

'Really?'

'Yeah, strange, I know. Since we were kids she always took special care of Johnny . . . at least when our father wasn't around. As a kid I thought she liked Johnny more than me, but later I decided she was trying to atone to him for not shielding him from the old man's constant cruelty. She sure never offered to clean *my* place. I mean . . . not that I want her to. I have a service that—'

'Right. Just get the key from her.' Richard was looking away, watching people come down the hallway, headed for various courtrooms. 'I gotta go. My client's facing jail time.'

'Yeah, well, good luck,' Kirsten said. 'And when you get that key, call me. I'd like you to be with me when I go. Tomorrow if you can. Or Saturday?'

'It'll be a few days. I'm leaving straight from court for Florida. Got a drug case that just blew up big time, and there goes the weekend. Be back sometime Monday.'

'Damn. OK, talk to you Monday then.' Johnny's house wasn't *that* urgent, anyway. She watched as Richard joined his client and her family, and they all disappeared into the courtroom.

On her way to the elevators she thought of the look on that mother's face, and couldn't imagine the depth of the fear the woman was feeling. She knew, though, what it was like to have to face the future . . . and to be scared about it.

'It's me,' Kirsten said, surprised she'd gotten through to Father Watson without even having to stretch the truth. She'd left the courthouse and was walking north on Dearborn, cell phone to her ear. 'Sorry to bother you.' That part *was* a bit of a stretch.

'Actually,' he said. 'I was wondering when I'd hear from you again.'

'You got a few minutes?'

'I have a pretty full schedule, but . . . when and where did you have in mind?'

'I'm on foot,' she said, 'and I'll be outside your office in . . . oh . . . ninety seconds.' She exaggerated a little to keep the pressure up.

'Oh. Well, OK, I'll meet you.' No argument, another surprise.

In five minutes she was at Chestnut and Rush, outside a gray gothic building – once a seminary, now full of arch-diocesan offices – just steps from Michigan Avenue's Magnificent Mile. And there was the soon-to-be *Bishop* Wayne Watson, coming out the door, black suit freshly pressed and roman collar gleaming. When he spotted her he looked a bit apprehensive, she thought, but not unhappy to see her.

'Where's a good place to talk?' she asked.

'I told my assistant I was going over to the cathedral. We can talk on the way. It's just a few blocks, at Chicago and—'

'Don't worry. I've been there.' Holy Name Cathedral was the site of Kirsten's first meeting with – of all people – Polly Morelli, back when she'd needed his help. 'I'm stuck,' she said, as they crossed at the light, heading west on Chestnut. 'It's this "connection" you talked about between the murders of Johnny O'Hern and Father Landrew.'

'I know. It was probably foolish of me to—'

'No, hold on. I'm not saying you're foolish. I mean, if we assume the CIA was at Fair Hope Clinic when Father Landrew was there, and Janice Robinson was in charge, then just being Johnny's sister makes Janice a *sort* of connection. But your next step . . . that it may have been Johnny who actually *killed* Father Landrew . . . that's a big leap.'

'It wasn't a "step" or a "leap", just a suspicion. And don't forget what Janice said about—'

'I know . . . about violent men being "useful". But that was a pretty generalized remark. Was there anything else?'

'I can't think of anything else specific she said.' As he spoke he smiled and nodded in response to a greeting from a passer-by, the third greeting he'd gotten in just a block. It had to be the roman collar. 'But,' he went on, 'she never visited her family, and she despised her brother, so why would she come to his funeral? Was she worried about something that might happen if she wasn't around?'

'Y'know,' Kirsten said, 'with a thought process like that, you should've been a cop.'

'I don't know. I guess I'm just looking for whatever might support my suspicious feeling.'

'Exactly,' she said. 'Cops do that a lot. Some, anyway. First they decide who's guilty, and then they look for things that'll prove it.'

'Yes, well, the police . . . that's another thing. Officer O'Hern was one of the detectives who worked on Father Landrew's murder.'

'He *was*? How do you know that? I thought Janice didn't answer you when you asked if her brother worked on the case.'

'She didn't, but I already knew the answer. That's why I asked her.'

She stared at him as they waited to cross another street. 'Like I said, you should've been a cop.'

'Me?' This time he actually smiled at her, and pointed his thumb toward his own chest. 'You want someone like *me* responding if a crook's breaking down your door?'

'Not really. I mean . . . no offense, but . . .'

'I wouldn't either,' he said, and she recalled how in their first two meetings she'd had to fight like hell to get him to open up. Today, maybe because he'd already told her what was scaring him, he seemed more at ease. 'Back when I first started worrying about all this,' he said, 'I called the police and asked for whoever was in charge of Larry's . . . Father Landrew's . . . case. I got the names of two detectives. One was John O'Hern. The name, of course, meant nothing to me, but I called him. He never called back, though, so I called the other name, a man named Maddox.'

'Maddox? *Zane* Maddox?'

'I didn't get his first name.'

'Was he African-American?'

'Well, he sounded that way on the phone. Why? Do you know him?'

'Not well,' she said, 'but I was a police detective myself, and it's surprising how many names I still recognize. Anyway, go on.'

'Maddox said he'd been the lead investigator in Father Landrew's case for the first week or so, before it was re-assigned to O'Hern. I told him I couldn't reach O'Hern and he apologized for that. He said he'd try to answer any questions I had. I don't know what I expected, but he didn't tell me anything that hadn't already been in the news. He said the case was still open, and there were no suspects.'

'Did he say why the case got reassigned? Or anything about O'Hern?'

'No. And, like I say, the name O'Hern meant nothing to me, so I didn't ask.'

By then they'd reached the cathedral, on State Street just south of Chicago Avenue, and stood at the foot of the broad stone steps leading up to the doors. 'OK,' she said, 'so O'Hern worked on the case. That adds to the connection, for sure. But it doesn't mean he killed the priest.'

'I agree. And I can't think of anything else I haven't already told you. So, considering it now, I . . .' He paused, looked away, then back at her. 'I was about to apologize for calling you. But the thing is, I'm glad I called. Yes, maybe I let my suspicions run away with me, but the whole business . . . the CIA, Father Landrew's murder, what Janice Robinson said, all of it . . . I had to tell *someone*. And I'm glad it was you. You were willing to listen, to at least take me seriously.'

'Yeah, well, my husband's a murder suspect. I'm taking everyone seriously.'

THIRTY-ONE

A dentist's office seemed an odd place for a lawyer-client conference, but Renata Carroway obviously liked to make the most of every minute in her day.

The building was right downtown, on Michigan Avenue between Madison and Washington, and when Dugan arrived at four o'clock she was there on the tenth floor, reading what looked like police reports. The lighting was dim and the furnishings in the tiny waiting room hadn't been upgraded in, say, fifty years.

'Place seems deserted,' he said.

'Dr Burke's in the back with a patient.' Renata was shoving the reports into a manila folder. 'He works solo, and his receptionist retired a year ago. I've been coming here since I was a kid, and I'm waiting for *him* to retire, too, because I can't bear to tell him I'm hooking up with a younger dentist. Anyway, my appointment's at four fifteen, so we've got a few minutes. I told you to have Kirsten here, too. Where is she?'

'I don't know,' Dugan said. 'She seems to have her phone turned off. So . . . how's the case look?' Even as he asked, he wasn't sure he wanted an answer.

'Looks like it always did. Like a bullshit, circumstantial case, with the cops determined to go forward.'

'I guess you couldn't talk that guy Newhouse out of any police reports.'

'Nope. He's sticking to procedure. No reports until charges are filed and the discovery rules kick in.'

'Uh-huh,' he said. 'So . . . what's left to discuss?'

'I wanted Kirsten here, dammit.' Renata looked at her watch. 'I need to talk to her about her investigation.'

'Yeah, well, if I could talk to her about that, then I could fill you in. But you told me not to discuss my case with anyone but you.'

'I know exactly what I told you, and I have a pretty good idea how well you follow directions. So, is she getting anywhere? Nothing like producing the real bad guy to make a difficult case go away.'

'A few days ago you told me the case against me "sucks". A few minutes ago you said it was "bullshit". How did it suddenly get to be "difficult"?'

'You know as well as I do. There's no homicide case that's not "difficult". You never know *what* a jury will do. And a bench trial? You just hope for a good judge . . . who's having a good—'

'*Haahh . . . haaah!*' The cry came from deeper in the office.

'What do you think?' Dugan asked. 'Laughter . . . or pain?'

'Beats me,' Renata said, 'but I'll go with laughter.'

'And I'll go with the case against me being bullshit.'

'Fine, so tell me what's going on from Kirsten's side.'

'Nothing substantial yet, really.' He gave her a quick rundown on the various angles Kirsten was following. When he finished he said, 'Everything points to a pro, so take your pick: an Outfit hit? the CIA? a bent cop?'

'With those your choices, you better hope it's the bent cop. But how about someone with a more personal grudge? Family, maybe.'

'Kirsten hasn't ruled anything out,' Dugan said. 'And even

though she's AWOL today, you'll hear whenever she turns up anything solid. What about that Asian-looking woman O'Hern picked up at the bar? Have the cops ID'ed her?'

'I asked Newhouse. He wouldn't give me a real answer, but he and I go way back, and I think I'd know if they did.' Renata sighed. 'That's one thing I wanted to talk to Kirsten about. We can't depend on the cops finding the woman, and she could be crucial. The time parameters are a little uncertain, but it seems O'Hern and she either parted ways right away and he went home alone . . . possible, but unlikely . . . or else she was there when the shooting went down.'

'Maybe she shot him,' Dugan said.

'Not likely. By all accounts O'Hern was a very careful, very suspicious guy . . . and he knew he had enemies. She'd have had to get out of the car, go around to his side, and then shoot him in the face before he could do anything. It's more likely she managed to run when someone approached the car.'

'Or the killer *let* her get away. A real pro might not be interested in her at all, if he knew she couldn't identify him. Problem is, if she got away, why hasn't she come forward? Does that mean she's an accomplice?'

'She *could* be,' Renata said, 'but that's also not likely. She's probably just scared. Or doesn't want to step up and announce she's a hooker.'

'Or that she *isn't* a hooker, and her husband was out of town.' Dugan shook his head. 'Too damn many *maybes* here.'

'Which is why I'm hoping Kirsten turns up a hard fact or two.' Renata checked her watch again. 'Meanwhile, it's twenty after already and my appointment was—'

The door from the inner office burst open and a tall, gray-haired man in a business suit came out. He was stooped over as he walked, and he had a hand pressed flat against his check. A cheerful male voice called out after him, 'Same time next week, Roger. And don't forget. Take those pain pills . . . as needed.'

'Right, I got it,' the man called back. Then, in a lower voice, he added, 'Christ! How'm I gonna *forget*?' and went out into the corridor.

A kind-looking elderly man in a white coat appeared in the doorway to the inner office. 'Ah, Renata,' he said, 'sorry to keep you waiting.'

'That's all right. I've got time.' She grabbed her briefcase and stood up. 'I'm only here for a cleaning.'

'And a check-up,' the dentist said. 'And some pictures. You never know what a few X-rays'll turn up.'

Dugan stood, too. 'Lotsa luck, Renata,' he said. 'And don't forget to smile for the camera.'

THIRTY-TWO

Kirsten had skipped the meeting with Renata Carroway, figuring Dugan could answer whatever questions the lawyer had. After she left Father Watson at the cathedral steps she'd had to hurry and corner the artist, Virginia Plante, and talk her into an evening session with Dugan.

By six o'clock the three of them were in Dugan's office, working on the sketch of the thug he threw in the river. They'd been at it for forty-five minutes and Virginia was still asking questions and making changes to the drawing.

Kirsten could tell Dugan was losing interest.

'That's about it,' he finally said. 'Not perfect, but close.'

To Kirsten the sketched face looked about as generic as Parker Gillson predicted it would. 'What do *you* think, Virginia?'

'Well, it's a start, but not the likeness we'll get if we keep going. Plus, you said there were *two* men.'

'Yeah,' Dugan said, 'but one oughta be enough.'

'I know the process is tedious,' Virginia said, 'and the truth is, it works better when you're not fatigued. I guess we could pick up again tomorrow, but I don't know what time. I have to be in court at nine.' A freelancer who'd been recommended to Kirsten as one of the best, Virginia didn't use a computerized system. She relied on charcoal pencils, lots of sketch paper, and her own method for pulling details from a person's memory that the person hadn't been conscious of. 'It's all *in* there,' she said, pointing the tip of her pencil at Dugan's forehead. 'It just takes patience to get at it.'

'It might be *in* there,' Dugan said, 'but—'

Kirsten's cell phone rang and she answered it. It was Dea Hannson.

'My husband gave me your card,' Dea said, 'and I'd love to meet and talk about a photo shoot. But I can't. I'm on my way out of the country.'

Three minutes later Kirsten was headed for the elevator, with Virginia's last unfinished drawing in her hand and Dugan on her heels.

'Slow down a minute,' he said. 'I thought the woman told you she couldn't talk now.'

'She did. Her mother's quite ill, in Sweden, and she has to be at O'Hare by eight. I'll try to catch her going out the door.'

'Great,' he said. 'I'll come with you.'

'No, you need to finish at least one sketch with Virginia.'

'I can do that tomorrow. You need me to keep Dea's husband occupied while you talk.'

'God knows what time that artist will be free tomorrow, Dugan, if at all. Besides, I'll catch her as she leaves. Her husband won't be going with her.'

'How do you know that?'

'Because he's a real creep. He couldn't care less about her mother. Besides, she said "*I* have to pack and get a cab," not *we*.'

'Still, I'll come with you.'

'Dugan, please, we *need* a completed sketch. Two of them, if possible. And I might not even catch Dea.'

Dugan gave in and Kirsten rode the elevator down and went outside and got a cab. The driver was young and Middle Eastern, with pretty good English. During the ride she explained what she wanted, and within fifteen minutes the cab was double-parked in front of the brownstone on North Clark, and Kirsten was ringing Dea Hannson's doorbell.

A thirty-something blonde woman, with a deep sailor's tan, opened the door and Kirsten said, 'Ms Hannson? Your cab's here. See?' She pointed. 'I'm assisting the driver. I'll help with your bags, please.'

'But I only just called, and—'

'Right.' Kirsten grabbed the larger of two bags sitting just inside the door. 'I'll get this.' The bag weighed a ton, but she pretended it was nothing and carried it to where the driver waited beside the cab's open trunk.

Dea followed, and by the time both her bags were safe

inside the trunk Kirsten was holding the cab door open and inviting her to get in. She did, and Kirsten got in beside her. As they pulled away the driver asked, 'Which airline, Miss?'

'What? Oh . . . uh . . . American.' She turned then to Kirsten and said, 'Your voice. Wasn't it you I just called a little while ago? I mean . . . who *are* you, anyway?'

'I'm the one you talked to. And I already paid for the cab, including the tip.' Kirsten handed Dea another business card, this time one that said *Wild Onion, Ltd.* 'I'm an investigator. I could give you lots of references, to check up on me, if we had time. But under the circumstances . . .' She shrugged. 'I *did* get this cab to your place in a hurry, right? And I look trustworthy, don't I?'

'I guess so, but I . . . what is it you want from me? My husband said something vague about me helping a friend of yours.'

'Right, the guy you pulled out of the river a couple days ago. I mean . . . sorry to be so mysterious with your husband, but I didn't want to go into it with him because . . . well . . . I thought maybe you'd prefer I didn't.'

'Oh . . . yeah . . . thanks.' Dea had a guilty look on her face. 'You know, I've been worried about that whole incident since it happened. Like, should I go to the police? Or talk to someone about it? But then I think . . . what's the point? Nobody really got hurt or anything. But . . . it just bothers me. He *is* OK, right?'

'Look, Dea, I have to tell you. The guy you helped, he's not actually my friend. He's just someone I . . . well . . . I'm looking for.'

'Damn, I *knew* there was something weird going on. How could a grown man lean over the railing and *accidentally* fall into the river, like he said? He must've jumped, right? Except he didn't seem suicidal to me. He seemed . . . he wasn't very nice at all. I hope you're not going to tell me he wants his money back.'

'I don't even know him,' Kirsten said. 'But what money?'

'He gave Barna . . . he gave my friend and me each . . . well . . . some cash. Not that he seemed really grateful, though. He seemed mostly pissed off. I mean, not at *us*. Anyway, he said he wasn't hurt and we should just put him ashore and then keep on going, not stop and talk to the police if they came, or the media or anyone . . . which was fine with us. Damn, did someone *throw* him in?'

'I wasn't there, Dea. I didn't see what happened. I'm just working on a case and I need to identify the man.'

'God, he's a *crook*, isn't he? I knew it. I—'

'Whether he's dishonest or not has really nothing to do with my case. I just need to know who he is. Did he tell you his name?'

'Are you kidding? He barely spoke. All he wanted was to get on dry land and get away from there.'

'That figures.' Kirsten took Virginia's sketch from her bag and unfolded it, 'Someone else who saw the guy has been working with an artist. This isn't finished yet, but does it look like him?'

Dea took the drawing and held it near the window to catch the light from outside the cab. 'Well, I mean, it's the right shape of face and the right hairline and all. But somehow it doesn't show really what he *looks* like. It misses the . . . the *meanness*.'

'Right. Originally, I was hoping I could get *you* to help the artist create a better likeness. But since you're leaving for . . . Oh, forgive me. I'm really sorry to hear about your mom.'

'Yeah, thanks.' Dea's guilty look was back. 'She's not *that* sick, you know? I just need to . . . to get away.'

Kirsten suddenly wondered whether Dea was going to Sweden at all, but decided not to press her luck by asking. 'So you have no idea who the guy was?'

'I told you, he hardly said anything. We left him at a place under the next bridge from where he could take some stairs up to street level, and he was gone.'

'And that's it? Nothing else was said?'

'Well, like I told you, he gave us the money, and asked . . . well, he *ordered* us, really . . . not to talk to anyone. I mean, he didn't actually *threaten* us, not explicitly, but . . . I don't know.'

'Yeah, well, you don't have to take *my* advice, Dea, but I think the best thing is to do what he said. Whoever he is . . . and I really don't know yet . . . there's no sense making him upset with you. But . . . you're sure there was no other talk?'

'Not that I . . . well, his cell phone was wet and wouldn't work, so I let him make a call on mine.'

'Really? Did you hear what he said?'

'No, he turned away. I *did* hear . . . like . . . one word. "Stunt", or "stump", or something. That's it.'

'OK, well, call me if you think of anything else. I'm gonna have the driver let me off up here somewhere, and then he'll take you on to O'Hare. Don't forget, I've already paid him, and . . .' Kirsten paused as she fumbled through her purse. 'Damn! Um . . . I hate to impose on you more than I already have, Dea. But could I possibly . . . use your phone?'

THIRTY-THREE

Dugan was alone in his office when his cell phone rang and ID'ed the caller as Dea Hannson. He took the call. 'Hey, Dea,' he said. 'It's been *way* too long, babe.'

'Very funny,' Kirsten said. 'The cab's about to exit the expressway and drop me off. Then he'll take Ms Hannson here to the airport. How're the sketches coming?'

'Not bad. Just the one, though. Virginia left a few minutes ago. What about your end?'

'Looking up, but I'm hungry. There used to be a Bulgarian place not far from—'

'*Bulgarian?*'

'Yeah, at Foster and Harlem. I'll meet you there . . . if it's still there.'

'It'll take me a while, and if I don't see the place I'll call you. On your own cell?'

'Yeah, that'd be great. Gotta run.'

Dugan hung up. Obviously, Kirsten had caught up with Dea Hannson and they were already halfway to O'Hare. She must have made some progress, too, because things were 'looking up'. He could always count on Kirsten.

But *Bulgarian* food?

He took a cab, made one quick stop along the way, and found the restaurant near where Kirsten said it should be.

It was a small place and jammed with people, and the walls shook with what Dugan had to assume was Bulgarian rock.

The bar was in the front and the crowd seemed mostly recent immigrants. He elbowed his way through – not an easy task – to a door in the rear that opened into a separate dining room. Kirsten was there, sitting at one of about a dozen tables, most of which were filled with family groups. He waved hello and then turned right around and bullied his way back to the bar, where he got two bottles of a Pilsner called Zagorka.

He carried the beers back into the dining room. The music was less deafening here, and he joined Kirsten. She was nursing a huge white mug of coffee and had already finished eating.

'That's a shock,' he said. 'Most places like this, you wait forever to get served.'

'Yeah, well, no exception here. But they *do* have a male waiter who pops in about once every half hour, and I . . . well . . . sad to say, I flirted a little.' She cocked her head and batted her eyes to show how it was done. 'It worked,' she added, 'and pretty soon he brought me some wonderfully delicious bread and a moderately OK salad. So . . . if you want something to eat, maybe I can—'

'No need. I picked up a burger and fries and ate on the way. No drink, though. Which is why I'm so thirsty.' He took a long pull on one of the Zagorkas. 'Not bad,' he said. 'So . . . how'd it go? Why'd you use that woman's phone to call me?'

Kirsten summarized her cab ride with Dea Hannson. 'When she told me how the thug's cell phone wouldn't work and he used hers to make a call,' she said, 'I decided to borrow hers, too. I fumbled around with it for awhile, first like I wasn't sure how to use it, then like I couldn't quite remember the number I was calling.'

'And she didn't catch on?'

'She's not the suspicious type. And . . . if she *had* asked what I was doing, messing with her phone, I'd just have told her. I'm sure she'd like to know who the guy in the water was, too; although I think she's better off in the dark. Anyway, I got to her phone log. Out of the last ten outgoing calls, eight of them had names and no numbers, so they were people she called a lot. Of the two that had numbers without names, one was an 800 area code, and one was local. I clicked *select* on the local one and found out that call was made at about the right time on Tuesday afternoon.'

'And you memorized the number?'

'I did. Oh, and Dea's cell number, too. Just in case. It's different than the business number I originally called her on.'

'You memorized *two* phone numbers? Like . . . in an instant?'

'Of course. Can't you do that?'

'Uh . . . sure. I guess.' He downed some more Pilsner. 'And you did a name and address check for the number you're guessing my guy called?'

'I need a computer for that, and I didn't feel like waiting.'

'So you called the number.'

'Yep,' she said.

'And?'

'You said the *partner* of the guy you threw in the river was short and thick and solid, right?'

'Uh-huh. A walking beer keg. So?'

'So . . . I call the number from Dea's log and a guy answers. I say, "Is this Stump?" He says, "Yeah, who's this?" I say, "Phone company, sir. Random service check," and then I end the call. *Your* beer keg's gotta be *my* Stump.'

Dugan shook his head. 'And he checks his phone log and sees it's you that called, and now they know we're on to—'

'Nope.' She lifted her mug and sipped some coffee. 'I told you I flirted. And that it worked.' She nodded at Dugan, then lifted her chin and gave a cute little smile and a finger wave to someone beyond his shoulder.

Dugan twisted around and saw a guy coming their way. Close to seven feet tall, he wore a white apron tied around a fifty-inch waist. He had a grin on his face, and was clutching what must have been Kirsten's check in one huge paw.

'He let me use his phone,' she said.

THIRTY-FOUR

'My God, Park,' Kirsten said, 'it's barely noon. How do you *do* it?'

'If I told you, I'd—'

'You'd have to kill me, I know. You need to expand your cliché repertoire.'

She'd caught him at eight that morning, picking up coffee and a doughnut in the lobby of One Prudential Plaza before he went up to his office, and all she'd had for him was the artist's sketch of the guy in the water, and that he'd been teamed with a man called 'Stump'. Now here they were, sitting on a bench in the sun with their backs to the Chicago River, drinking coffee – Park was always drinking coffee – and watching people stroll by along Wacker Drive just west of Michigan Avenue.

'No lunch today?' she asked

'How often you think I miss lunch?'

'Once a year?'

'Not even. I got a meeting over there at twelve fifteen.' He gestured vaguely with his cup to the west and across Wacker.

'The church?'

'Right. Then lunch.' He sipped some coffee. 'Your mope's name's Hecky Pasco. He and his buddy, a slow thinker named Marlon "Stump" Stolecky, do freelance piece work, these days mostly for a dirtbag named Vincent Rondo.'

'Rondo I've heard of,' Kirsten said. 'Supposedly a connected guy. Charged with attempted murder a couple years ago. Went after a soldier just home from Iraq, right?'

'Allegedly,' Park said. 'Seems this young Marine wandered into the wrong bar, had a couple too many, and said something to . . . or maybe about . . . Rondo's wife. Or maybe it wasn't the Marine at all who triggered things, but the cute, flirty little wife. Anyway, Rondo got pissed off. Or maybe he didn't. For sure, though, there was an altercation. Everyone agrees on that. And only one person got hurt.'

'The Marine,' Kirsten said.

'Right. Guy's a permanent vegetable. Rondo walked. Plenty of people there at the bar, mostly Rondo's group, and . . . surprise . . . no one actually saw just what happened.'

A bus stopped at the curb and a bunch of Japanese tourists got out and gathered around a woman who led them eastward, probably toward the tour boat dock on the river, below Michigan Avenue. 'What about the wife?' Kirsten asked. 'She testify?'

'Not available. Took a year to get the case to trial, and in the meantime she died. "Accidental overdose" was the ruling. A mix of anti-anxiety meds and sleeping pills. Rondo didn't seem to take it too hard.' He shook his head. 'Nice people you deal with.'

'I know. I should choose my enemies more carefully. You get an address?'

'Not yet. Not a street address. But he's got himself a yacht . . . it's a power boat . . . and I understand he pretty much lives on it . . . day and night . . . from May till late October. Calls the thing "*Va Bene*", and keeps it in Monroe Harbor. Hell, I can see part of the harbor from my office window. I'd wave at him for you, 'cept I'd never pick out which little speck his boat is.'

'I need to get closer than that,' Kirsten said. 'I need to pay him a visit.'

'You'd need an invitation. And you'd have to find him. The boats are all tied up separately to these . . . these *cans*. That's what they call 'em.'

'Mooring cans,' Kirsten said.

'That's it.' Park stared at her. 'How do you know that?'

'Long story. I took sailing lessons one summer, and they talked about "mooring cans" all the time.'

'Sailing? Really?'

'Yeah, in high school. And in college I played soccer and softball and rowed on the crew team, but let's get back to Rondo's boat.'

'Right. Well, I couldn't get the exact location, but he's supposedly somewhere in the row of cans farthest from shore.' Park paused and leaned forward. 'By the way, invited or not, it would be very, very stupid to go there, and especially alone.'

'Oh, absolutely. I agree. That's why I'm not going at all. Ever. With or without support. Got it?'

'Yeah, I got it.'

'Just out of curiosity, though . . .' She swirled her cup around as though there were anything in it to mix with the coffee. 'I don't know much about Monroe Harbor, but it's big. And don't they have a shuttle boat to take people out to the yachts and back?'

'They do. I mean, lots of people use dinghies to go back and forth. But the shuttle boat . . . a "tender", they call it . . . runs all day and half the night. You gotta bet Rondo's made it clear no one's to be brought out to his boat without his OK. That's why I say a person would need an invitation. And lots o' luck putt-puttin' up to his yacht in a little dinghy. Not that you're even thinking about it.'

'Uh-huh,' she said. 'But what's with you and all this "cans" and "dinghies" and "tenders" stuff? You into the yachting scene now?'

'Not me.' Park drank some coffee. 'But I know a guy with a boat in DuSable Harbor, right next to Monroe. I been out on it a few times.'

'Really? Who's the guy?'

'Name's Cameron Springer. Maybe you—'

'Cameron *Springer*?' Kirsten asked. 'The bankruptcy lawyer who does all that goofy late-night TV advertising? How he'll "*sprinnnng*" me out of that "dungeon of debt" I'm locked in?'

'That's him.' Park grinned. 'Can't be but a handful o' black folks with yachts in the city harbors, and he's one. I first met him when I served a subpoena on him. Handed it to him right out there at the harbor. And guess what? He invited me on to his boat.'

'You hand a guy a subpoena . . . you're lucky he doesn't push you off the dock.'

'He knew it was coming,' Park said. 'Subpoena for records, and not even *his* records. Stuff he was holding for someone. He didn't care. So anyway, he invites me aboard.'

'And you went.'

'Hell, yes. Boat's name is *Chapter 11*, and it's got two bedrooms, two bathrooms . . . "heads", they call 'em . . . and a full kitchen. He loves that thing. And loves showing it off. Even offered me a beer. I told him I don't drink, and he said he doesn't either, but keeps the fridge stocked for guests. Turns out he's an alcoholic. So we got a lot in common. We hit it off pretty good.' In fact, Park hit it off good with just about everyone.

'So . . .' Kirsten paused, while an idea took shape. 'Did you take the tender back and forth, or does Springer have one of those dinghy things?'

Park smiled. 'He's got a "dinghy thing". But DuSable Harbor . . . where he is . . . is smaller, and set up different from Monroe. Boats in DuSable are lined up side by side, like in a parking lot. Tied to long piers sticking out from shore. Each pier's got a gate, and you just unlock the gate and walk down to your boat.'

'And are you still in touch with Springer?'

'From time to time. Last Fourth of July he had a bunch of us out to the boat to watch the fireworks. Guy's sort of an oddball. You can tell that from his TV ads. But a good-hearted guy. A real free spirit.'

'Really? Free spirited enough to do a favor for a friend of yours? I mean, hypothetically.'

A few minutes later they split up, Park to go to the downtown Christian Science church for what Kirsten was sure was an AA meeting, and she to grab a cab and head for the lakefront. It was only a fifteen- or twenty-minute walk, but she was in a hurry.

Her circle of possible suspects was shrinking. She'd been hopeful about Richard's theory that some cop co-conspirator of Johnny may have killed him to shut him up about shaking down drug dealers, but that was going nowhere. Of the crew that worked with him when he was on a narcotics task force, one had bought the farm in a shootout, one died in a car accident in Florida, and one was retired and living in Baja California. Besides, there'd been a major internal investigation not long ago, which resulted in a handful of narcotics guys doing hard time. Johnny and his crew were untouched. Which didn't mean innocent, of course. Just untouched.

She still had the real estate developer, Barry Zelander, as a possibility. And at least three out of four of Johnny's own family members couldn't be ruled out. Her sights right now, though, were set on Vincent Rondo. If he'd sent those two thugs to scare her away, it was because he wanted the O'Hern investigation to stay focused right where it was. On Dugan. And away from the real killer.

According to Park, Pasco and Stolecky 'mostly' worked for Rondo, which didn't mean they couldn't have been hired this time by someone else. Still, something told her Rondo was her man, although she wouldn't identify him to Polly Morelli. That creep's sole interest was in protecting his own ass. If he determined that Rondo, one of his top lieutenants, was a liability, he'd do whatever he thought best . . . for himself. And how would that help Dugan?

So no Polly. Not yet.

And the cops? What she had for them was that someone

wanted to keep her from looking into O'Hern's killing. Probably Rondo. Probably because he himself had ordered the hit. Probably because . . .

Anyway no cops, either. Not yet.

For now she'd take a walk along the lakefront, scope out the two harbors, DuSable and Monroe, and trust Park to have good luck with Cameron Springer. Because with nothing but *probably this* and *probably that*, her next step was to get out on the water and rock the boat . . . and see whether any facts fell out.

THIRTY-FIVE

It had been a warm afternoon, but by evening clouds had moved in and the temperature was dropping, and around midnight the rain started. Barely a hint of a breeze, though, to go with a soft drizzling rain. Kirsten was dressed for it: hooded rain jacket down to mid-thigh, black jeans, black running shoes, thin leather gloves. She was out in the dark in DuSable Harbor, aboard Cameron Springer's forty-foot power boat, the *Chapter 11*.

She'd called on her cell at eleven and Springer had come and opened the gate to Pier E and led her to the boat. It was a pretty long walk, since the pier must have been about a hundred and fifty yards long and his slot, number 28-S, was the third from the end.

Springer himself was friendly enough. He'd helped her aboard and shown her the dinghy – a tiny, two-person inflatable boat made of rubber, or PVC or whatever – and how it was tied up to the rear of the yacht. 'The stern,' he'd said. And not long after that he'd wished her, 'Good luck with . . . you know . . . whatever,' and gone back down the pier and out the gate. Park said he'd told Springer only that a trusted friend needed to borrow a boat – not a yacht, just a dinghy; and no motor, just the oars – and made vague reference to a clandestine romance. It was clear Springer didn't know, and didn't want to know, who Kirsten was. He may have been 'sort of an oddball', as Park said, but he was no dummy.

When he was gone she'd sat under a canopy on deck, shielded from the light rain and inhaling the not-unpleasant odors of the harbor: the slightly fishy smell of the lake itself, stirred up by the rain; but also barbecue smoke and grilled fish, fresh paint and varnish, gasoline and diesel fuel. She knew there were eight piers in all, A through H, and with thirty slots on each side of each pier there must have been mooring for well over four hundred boats. With the close of the season drawing near, though, about half the slots were empty. Sailboats seemed popular here, outnumbering power boats two to one.

She sat there for half an hour and, for the most part, nothing happened. At one point there was a little commotion over on Pier D, when several chattering people climbed out of a boat and walked down toward the gate, but otherwise there didn't seem to be any action on any of the boats or piers.

The lights in the tall buildings of the Loop seemed distant through the drizzling rain, while here in the harbor low lights glowed softly from posts placed every few yards along the length of each pier. On the shore stood tall poles with security lights, and twice she saw a man she thought was a security guard walking his rounds, but no way could he see her this far out in the dark. She knew there was a Coast Guard station just north of the harbor, but there was no sign of any boat patrolling the area.

Occasional snatches of music drifted her way, and on a few of the boats lights showed behind curtained windows. Hulls knocked gently against docks, ropes creaked, pulleys clanked against masts. The whole lake looked pretty calm, but even more so here, inside the breakwater. She checked her watch. Six hours till sunrise. She went down to what Springer had called his 'guest stateroom', took off her gloves and her jacket, and lay down on a bunk against the wall.

The alarm on her watch woke her at four o'clock and a few minutes later she was standing on a ledge – a 'swimmer's platform', Springer called it – that stuck a few feet out from the rear of the yacht. She stared down at the inflated dinghy, bobbing softly on the surface of the water. The weather hadn't changed: light drizzle, very little wind.

Maybe two more hours of real darkness left. And if that

wasn't enough time to find Rondo's boat, she'd have to think of something else.

With very light wave movement, she was still dealing with two unstable, out-of-sync surfaces – one bobbing up when the other went down – as she struggled to step from the platform into the dinghy. It didn't help that the rain made every surface slippery.

With both hands holding tight to a railing along the edge of the platform, she crouched deeply and, right foot first, stepped backwards down into the dinghy. When her foot touched the bottom she used that leg to pull and hold the dinghy tight against the yacht, then stepped her left foot down. Finally, with both feet firmly inside the dinghy, she pushed off from the railing and shifted her weight backwards . . . and the dinghy suddenly tilted deeply to her right. Water sloshed over the side and she instinctively leaned to her left, tilting the boat the other way . . . and somehow *both* feet slid out from under her. Like a clown at an ice show she flailed her arms in wild circles, but there was nothing to grab hold of, and she totally lost her balance and fell backwards. Fortunately, she landed on her rear end *inside* the little boat, and though the damn thing wanted desperately to flip itself over, it was tied to the yacht in two places, so it couldn't.

She sat there for a few seconds, feeling cold water soak through her jeans, then struggled to her knees. She crawled forward and, stretching her arms and chest across the slick, rubbery side of the dinghy, she worked on untying it from the yacht. For something that looked like a life raft, the thing was pretty unstable, wobbling from side to side with every slight movement she made. She had to take off her gloves to do it, but she got it untied, dropping the ends of the ropes on the bottom. Remembering how to re-tie the thing was another problem she'd leave for later.

The dinghy sat in the water barely a foot from the yacht, tilting from side to side as she put her gloves back on and then crawled, backwards, until she hit the edge of a hard bench seat. Once she got herself sitting on that, the world stopped rocking so much and she relaxed. She was a good swimmer and fear of drowning wasn't the problem. But she sure didn't want to be dumped in the water, fully clothed, and then have to figure a way to climb back into this dinghy . . . without drawing attention to herself. Besides, she didn't want her cell phone dunked under water . . . or the Colt 380.

She lifted one of the aluminum oars out of its lock, used it to push herself farther away from the yacht, then fit the oar back into place and started rowing. Pulling on just one oar at first, she turned the front of the dinghy to face east and then rowed out past the end of the pier, where she turned again and headed south along the protected inner side of the breakwater.

In the softly falling rain the dinghy moved easily over the water. Her crew team days were ancient history, but she'd kept up her rowing – these days on those boring machines at the Y or the health club – and was in at least as good shape now as then.

It was dark enough so that only someone watching very carefully would spot her. Not so dark, though, that she couldn't see what she was doing. She headed south, parallel to the breakwater – the outer edge of the harbor – and even though she faced the rear of the dinghy as she rowed, by keeping the breakwater a couple of yards to her right she didn't have to twist around every few seconds to see where she was going.

She passed the end of Pier F, then G, and finally H, the last pier in DuSable Harbor, a one-sided pier because it was built close against the wall of a wide concrete levee that stuck out from the shore. Once part of the intricate system that controlled the flow of the Chicago River into and out of the lake, the levee served now merely to separate the two harbors. It stretched almost out to the breakwater, leaving a space just wide enough for yachts to pass out of DuSable into Monroe, giving them access to the harbor mouth and the open water.

She rowed past the levee and into Monroe Harbor, passing the stern of a much larger boat. A *ship*, really, over a hundred yards long and rising four stories above the water, it was moored along the south edge of the levee. This was the floating home of the Columbia Yacht Club. She'd been on it once, for a wedding, and remembered its elegant bar and dining room, its party salons, and its unbeatable view of the city skyline and lakefront. Now, though, in that gloomy midnight drizzle it looked abandoned, forsaken; a ghost ship, dark and silent.

She lifted the ends of the oars from the water and placed them inside the dinghy. Then, struggling not to capsize and flip herself into the water, she eased off the seat on to her knees and maneuvered around until she was facing out over the front of the boat. She knew, of course, that kneeling on the bottom and facing forward would make rowing much more difficult. She would have to push – not pull – on the oars to propel the dinghy. But, looking for Vincent Rondo's boat in the dark, she'd rather be facing forward.

Monroe Harbor lay before her, much of it not even vaguely visible. She knew it was maybe ten times larger than DuSable, with mooring for a thousand boats, widely spaced and spread out over the water, not lined up in tight rows against piers.

That afternoon as she'd walked the shoreline she called the harbor office asking for help, claiming she couldn't remember the mooring spot of a friend she was supposed to visit, and that the friend wasn't answering his cell phone. Not surprisingly, that got her nowhere. She'd considered searching out some talkative harbor employee, maybe someone on the crew of the 'tender'. But she didn't want people remembering that she'd been nosing around, asking about Vincent Rondo.

So she was left with Parker Gillson's information that the *Va Bene* was a power boat, not a sailboat – eliminating maybe half the boats here – and that it was moored 'somewhere in the row of cans farthest from shore'. There was also the fact – though not as obvious here as in DuSable Harbor – that a lot of the mooring spots were empty.

In her flimsy inflatable rowboat she felt very small, and vulnerable, but she lowered the oars and pushed ahead, going south, keeping the breakwater beside her. It had to be a half-mile to the flashing red light that signaled where the breakwater ended and the harbor mouth gave access out to the lake. Well beyond that, less visible, a green light flashed where the breakwater started again and stretched another half-mile, angling toward shore and protecting the south half of the harbor.

That could mean a lot of searching . . . and a lot of rowing.

And she was wet, and getting cold, and not so sure any more that trying to rock any facts out of Rondo's yacht – if she ever found it – was as good an idea as it had seemed when she'd been at lunch.

As far as she could tell she was the only person awake, and hers the only moving boat, in the harbor. She took comfort in that because, while it probably wasn't illegal to row around out here in the rain a couple of hours before dawn, it sure as hell would have piqued curiosity in anyone who spotted her.

The yachts here were tied by their front ends to buoys – the so-called 'mooring cans' – bobbing on the surface, with each can attached by a chain to a heavy chunk of concrete on the lake bottom. There had to be over five hundred boats still in the harbor, but she was taking Park's 'row farthest from shore' at face value, and was looking only at power boats – not sailboats – in that row, which meant the row closest to the breakwater. She had a powerful, thin-beamed LED flashlight to help her see their names through the misty rain.

It was slow going.

Row. Stop and lift the ends of the oars inside the boat. Get out the flashlight and check the name. Put the flashlight back in the pocket and the oars back in the water. Row.

She finally finished the outermost row along the north half of the harbor and paused just short of the flashing red beacon at the end of the breakwater. She'd found power boats named *Slo-Mo-Sean*, *Country Cussin'*, *Bare Naked Truth*, *Hell's Belles*, and over a dozen others. But no *Va Bene*. Ahead lay the channel into and out of the harbor, fifty or sixty yards of open water; and after that the green light where the breakwater started again.

No use quitting now. She would cross the channel and do the outside row on the south half of the harbor. If she didn't find Rondo's boat she'd call it a night, and in the morning tell Parker Gillson how wrong he'd been . . . for once.

Still on her knees, she started her clumsy, push-forward rowing again, her eyes on the green light blinking in the distance. The light was tiny, but seemed more clearly visible now. *Damn! When did the rain stop?* She slid her jacket hood off her head and felt the breeze against her cheek as she pushed forward into the channel.

The sudden chop that hit when she moved into unprotected water took her by surprise. The waves coming in looked gentle enough, but set the dinghy bouncing up and down, with water splashing over the sides. She managed to get it stabilized, but it was clear she needed to get back up on the seat and in position to row properly, or it would take her forever to get across the channel.

She lifted the oars into the boat and, struggling to maintain stability, eased herself around and up on to the seat. Aware at once that the choppy waves washing in through the harbor mouth had carried her inward, past the first row of moored boats, she took up the oars again . . . which is when she saw that Park's information *had* been off, but not by much.

The name, *Va Bene,* written in white across a dark stern, glowed red and then disappeared, with each on-off flash of the harbor light. The boat was tied to a buoy at the end of the *second* row in from the breakwater. Just ten yards away now, but she'd have missed it for sure if she hadn't been pushed off her route.

The *Va Bene* was an old boat, but in decent shape, and if the *Chapter 11* was forty feet long, this one had to be fifty. The swimmer's platform at its stern was larger, too, with a ladder mounted at its edge, like a pool ladder. And the pilot house was higher up, allowing the brave Captain Rondo to better scan the horizon. Just then, though, like the rest of the boat, the pilot house tower was wrapped in deep darkness.

He might be captain of his ship, but Rondo wouldn't be out here alone, without paid muscle. But muscle awake and alert an hour before dawn? Not likely. And even though some sort of motion detector system was possible, she'd take her chances on that, too. Park had told her Cameron Springer didn't have an alarm, and that most people didn't, not in the Chicago harbors, anyway; and especially not if they were tied to a mooring can out away from shore, because the wave action could so often set alarms off.

She rowed a few strokes closer, then paused. She saw no one, heard nothing but the soft rhythmic slosh of water against the dinghy and the hull of the overpriced water-toy in front of her. She eased up to the swimmer's platform, tied the dinghy to the ladder, and boarded the *Va Bene*.

THIRTY-SIX

Kirsten wasn't surprised to find no one on the deck, or up in the pilot house. Now, as the boat rocked gently on the surface of the harbor, she stood in an open door at the top of a stairway leading to the area below deck. There was another open door at the bottom, and beyond that it was dark, with no sound of anyone talking or moving around. For all she knew Rondo was rolling dice in a casino in Peoria, and she was all alone on his yacht.

But she didn't think so.

And she certainly hoped not. She hadn't gone to all this trouble to look around some mid-level Outfit guy's empty cage. The chances there'd be evidence of a hit on Johnny O'Hern lying around this boat were less than slim. What she wanted was a bit of a chat with a guy who thought he could scare her away with a half-assed threat.

She switched her flashlight from narrow beam to wide, but didn't turn it on yet, and then – the light in one hand and her Colt 380 in the other – went silently down the stairs. At the bottom she stood to the side of the doorway and, when she heard nothing, eased her head around the door frame and looked in.

She pulled her head back, nearly gagging on the stench of stale cigar and cigarette smoke. She hadn't seen a thing in the darkened room.

She silently counted to three and then, raising the gun and hitting the switch on the flashlight, she stepped into the doorway and swept the beam across the small room. No one was there. One side was a sort of parlor, with a sofa and a flat-screen TV that was way too big for the space. The other side was a dining area, with a table and chairs; and beyond that was a tiny kitchen. The décor and furnishings were upscale and elegant, but the place was a mess, with magazines, newspapers and empty Bud Light bottles – she stopped counting at nine – strewn everywhere. Five or six cardboard take-out cartons sat open on the table, plastic forks sticking out of the congealing remains of Moo Shu pork and curried shrimp. A dozen cigarette butts – none showing lipstick, she noticed – sat crushed into an old-fashioned brown-glass ash tray on an end table by the sofa.

She stood still and listened . . . and heard something. Someone moaning, maybe sobbing? But no, the sounds were too even, too regular. She went across the room and into a short hall – five or six feet long – with three doors: one on each side, both closed; and one at the end, half-open and revealing possibly the world's tiniest bathroom.

Behind the closed doors, she was sure, were staterooms, and from the sounds of the snores and ragged snorts – what she'd first taken as moans and sobs – she guessed there was probably just one person, a man, in each room. But however many there were, and whether male or female, they sounded seriously asleep. She didn't try the handles to see if the doors were locked. She wasn't ready yet for that.

She holstered the Colt and went back on deck and from there up to the pilot house, and to the boat's control console. She noticed first that the *Va Bene* had a key-turn ignition, and that the key – with another key hanging from the same ring – was in the slot. Careless, yes; but not really so strange, not with the owner on board. Farmers left keys in their tractors and trucks, too, at least when they were on the property. Anyway, she wasn't out here to steal a yacht, even if maneuvering this one out of the harbor and sending it – and its captain – out into the middle of the lake was an intriguing idea. No doubt she could manage the pilot's wheel, but the *Va Bene* had too damn many electronics. There were radar and radio controls to consider, read-out screens to monitor, buttons and levers to push and pull. Plus, she'd have to untie the dinghy and row to shore, or jump ship and swim; not at all intriguing ideas.

Anyway, she'd developed a plan, and none of that was part of it.

There was one little control panel in particular she was looking for among all the dials and gadgets. She found it, and then she removed the companion to the ignition key from the ring and took it with her, and crept down to the deck again. The key fit the door at the top of the stairs leading below deck. She thought for a few seconds, then decided to leave that door unlocked and open. She grabbed a couple of flotation cushions from a bench and took them with her back to the pilot tower. Up there she could stay out of sight, and still see anyone coming on deck from below. She made a seat with the cushions on the floor . . . and settled down.

She didn't really *have* to wait, but a confrontation at dawn seemed more dramatic, somehow. Not to mention that daylight, and the probability of witnesses around, would facilitate her departure. And staying awake would *not* be a problem. She couldn't have slept if she'd wanted to, not with every nerve in her body on high alert.

She sat on the cushions and waited, and as the minutes crawled by, very slowly, very quietly, a question crept into her mind, and wouldn't go away: *Plan or no plan, what the hell am I doing here, sitting on a mob guy's yacht, waiting for sunrise?*

It was more than just uncertainty. It was fear, too. But not fear of Vincent Rondo and whatever dim-bulbed mope he might have around to keep him safe. No, this was a much more worrisome fear. A fear tied to her own yearning.

That yearning . . . for a child . . . had been consuming her for what seemed a long, long time. She could feel it in her belly . . . feel it deep in her empty, waiting womb. So then, what business did she have rowing out in the dark and sneaking on to a boat, waiting to confront a guy with the conscience of a weasel?

The answer was that if this was what it took to smoke out Johnny O'Hern's killer and protect Dugan from a murder charge, this is what she'd do. She was more and more convinced that this particular weasel was behind O'Hern's murder. But there was something else, too. This guy had threatened to hurt her, to scar her, and she wanted to show him – and herself, too, she was aware of that – and anyone else who might hear about it, that she wasn't so easily frightened away.

As she stared down at the deck below, she was unable to shut down her chattering mind. She wanted to be a mother. But she also wanted to be right where she was just now, on this yacht, waiting. This was the sort of thing she did, and she wouldn't have it any other way – even when it meant pushing herself beyond the boundaries of so-called 'common sense'.

And wouldn't a child change everything? Change not only

her days and her nights, but her hopes and her dreams? A child needs a mother always close at hand . . . to cuddle away the nightmares, to kiss away the scrapes and bruises, to wipe away the tears. Kirsten wasn't always there for Dugan, but that was different. Dugan understood, and made a choice. He chose to accept her absences as part of the total package, freely. Children, though, don't get to choose. Children have to take what life hands them . . . what their *parents* hand them.

A baby meant the life she'd been living was over. Most women longed for that. Could she handle it? Which brought her face-to-face with the fearsome question: Did she really *want* to be a mother?

By six o'clock a strong breeze had appeared out of the northwest and the cloud cover over the city had been broken into chunks of gray, scudding across a brightening sky. Out over the lake, though, the horizon was still just a guess, hidden in fog, until finally, at six thirty, the first tiny sliver of blood-red sun slid into view, revealing the water's edge. She watched as, with surprising speed, the sliver rose, growing into an ever-larger slice, and finally a perfect circle. That blazing disc quickly burned through what was left of the curtain of cloud, and she had to turn her eyes away.

She wondered when Vincent Rondo had last seen a sunrise . . . or if he'd *ever* seen one.

She waited a little longer, and at a few minutes past seven made a call on her cell phone. A man answered and said others were calling too, and it would probably be seven thirty or a little after. 'That'll be great,' she said. 'I'll be watching for you.'

It was a Saturday, and she could hear the city, and the harbor itself, stirring into life. A few early risers were moving about on the decks of their boats. When a dinghy set out from a yacht in the south half of the harbor and headed toward shore, and the sound of its outboard carried easily over the water, she knew how right she'd been to use the oars in the night.

Other than that motor, though, what little activity there was in the harbor was quiet, calm, peaceful. The sun had slowed to its usual snail-like crawl up the sky, and nothing at all stirred on the *Va Bene* . . . until suddenly a man lurched through the doorway below her and stumbled out on to the deck.

Back to bed, dammit! It's not time yet.

She'd seen a picture of Vincent Rondo, a slim, slick, too-handsome guy, and this short, squat mope – with his baggy white T-shirt, green boxer shorts, and huge, hairy bare feet – wasn't Rondo. This had to be Dugan's fireplug, aka Marlon Stolecky, aka 'Stump'.

If Stump had turned and started up her way, she'd have had to switch to Plan B. But he didn't.

In fact, he was clearly not operating in 'greet-the-new-day' mode. She couldn't see his face, but his bent-over body said 'bellyache, hangover, half-dead'. Still, there he was, out of bed and shuffling determinedly across the deck toward the railing. Assuming he wasn't going to do the right thing, and throw himself overboard, he was probably on his way to puke his guts out into Lake Michigan.

But first things first. He got to the railing, looked to his left, looked to his right, then reached down to his crotch . . . and took a piss off the side of the boat. Kirsten almost threw up herself. Then, when the mutt had finished and tucked himself away, he leaned over the railing and emptied his stomach where he'd emptied his bladder.

He heaved and vomited until there was nothing left to spew out, then choked and retched some more. Finally he turned and, with his chin to his chest as though he were studying the traces of vomit on his shirt, shambled back across the deck and went below.

She gave Stump a couple of minutes to settle in again, and by then it was almost seven fifteen. Time for Rondo's wake-up call. She went to the pilot's console, switched on the ignition, and studied the little control panel she'd located earlier. The label on the panel said *Kahlenberg Model O2M*, and the touch pad had twelve different choices. Some were to be expected, like *ON* and *OFF*, *AUTOMATIC* and *MANUAL*, *FOG* and *ALERT*. But a few were more interesting, like the choices in a row across the bottom: *TUNE 1*, *TUNE 2*, and *TUNE 3*.

She pushed *ON* and a little green light glowed. Then she pushed *ALERT*, and at once the most godawful, ear-piercing blare screamed from the cluster of five chrome-plated bugles mounted on the roof of the pilot house. Short, sharp blasts, one after the other, again and again, until she hit *OFF* and it suddenly stopped. Right away, though, she hit *ON* again, and then – wondering what melody was coming – hit *TUNE 3*, at which the screaming bugles launched into what had to be the best version of *Yankee Doodle* possible, using just five notes.

The horns finished a chorus, then repeated it, over and over. Like one of those annoying ice cream trucks. But a hundred times louder. She was sure they were hearing *Yankee Doodle* from the south end of Monroe Harbor to the north, and in DuSable Harbor as well, and maybe all the way over on Michigan Avenue. She couldn't see him, but some guy from one of the other boats was yelling hysterically. '*Turn it off, dammit!*'

By the end of the first replay, though, Kirsten had already left the pilot house and was down on deck, about ten feet back from the door to the steps coming up from the staterooms below. She took a shooter's stance, holding the Colt in two hands, aiming it at the narrow doorway.

She heard a man come shouting and cursing his way up the stairs. '*Fuck!* Goddammit, Stump.' He appeared in the doorway, but was looking away, yelling down the stairs. 'What the *fuck* is—' He stopped when he turned and saw her.

The slim, slick Vincent Rondo had a little round belly on him. His face was puffy, and his hair stuck out in various odd directions. He had a nice tan, though, which, along with some too-tight yellow Jockey shorts, was all he was wearing.

He opened his mouth, but snapped it shut when she took a step forward, holding the gun steady, trained on the bridge of his nose.

She stepped even closer. 'If you wanted to scare me off,' she said, raising her voice to be heard over the incessant, maddening *Yankee Doodle*, 'you made the wrong choice.'

He shook his head as though trying to shake away a bad dream. 'What the fuck are you talking about?'

'I'm saying if you have a message for me, you don't send mopes like Pasco and Stolecky . . . to my husband.'

He stared at her. 'You're out of your fucking mind, lady. I haven't seen Hecky Pasco in . . . I don't know . . . a month, at least.'

'You're lying,' she said. 'But now you can deliver your message in person.' She took another step closer. 'Before you die.'

THIRTY-SEVEN

Dugan could hardly believe what Kirsten was telling him. He knew he ought to be angry with her for being so reckless, but amazement crowded out everything else. 'Did you *know* you were gonna say that?'

'The part about him delivering his message in person . . . yes,' she said. 'The other part, about him being about to die, that just popped out.'

'Because . . . I mean . . . it doesn't sound like you.'

'Yeah, well, I was tired, and frustrated. It was a long night and while I was waiting I started having all these feelings run through my mind. You know, all sorts of . . . *stuff* . . . and . . .' She shook her head, and it was clear she was wishing she hadn't brought it up. 'And then the creep's acting like he doesn't know what the hell I'm talking about, and . . . and I just kinda lost it.'

'Yeah, that happens.' It was late Saturday afternoon and they were in her car, headed north on Lake Shore Drive. He wanted to hear the rest of the story, like how she got away from the damn boat, but what she *wasn't* telling him might be more important. 'But that "stuff" running through your mind. What *kind* of stuff?'

'Nothing. Pre-dawn jitters.' She waved her hand, brushing the topic aside. 'Anyway, the idea was to get Rondo to admit he sent two goons to scare me away, and to shake him up and see what else I could get out of him . . . or what he might do later. But right then there wasn't much time. The boat I called to pick me up – the tender – was on its way, and three or four other boats were coming, too, because those damn horns were driving everyone nuts. So I finally just backed Rondo and Stump down the stairs and locked the door. Then I had to run up and shut off *Yankee Doodle*, and then untie the dinghy, and—'

'Hold on.' Dugan raised his finger. 'Didn't you know Rondo and the mope might have had guns down there? They could've shot their way out, and then shot *you*, and claimed you broke in and . . .' He gave up. 'Jesus.'

'No way they'd do anything like that. They *knew* there'd be boats coming, and Rondo didn't need a shooting on his yacht, and all the attention that would bring.' She took the Foster Avenue exit off the Drive. 'Anywhere you wanna go in particular?'

'No,' he said.

He'd woken up that morning to find Kirsten in the kitchen making coffee. She'd been out all night. She said she was too tired to talk, the coffee was for him, and she was going to bed. He went to his office, and when he got home it was three o'clock, she was still asleep, and they'd both missed most of a beautiful sunny Saturday. He'd woken her up and insisted they go for a drive. No destination in mind, and not especially good for the environment, but he'd needed to get out and go somewhere. And she'd looked like she needed to talk.

So here they were, and at the end of the exit ramp she turned right and drove through the park, past busy soccer fields and basketball courts, and lots of people of all ages, jogging, cycling, pushing strollers. Near the lake, a parking slot opened up in front of them and she pulled in, and they sat there and he listened to the rest of her story.

She told how she'd apologized to the people on the tender for the noise, and explained that it was her fault and that she'd hit the wrong buttons and gotten confused, and it had taken a few minutes to figure out how to get the horn turned off. The guy in charge agreed to tow the dinghy to shore, and she'd left word with Springer's voice mail where to find it. 'And then,' she said, 'I headed for home.'

'So what's next? We wait and see if Rondo's shaken up enough, and dumb enough, to do something to give himself away?'

'He's dumb enough, but . . .' She sat and stared out the windshield. 'I don't know what's next.'

'You still seem a little tired,' he said, 'or . . . *subdued.*'

'I guess I'm feeling a little let down. The thing is, I shouldn't be. I went to a lot of trouble last night, and it was all worth it. I learned something very important, even if it was something I didn't expect to learn.'

'What? That Vincent Rondo has a pot belly?'

She gave a half-hearted smile at his attempt to cheer her up. 'I saw his reaction when I challenged him,' she said. 'And Stump's, too, he was right there behind him.'

'And?'

'By the time I locked the two of them down below deck, there was no doubt in my mind. Whoever sent Stump and Pasco to talk to you, it wasn't Vincent Rondo.'

They'd been trying to improve their dietary habits – obviously easier for Kirsten than for him, Dugan thought, which was unfair – but he prevailed that evening and they ended up at a bar he'd heard about called Candlelight, up north on Western Avenue. He washed down his two-thirds of a pepperoni and green pepper pizza with a couple of Smithwick's. Kirsten stuck to water. She seemed preoccupied and they didn't talk much. Which was fine because there was a Bulls game on.

Later, on the way home, she still seemed lost in her thoughts and he was wondering how old babies had to get before they could eat pizza, and—

'*Hey!*'

His head jerked up. 'What?' He hadn't even known he was dozing.

'I was talking,' she said.

'Of course you were, and I was listening.'

'Bullshit.'

'You'll have to clean up your language,' he said, 'when the kid gets here. But anyway, you were . . . ah . . . you were saying you couldn't believe we weren't pregnant yet, me being such a strapping fine—'

'I was talking about Polly Morelli, and whether I should tell him it wasn't Rondo who sent those guys to scare me off.'

'Right.'

'So . . . ?'

'Oh, you want my opinion?' He took her deep sigh as a *yes*, and said, 'You never told him Rondo *was* the guy, did you?'

'No.'

'So why tell him he wasn't?'

'Because he'll find out sooner or later that I went to Rondo's boat, and he'll figure I'd only do that if I thought Rondo was the guy who didn't want me looking for Johnny O'Hern's killer.'

'And that would have been,' Dugan said, 'because *Rondo* killed O'Hern, probably to keep him from talking to the feds.'

'And Polly doesn't need a top guy the feds are looking at.' They were off the expressway now, and she stopped at a light. 'The thing is . . . I was wrong, and I may have created a big problem for Rondo.'

'So . . . ?' Dugan yawned. 'He's the one joined Polly's team. It's not up to you to cover his ass. Let the two of them talk it out.'

'Polly's not real good at talking. I need to tell him I made a mistake.'

'There,' Dugan said. 'Aren't you glad you got my opinion?'

'Well, sometimes I need— Damn.' They'd just rounded the corner on to their street. 'We've got company.' She slowed almost to a stop and pointed through the windshield.

He looked ahead and saw a car double-parked in front of their condo building. A plain, four-door sedan, and he knew as well as she did that it was a police vehicle. 'I suppose,' he said, 'that they don't have be looking for *us*.'

'No, they don't *have* to be. And that car that's been behind us for the last five or ten minutes? That could just be a coincidence, too.'

THIRTY-EIGHT

Traffic was light on their street and Kirsten considered just swerving around the double-parked car and continuing on, but what good would it do? So she drove closer to it and stopped, and was surprised when the car behind them, a silver-colored Ford SUV, was the one that pulled out into the oncoming traffic lane and kept on going. The two people inside, a man and a woman – with the woman driving – were deep in conversation and gave no glance at her and Dugan . . . or at the unmarked, either.

She turned to see Dugan putting his cell phone to his ear.

'Hey,' she said, 'what—'

Holding up a palm to shush her, he spoke his name and gave their location. Meanwhile, two forty-something white men in sport coats got out of the car in front of them. She didn't recognize either of them, but they were cops alright.

'We're in our car, a Toyota Camry,' Dugan said into the phone. 'Two men have us blocked in and— My God, they're coming *at* us.' He turned and winked at Kirsten while he said, '*Hurry!* I think they have *guns*.' He paused. 'Yes . . . thank you, ma'am. Yes . . . yes, we'll be right here.' He dropped the phone on the floor and spread his hands – palms down, fingers splayed – flat on the dashboard in front of him.

Kirsten kept her hands in plain sight, too, resting on the top of the steering wheel. 'Are you crazy?' she said. She didn't lower her window.

'Well, they *could* be imposters, right?'

'Yeah, right.'

'The woman said not to panic, they have units right here in the area.'

By then the man who'd come from the driver's side of the unmarked was rapping his knuckles on her window, and making an *unwind-the-window* gesture. The guy on Dugan's side did the same.

'Who *are* you?' she asked, loud enough for the guy to hear.

Dugan didn't say anything, and neither of them moved their hands.

'Open the window, ma'am,' the cop on her side said, and he pressed his star flat against the glass. He bent over and stared in at her, while she peered at the badge as though trying to determine whether it was real.

'Uh-oh,' Dugan said, and she looked across and saw that Dugan's cop had taken a step back from the car. The guy had a gun in his hand – a Glock, she thought, nine millimeter – the barrel angled down toward the pavement. 'The guy's nuts,' Dugan said.

'I second that,' she said, and then, very slowly, moved her left hand to the button and lowered her window. 'Evening, detective,' she said, looking up at him.

'Step out of the car, please, and—'

'*Drop the gun, sir! NOW!*' That shout came from the side-walk, and a very large uniformed police officer stepped into view. He must have come through the gangway alongside Kirsten and Dugan's building. His gun was raised, and was pointed at the cop on Dugan's side of the car.

Just then a blue-and-white careened around the corner ahead of them . . . no siren, Mars lights flashing . . . and came their way. Dugan still didn't move his hands. The plainclothes cop on his side lifted his arms out wide from his body, about shoulder height. He leaned to set his weapon gently on the hood of Kirsten's car and, hands still raised, turned toward the uniform on the sidewalk. 'Police,' he called. 'ID's in my jacket pocket.'

Two other patrol cars roared up and screeched to a stop. Car doors opened and slammed shut, and a man yelled, ''S'all right, Gomez. Relax. They're police. Everyone ease up.'

'Everyone, that is, but you and your heroic boyfriend here,' Kirsten's cop said. He gave a little wave toward Dugan, whose palms were still glued to the dashboard. 'You two get outta the car, and keep your hands in sight.'

It wasn't even nine o'clock yet and, although their street was residential, it wasn't far from lots of night life, so Kirsten wasn't at all surprised at how quickly three squads with flashing lights – and a little shouting about guns – drew a crowd of twenty or so people.

Really, though, there wasn't much to see.

Dugan announced right away that he was the one who'd called 911, and it was clear to Kirsten that inside of a minute there wasn't a cop there who believed that she and Dugan hadn't recognized the unmarked car as a police vehicle, or that they actually feared an attack. But what could they do about it? After all, the two detectives, Larking and Wizinski, *hadn't* been in uniform, and Larking's display of a weapon was, at best, only *arguably* legitimate under the circumstances.

All but one of the uniformed cops were gone within five minutes. The only one still on the scene was a sergeant, and he was in his car, writing on a clipboard.

'OK,' Wizinski said, 'now that everyone agrees about who everyone is, we got some questions to ask.' He looked around. Only a few of the gawkers were left. 'You mind if we come up to your place? Everyone'd be more comfortable.'

'I'm sure everyone would,' she said. 'But let's meet somewhere else, at your convenience. Say . . . tomorrow? We've had a long day.'

'Right,' Dugan said, 'and I always like to straighten the place up before we have company.' He shook his head. 'Besides, I'd have to call my lawyer, and she'd have to—'

'No problem,' Larking interrupted. 'We only need to talk to *her*, anyway.' He nodded toward Kirsten.

'Really,' she said. 'What about? Or is that something you can't divulge.'

'We can "divulge" this much, sugar,' Larking said. 'It's about a guy named Vincent Rondo. Him and an associate of his. They were shot a few hours ago.'

'Oh, I . . .' She struggled to catch her breath. 'Is he . . . are they . . . ?'

'Yeah,' Larking said. 'We can "divulge" that they're dead. Both of 'em. Brings a salty tear to my eye, y'know?'

'We need to talk to you,' Wizinski added. 'Now.'

She took out her keys, removed one from the ring, and gave it to Dugan. 'I guess you better park the car.'

She led them up to the condo, after all. She even offered coffee, which they declined.

Wizinski, whose business card said he was assigned to Area Five homicide, asked the first question. 'How well did you know Vincent Rondo?'

'I didn't know him at all. I knew *of* him.'

'Had you ever met him?'

'Yes.' Either they already knew she'd been on his boat that morning – and that's why they were here – or they'd find out pretty easily. So she told them how she'd heard about a guy who had a rowboat, and she borrowed it and went out and woke Rondo up.

'And why did you do that?' Wizinski asked.

'Someone sent two men – thugs, really – to threaten me with serious bodily harm if I didn't stop looking for Johnny O'Hern's killer. When I discovered the men usually worked for Rondo, I assumed he was the one who sent them. I wanted to talk to him.'

'You weren't . . . afraid?'

'I don't like to be threatened. More importantly, I wanted to find out what his interest in the O'Hern murder was. Turns out he's not . . . or he *wasn't* . . . easy to get in touch with, so I went out to see him, uninvited.'

'And now he's dead.' This came from Larking. 'Quite a coincidence, wouldn't you say?'

Kirsten kept her gaze on Wizinski. 'Do you have any more questions?'

'Yes,' he said. 'When you—'

Kirsten's cell phone rang and she reached for her purse.

'Let it go to voice mail,' Larking said. 'We're in a hurry.'

She opened the phone. 'Hello?'

'It's me,' Dugan said.

'I know.'

'Everything OK?'

'Peachy.'

'You want me there?'

'I'll call you when. 'Bye now.'

'Love ya,' he said.

'Ditto.' She flipped the phone closed and looked at Wizinski. 'You were asking?'

'Who have you talked to since the time you left the boat . . . until now?'

'Let's see . . . I was picked up by the harbor tender . . . that's a sort of taxi boat . . . and I told everyone the horn going off was my fault and I was sorry for all the noise. Then I took a cab home. That's the only people I talked to all day. Except my husband, of course.'

'Did your husband know you were going out to see Mr Rondo?'

'Nope.'

'The guy you borrowed the rowboat from?'

'Nope. Nobody knew but me.' Even Parker Gillson, she told herself, didn't *know*.

'So you went out to talk to Mr Rondo. Mind telling us what you talked about?'

'I woke him up . . . him and another guy, a guy he called "Stump". As far as I know, they were the only two on the boat besides me. The conversation was pretty brief. I asked Rondo why he tried to scare me away from finding O'Hern's killer. He said he didn't know what I was talking about. I quickly became convinced that he wasn't the one who sent the men after all. So I left . . . on the tender . . . about seven thirty.' She paused, then added, 'I take it he was killed somewhere in Area Five, and not on his boat.'

'Maybe you can catch some of those details on the news,' Wizinski said. 'So . . . when you left . . . what was Mr Rondo doing?'

'He was down below deck, and I didn't see what he did.

He might have gone back to bed. Both of them looked like I'd woken them up from a pretty sound sleep.'

'Do you know of anyone who might have had a motive to kill Mr Rondo?'

'Word on the street was he had ties to organized crime. So . . .' She shrugged. 'Maybe that had something to do with it.'

THIRTY-NINE

As soon as the detectives were out the door, Kirsten called Dugan. 'They're leaving.'

'I don't really like driving this Camry,' was his answer. 'It's kinda small, isn't it?'

'No, you're kinda big. Anyway, it's not your vehicle. It's mine. Where are you?'

'I'm down the street, a block and a half away. I haven't seen them come out, but . . . ahh . . . there they are. They're getting into their illegally parked car and driving away. So I guess I can— Oh-oh, looks like the night's still young.'

'What do you mean?'

'I have a suggestion.'

'Dugan, would you tell me what—'

'To quote that gun-happy detective, "I can *divulge* this much, *sugar*." Our doorbell's about to ring. And before it does, I suggest you leave the apartment . . . by the back way. I'll pick you up in the alley. And we can *divulge* all over each other.'

'Damn, are you *sure* some— Oops!' The doorbell rang and she almost dropped the phone. 'The alley,' she said. 'I'm on my way.'

He picked her up and they were moving before she had the car door closed. 'They might be coming to check the back,' Dugan said.

'*Who* might?'

'That car you said might have been tailing us? That was a Ford SUV, right?'

'Yeah, an Explorer . . . or Expedition . . . whatever.'

'Well, it came back.' He explained that after she and the

police detectives had gone inside, he'd circled around and ended up back on their street. 'I found a place by a hydrant,' he said. 'That's when I called you the first time. Then I waited, and finally you called me. While we were talking I saw the cops leave, and then right away the SUV showed up again . . . like *they'd* been watching, too. They double-parked, same as the cops. But the driver stayed in the car while the other guy got out and headed for our building.'

'The *other* guy?' she asked. 'Are you sure the driver was a man? Because the driver in the one that passed us was a woman.'

'Oh. Well, it hadda be the same SUV, so I must have assumed wrong. You know what they say: "Look for the *ass* in every assumption," and—'

'Hold on,' she said. 'Stop the car.'

He stopped. He'd taken the same circular route he'd described to her, and they'd just turned back on to their own street. And there was the silver SUV, in front of their building, a block and a half away. 'At least,' he said, 'if one's a woman, you can bet they're not Outfit people.'

'Another assumption, but this time I agree.' She leaned forward and squinted. 'I *think* they're both in the car. Uh-huh . . . OK, they're leaving,' she said. 'Hurry up.'

'Hurry up *what*?'

'Follow them.'

'You're kidding. We just *avoided* them.'

'And what? Whoever it is, you think they won't ever come back?'

He put the Camry in gear. 'What I think is I was right when I said the night's still young.'

Eventually the SUV led them south on LaSalle, then west on Chicago Avenue. 'I don't think I ever actually *tailed* someone before,' Dugan said. 'Am I staying too close?'

'Don't worry about it,' she said. 'You're doing OK . . . for an amateur.'

She wasn't about to tell him the truth, which was that he was doing great. He managed to keep at least one car between them and the SUV. He hadn't gotten caught by any red lights, either.

A man and a woman in a Ford SUV. Who the hell were

they? Why would they show up right after the homicide guys? Whoever they were – neither cops nor mob people, she was certain – they didn't appear to know they were being followed. They'd been headed west on Chicago Avenue now for over a mile, past the river, where the smell of chocolate from the Blommer factory wafted in even with the car windows closed, past Halsted and into an area once mostly warehouses and industry, now turning more residential.

Traffic was thinning out, and Dugan hung back almost a block, still keeping a car between them and the SUV. Finally, approaching a red light at Ogden Avenue, the SUV's left turn signal went on . . . which is when Kirsten decided she knew who the two people were.

Dugan slowed down. 'There won't be many cars on Ogden. So after we make the corner I'll pull over, let 'em get ahead a little.'

'No need for that.'

'But they'll spot us for sure, especially if they make a turn or—'

'Doesn't matter,' she said. 'I know where they're going. Let's go home.'

'No way. Now I need to see if you're as smart as you think you are.' He stayed behind the SUV and when the light changed he followed it onto Ogden.

One of Chicago's infrequent diagonal streets, Ogden cut south-west across the city's mostly rectangular grid. This section was four lanes wide, with no parking on either side, and at that time of night it was almost deserted. Dugan hung back four or five car-lengths and both vehicles cruised along in the curb lane, making maybe forty miles an hour, with stop lights every couple of blocks.

She gave it a few minutes and then said, 'I have a better idea. Pass them up.'

'What?'

'If they haven't spotted us by now, they're asleep. Just get ahead of 'em.'

'I don't get it, but . . .' He stepped on the gas and they swept past the SUV.

'Are they following us?' She didn't want to turn around to look.

'Nope.' He glanced up at the rearview. 'I mean, they're still there, but they didn't speed up.'

'Try to make that light up there,' she said, pointing.

He accelerated and went through on yellow. 'Our friends didn't make it,' he said. 'They're stopped.'

'Good. Keep going and hang a left at Roosevelt.'

Just past Juvenile Court he took a hard left onto Roosevelt Road, an east-west street where traffic was a little heavier. When he'd gone about a block she said, 'Pull into the right lane.'

'Whatever you say, boss,' he said, following her direction, 'but it's a *Right Turn Only* lane. It's for the entrance to that place.' The office building he pointed at was just a few years old, ten stories tall and looked about ninety per cent glass. It was set well back from the street, beyond a wrought-iron fence and a lawn dotted with a few newly planted trees. 'We're just a block or so from the U. of I. Med Center, so I bet that's some kind of medical—'

'Are they still behind us?'

'I think so.' He glanced up at the rearview. 'Yeah, that's gotta be them.' He paused. 'And hey . . . they're getting into this lane.'

'Right. Pull forward, and stop just before the entrance. Don't turn in, though. We don't want to be trespassing.'

'OK, but . . .' He drove a little farther. 'Oh, I see.' He stopped the car and put on the hazard lights. The sign on the wrought-iron fence said: *Federal Bureau of Investigation, Chicago Region.*

'It's me they want to talk to, so you stay here.' She opened her door, then reached back to the driver's side and turned off the engine. 'Save the planet,' she said, and got out and walked back toward the Ford SUV stopping behind them.

The man and the woman who got out of the Ford were the two Kirsten had seen drive past in front of their condo. The man stood by the front bumper on the passenger side, feet planted wide, hands on his hips, holding his suit jacket open, like – who was it? Doc Holliday? – ready to draw. The woman, a tall, athletic-looking blonde in a light blue rain coat and brown flats, came forward. She raised one hand, palm out.

'Stop right there,' she said, and with her other hand held up an open ID wallet.

Kirsten stopped maybe ten feet from the woman. 'Excuse me?' she said. Several cars sped by, headed east on Roosevelt. The westbound lanes were on the other side of a median strip. 'Is there a problem?'

'Your car, it's blocking the entrance to the building.'

'Actually,' Kirsten said, glancing back at her Camry, 'it's blocking just the turning lane. There's lots of room to drive around and into the entrance.'

'Your *car*,' the woman repeated, pointing, 'it's blocking—' She paused, and the sudden surprised look on her face made it clear that she'd finally recognized the Camry, and realized who Kirsten must be. 'And,' she said, 'we want to talk to you.' She thrust the open wallet forward, punctuating her statement.

'Is that a badge?' Kirsten leaned forward and squinted. 'I can't read that thing from—'

'It says FBI,' the man called out. He had a high, unpleasantly harsh voice, and there was actually a swagger in his step as he came up and stood next to the female agent. Yes, Doc Holliday. He even had the appropriate scraggly mustache.

'Oh . . . *F-B-I*,' Kirsten said. 'Why didn't you say so? Um . . . what did you want to talk about?'

FORTY

Kirsten sat in the SUV – an Expedition, actually – and had her discussion with the FBI agents right out there on Roosevelt Road. It wasn't exactly a congenial conversation, and twenty minutes later she'd rejoined Dugan in the Camry and they were headed east.

'Well,' Dugan said, 'at least they didn't drag you into their new digs and waterboard you.' She wasn't in the mood to answer that, and finally he asked, 'How'd it go?'

'They're kind of pissed off,' she said.

'What, you mean about my blocking their turning lane?'

'Yeah, right.' She fastened her seat belt. 'They're tired, actually, and I think embarrassed, about not recognizing this car right away. I mean, they'd been following us earlier. Of course I have no idea for how long, so I guess I should be embarrassed, too.'

'Maybe they weren't following us at all. Maybe they just happened to arrive at our place the same time we did. Anyway, what's their beef?'

'That my "interference with a police investigation" got Vincent Rondo killed. And Stump Stolecky, too, although they don't seem so brokenhearted about Stolecky's death.'

'So why do they care about *Rondo*? I mean, it's a homicide, a terrible crime and all that, and the cops have to look into it. But why should the *feds* care? It's not like he was a great asset to the community.' He paused. 'Although . . . I guess you could say the same thing about Johnny O'Hern, and . . .' His voice trailed away, and she knew he was beginning to understand.

'O'Hern was a wart on the community's backside,' she said, 'but he had value to the feds. I got the impression Rondo had value, too, although they didn't say so.'

'Maybe he did, but you had no way of knowing that. You thought he wanted to scare you off, so you wouldn't find out *he* killed O'Hern because he knew O'Hern was about to rat him out. It all made sense.'

'Maybe,' she said. 'But the only evidence that it was *Rondo* who sent those two guys was that they *usually* worked for him.'

'So you had to follow up with Rondo . . . and you did.' They were getting close to the lake by then, and Dugan said, 'I'm taking the Drive.'

'Yeah, whatever.' She didn't care what route they took. She had gotten a guy killed – *two* guys – and there was no sign that either of them had anything to do with the murder the cops were trying to pin on Dugan. If Rondo was already in the feds' pocket, he had no reason to worry about O'Hern's—

'Hello?' Dugan said. 'Anyone home?'

'Yeah, sorry.'

'I was saying . . . those FBI agents . . . they're working overtime just so they can come to our house and yell at you for getting Rondo killed?'

'Not just that. They wanted to know why I went out to his yacht, what happened. I told them what I told the cops, how

I thought he sent Pasco and Stolecky because I heard they worked for him, and how, when I confronted him, he convinced me he didn't know what the hell I was talking about. They wanted to know who I talked to about Rondo. Again I told them what I told the cops. What they really wanted to know was if I told Polly Morelli I thought Rondo sent the thugs, although they didn't mention Polly by name. I said I didn't tell anyone what I thought. Not even you, until late in the afternoon. By then Rondo and Stolecky might have been dead already, I don't know.' She shook her head. 'Jesus, both of them, for nothing.'

'Look, you're *not* to blame for two mob guys getting blown away.'

'Well, the *FBI* agents blame me. And I blame myself. It's what I *didn't* do. I told Morelli I'd find out who sent those two guys. I should have contacted him right away, told him it wasn't Rondo. He was bound to hear about my yacht visit. I just didn't think he'd hear so soon, and then *act* so soon.'

'Actually, you don't *know* that Morelli had anything to do with Rondo's death. You're assuming it, like me thinking that SUV had two *men* in it.'

'But I'm convinced it *was* him. And those agents are convinced, too. I think it's Morelli they're after, and now they've lost two informants . . . first O'Hern, now Rondo.'

'Poor babies. Now they gotta find somebody else. And you know what? That's their *job*. They don't need to waste my tax dollars being pissed off at *you*.'

They followed Roosevelt Road to where it emptied into Lake Shore Drive, just south of downtown, near the Field Museum, and took the Drive north. She stared out at the lake, thinking what a great father Dugan would make, and wondering whether she was suited at all to being a mother, when she suddenly realized they were going past Monroe Harbor. Vincent Rondo's yacht might still have been out there, bobbing gently on the water.

She sighed, and it came out louder than she intended, and with that she felt Dugan's hand on her shoulder. She put her hand on top of his.

'The Buddha had a saying about this,' he said. 'The Buddha said that whenever two FBI agents bawl you out because a couple of warts get scraped off society's ass, you just breathe in, and breathe out. Then you go home and have a glass of wine; or ginger ale, if you're trying to get pregnant. Then you turn down the lights . . . and try to get pregnant.'

'The thing is,' she said, 'they didn't just bawl me out. They *warned* me. Said I should stop messing in things too big for me. That if I kept "interfering with law enforcement" I'd find myself in big trouble.'

'Really. They said that? And did you promise to reform your life and be a good girl from now on?'

'No. I didn't promise anything at all.'

'I didn't think so. Let's go have that ginger ale . . . and make a baby.'

She leaned back and closed her eyes. What she *really* wanted was a dry Boodles martini and a long, soothing bubble bath.

FORTY-ONE

Kirsten got the bubble bath she wanted, and the next day, Sunday, she and Dugan spent the morning making love and making breakfast. Pretty much simultaneously. Then she spent the afternoon on the Internet, mostly. Among other things, it had occurred to her that possibly one of the two men Johnny O'Hern had killed in what were deemed 'questionable' shootings might have left friends or relatives with thoughts of payback. That theory didn't look promising, though. One incident happened over ten years earlier, and the victim was a crack dealer. The other incident was more recent, but the victim was a homeless man with no known relatives.

When she wasn't on the web, she was making phone calls and, through it all, wishing Dugan would leave her alone and go do something productive.

She called O'Hern's parents' number and Patrick answered and said his wife was at a church tea. Kirsten said that was great because *he* was the one she'd like to stop by and speak to, and he said – between rasping, labored breaths – that he'd 'call the fucking cops' if she showed up. She tried Richard O'Hern twice, to see if he could help her with his father – which she thought unlikely – and he didn't call back.

She also called Area Four police headquarters, and asked for Zane Maddox. He was off that day, and she got put through to his voice mail. She'd already talked about Maddox, a homicide detective, with Sandy Corrado, a friend from her department days, whose assessment was: 'Smart, tough, plays by the rules. No bullshit.'

That conversation with Sandy had been shortly after Father Watson told her that Maddox was originally the lead detective in the Landrew murder investigation, but that the case was pulled from Maddox and reassigned . . . to Johnny O'Hern. Interesting. Especially if it was true that Johnny's sister had been running a CIA operation out of the very clinic in Guyana at which Father Landrew, a frequent and outspoken critic of US policy, had spent a week volunteering.

The clinic *had* existed, and it *had* been near the Venezuelan border – she'd verified that – and the priest's murder *had* occurred within days of his return to the US. In addition, not long after that there'd been a failed attempt to overthrow the Venezuelan government. Of course there'd been other attempts, too, several before that, and at least one since, but it certainly was an interesting sequence of events.

At any rate, she was glad she didn't get straight through to Maddox. She was hoping he'd check out her credentials before he called back, and had suggested in her voice mail message that he talk to Sandy Corrado about her.

She was using the kitchen as an office, and had just hung up from that call when Dugan came in . . . for the fourth or fifth time since breakfast. 'Don't forget Polly Morelli,' he said. 'Have you reached *him* yet?'

'I don't have his number. Nobody does. People don't *reach* Polly. Polly reaches *them*.'

'Not always. A year ago you managed to get hold of him.'

'That was different. I was trying to save your ass from that crazy woman. And I had to drive clear out to Polly's place and pretty much get down on my knees and plead for an audience . . . like the creep was the goddamn pope or something.'

'He can't be the pope. The pope's Polish. Or no . . . this one's German, right?'

'Dugan, don't you have paperwork to do . . . at your office?'

'Hey,' he said, 'it's Sunday.'

'That's right. Think how quiet it'll be, how much you'll get done.'

'That stuff can wait. Don't forget, it's my ass you're trying to save *now*, too.'

'And think how much *I'll* get done,' she said, 'with you out of the way.'

'OK, OK.'

He left the kitchen and she went back to her laptop. But before she got very far he returned, in running shoes, jeans, and sweatshirt.

'I'll be at the lakefront,' he said. 'Gotta get back to my regimen. Five miles, maybe.'

'Uh-huh. Or maybe two,' she said, careful not to look up from her laptop until he closed the door behind him and was clomping down the back stairs.

He kept trying to pretend he wasn't worried about the potential murder charge hanging over him, but she knew he *was*. So was she. And they were both getting more worried as time went by, and as the list of possible suspects grew shorter.

She called Father Wayne Watson – more voice mail – and then went to work finding out what she could about Barry Zelander, the shady real estate developer who had a lot to lose, and who'd possibly started this whole mess.

Kirsten didn't sleep well Sunday night and at seven thirty the next morning she was already at the health club, working on her abs, when her cell phone rang. She jumped up and fumbled through her bag, trying to get to the damn thing before the call went into voice mail.

'Hello?'

'Maddox, Area Four Homicide. You left a message.'

'Yeah, I did. Thanks for calling back. I need to ask you about something. But first, did you check out my background? Did Sandy vouch for me?'

'I heard of you before. And yeah, Deputy Chief Corrado says you're OK people. Which doesn't mean I'll answer your questions. Anyway, what's it about?'

'I'd rather not . . . I'd rather talk in person. Whenever, wherever. You name it. Won't take long.'

'You got *that* part right,' Maddox said. 'Anyway, I'm on my way to pick up some witnesses, and I'll be at Twenty-sixth and

Cal all day. Jury trial. Room 402, Judge Merrick. Unless the airhead pleads out.'

'Great. I'll see you there. Around, say, eleven thirty?'

'Like I said, I'll either be there all day or I won't.'

Maddox was a heavy-set black man, and Kirsten found him pacing the hallway outside the courtroom. His waiting for her there was a good sign, since otherwise she'd have had to search him out in one of the rooms where cops and other witnesses sit around until they're called to testify. She offered him one of the two coffees she'd bought at the food vendor's truck – sometimes known as the 'Gangbangers' Grill' – parked outside the courthouse. Coffee wasn't allowed up here, but the rule wasn't always enforced, and a smile sometimes goes a long way. He took the cardboard cup and led her to a little room used by the assistant state's attorneys, and sometimes cops, to interview people. Another consideration he hadn't had to extend.

They sat on straight-back wooden chairs, at a small wooden table. 'Better make it quick,' he said. 'One of the ASAs might be needing the room. Plus, I could be called to testify any minute. Or . . . tomorrow morning, the way *this* damn case is going.'

She reached into her handbag and took out two sandwiches she'd smuggled in and laid them on the table. 'Ham and cheddar here,' she said, pointing. 'And this one's turkey and swiss.'

'Thanks,' he said, reaching for the ham and cheddar.

'Good. I'm trying to stay away from ham.' They unwrapped their sandwiches. 'OK,' she said, 'here's the deal. Anything you say here doesn't go beyond me. Period. And I'm hoping . . . and yeah, I know you have to do your job . . . I'm *hoping* what I say doesn't go beyond you.'

Maddox shrugged and spread his hands, half a sandwich in one of them. 'I'm guessing you're here on behalf of your husband, and I'm guessing you know I got nothing to do with the O'Hern case.'

'You're right. But I'm interested in another case, the Father Landrew murder. I'm sure you remember it.' He nodded, without expression, and she went on. 'I know you had the lead in that case, at first. But then it got suddenly reassigned. To our friend Johnny O'Hern.'

'Uh-huh. Cases get reassigned now and then.'

'But rarely,' she said, 'and there's always some reason, usually pretty straightforward and not a secret. The Landrew case, though, was front-page stuff, and I looked, and I can't find anything about that reassignment. So . . . did I miss something? Anyone tell the public what was going on, and why?'

He stared at her for a second or two, then said, 'If the public even *knew*, they wouldn't care.'

'Maybe,' she said. 'But the lead detective *would* care, and I can't believe you didn't ask for a reason.' He just stared at her, until finally she asked, 'Anyone say why?'

He leaned forward and rested his palms on the table. 'You mind telling me where you're going with this?'

She knew she had to tell him about her suspicions, but how detailed to get she wasn't sure. 'I'm thinking no one gave you a reason. Or if they did, you knew it was bullshit. You knew it wasn't the *real* reason.'

The faint hint of a smile on his face – whether deliberate or not – told her she was right, but what he said was, 'That's the privilege of rank. They don't have to explain.'

'What I think,' she said, 'is that someone outside the department applied pressure. Not because of any special problem with *you*, but because they wanted *O'Hern* to have that case. That possible?'

'Anything's possible.' He started on the second half of his sandwich.

'True enough. But I ask myself, "why?" I mean, Johnny O'Hern, for all his problems, *may* have been a first-rate investigator. I don't know. But I can't believe he got that case because somebody thought he'd do a better job than Zane Maddox.'

'Thanks.' He lifted his cup. 'But I never claimed to be the best homicide investigator in the world.'

'No,' she said, 'because that would be *me*.'

He laughed, to her great relief.

'I won't burden you with my theory as to who applied the pressure, 'cause it's only a theory. But I have a few questions I think you'll be comfortable answering.'

'We'll find out,' he said, 'won't we?'

'First, am I right so far? Was it odd that the case got reassigned, and that it went to O'Hern?'

'"Odd?" Yes, that's . . . safe to say.'

'And your partner? They take him off, too?'

'No. Thing is, he wasn't my usual partner. His name was Kriswell and he was new and . . . well, I won't say "dumb", but . . . green. He was put with me for . . . like a training experience. They left him with O'Hern.' He shook his head. 'For better or for worse.'

'So the case would be in O'Hern's hands. And Kriswell, the new guy, is he the kind that would let the experienced dick run things? Not second-guess what O'Hern did, or didn't do?'

Maddox frowned, then nodded. 'Yeah, or that's how he *was*, anyway.'

'So he's different now? Is he more—'

'I don't know how he is now. He left the department, last spring sometime. Moved to . . . where? Utah? Idaho? Somewhere out that way.'

'Oh.' She paused, regrouping her thoughts. 'OK then, back to the case, did the investigation seem to go the way you thought it should, once you weren't running it?'

'I'm not gonna discuss a police investigation. And what details would I have, if I wasn't working the case?'

'I understand, but . . . For example, were there angles you thought should be looked at that weren't, or any ideas . . .' She hesitated, then said, 'What the hell, what I want to know is whether Johnny O'Hern was put on that case so he could shut it down, so certain . . . possibilities . . . wouldn't be explored. Put it this way: were there things you would have done that he didn't do?'

'That's true in lots of cases other detectives are working on,' he said, which was a pretty clear *Yes*, Kirsten thought, for a non-answer.

'Like what things?' she asked.

He sipped some coffee, then set the cup down. 'Sometimes the way some people look at a case,' he said, 'gets narrowed pretty quick, and they don't look any farther. Say your eyewitness says the victim was killed by an armed robber. Sounds simple. Then you think: he's the only witness . . . is he reliable?' Maddox was clearly warming to his explanation. 'And you take a look at him. And then after him maybe you look a little farther. That's all I'm saying.'

'And O'Hern did nothing on the case, beyond what you'd already done?'

'It's still an open case,' he said. 'I'm not gonna second-guess another investigator.'

'But no new developments, no new progress, no— Well, damn. Look, if my husband is charged, and if his lawyer goes through all the hoops to get copies of those old police reports, which she will, and she'll succeed, would we find anything that O'Hern did, beyond what *you'd* already done?'

He waited a few seconds, then said, 'Nothing, not that I know of.'

'And if you'd—'

A buzz interrupted her and Maddox took his cell phone from his belt and answered it. 'Yeah?' He listened. 'On my way. I was finished here, anyway.' He ended the call and stood up. 'Sorry, gotta go.'

'Just one more thing, please.' Kirsten stood, too. 'If you'd stayed on the case, *would* anything more have been done?'

He'd already turned toward the door, but turned back to face her. 'I had some ideas,' he said, 'but it's not a perfect world. And whatever I did, that case might still be an open case today.' He lifted his hand, as though to block off any more questions. 'Thanks for the sandwich.'

FORTY-TWO

Zane Maddox was a cop. Kirsten wasn't. An ex-cop, yes, which put her maybe a step closer than a civilian, but definitely no longer part of the club – which, in some ways, she'd never really been. Still, Maddox the cop had given her more than what he might have . . . and everything he was going to.

She left the court building, convinced that the reassignment of the Landrew case to Johnny O'Hern had effectively shut the investigation down. Whether that was the *reason* for reassigning the case, and who was behind the decision, would be tough to establish. But it happened, and it made her wonder: Had someone decided now to slam the brakes on the O'Hern investigation, too? Just when Dugan was caught in the headlights?

Certainly, for whatever reason, the investigation seemed to have stopped short. No one 'looking a little farther'. Other than Kirsten.

She got her car from the parking garage and headed for downtown, reminding herself for the hundredth time that day that the case against Dugan was based on an unconvincing motive, and that any evidence the state thought it had would have to be so flimsy that if they ever actually *did* go to trial, there was little chance of a guilty verdict. Surely it couldn't be only she and Dugan and Renata Carroway who recognized that.

On Washington Street, in the heart of the Loop, the midday sun had brought the crowds out. Kirsten stopped for a light and watched people hurry to and from their lunches, and suddenly wondered whether any of them might turn up in the jury box if Dugan went to trial. She thought about that, and tried *not* to think about all the people convicted of crimes – some actually guilty, some not – who were sitting down to lunch that very day, having gone to trial absolutely convinced that the evidence against them was as weak and thin as the jailhouse coffee in their cups.

Her cell phone rang. She answered and a woman said, 'Hold on, please, for Father Wayne Watson.'

She waited, and he came on the line. 'I got your message and thought about it,' he said. 'Can we talk . . . in person?' He was clearly still worried about phone taps.

'Sure. Same corner as last time?'

'That's fine. Can it be . . . soon?'

'How's ten minutes sound?'

She drove north on State Street to Chicago Avenue, then east to Rush, and there he was, black suit and roman collar, walking near Chestnut, talking on a cell phone. She stopped and tapped the horn, and when he saw who it was he raised one finger, asking her to wait a minute. He finished his call, and came over and got in the car.

'That was quick,' he said.

'Yeah, but gosh, what if someone sees you alone in a car

with a *woman*?' She leaned over the wheel and peered around in all directions. 'And on *Rush* Street, of all places.'

He frowned. 'Do you *always* have to—' He stopped, then said, 'Oh. That's a joke, right?'

She smiled. 'Uh-huh.' She turned and went west on Chestnut. 'Heading to the cathedral again?'

'Yes, but only because there's a place there where you can park. Then we'll walk to where we're going. I got your message yesterday, and I went to the office and searched through our records on Fair Hope Clinic. I may have found someone for you.'

'Really. I figured I'd have to twist your arm again.'

'Not any more,' he said. 'I want to know what happened. I found a doctor who spent six months at the clinic, as part of a year's sabbatical.'

'Was she there when the CIA was there . . . allegedly?'

'She was certainly there when Father Landrew was. She's a— Hold on.' He was staring at her. 'How did you know this doctor was a woman?'

'I *could* say I'm a genius, but, y'know, there *are* only two possibilities. I almost always guess "female", which seems to surprise most men.'

'Anyway, her name's Castle.' He opened a little notebook he'd taken from his shirt pocket. 'Nora Castle. She's a trauma surgeon, and a professor at Northwestern Medical School. I reached her first thing this morning.' Kirsten stopped for a light and he looked up from his notebook. 'There's the cathedral parking lot.' He pointed. 'I'll give you a visitor's card that'll get you out.'

Five minutes later they were walking east on Chicago Avenue toward the Northwestern Medical Center lakeside complex, and Father Watson was telling how he'd called Doctor Castle and asked for her help.

'I was afraid she'd be too busy, or not interested, but as soon as I mentioned Fair Hope Clinic I could hardly shut her up. She *loved* her time working there, and said when she'd heard it was closed she called the archdiocese to see if there was any chance of it being reopened, but was told the decision was final. I said I was following up with some former volunteers, and asked if she could spare a few moments in the next day or so. She agreed, and I said I'd get hold of someone who's helping me . . . I said you were a "consultant" . . . and then get back to her. I just now had her on the phone again and she said she was at the medical school library and she'd see us right away. She sounds like a very enthusiastic, very high-energy person.'

'That's great, but . . . what did you say we were "following up" about?'

'I didn't. I'm leaving that up to you. But I'm coming along. I'm sure having an official from the archdiocese present will make her more willing to talk. And besides that, I want to hear what she says. Is it possible the CIA was really down there? I want to know.'

'So do I,' Kirsten said. 'But really, I'm not optimistic about getting an answer.'

And, more importantly, she was clueless about what to do if the answer was yes.

FORTY-THREE

The Galter Library, part of Northwestern's Feinberg School of Medicine, wasn't open to the public, but Doctor Nora Castle met them at the front desk. In no time she'd gotten them visitor's passes and led them inside and across a large room full of study tables . . . and not many students. Of medium height and somewhere in her fifties, she had black hair, smooth pale skin, and some sort of inner energy source that radiated waves that Kirsten could just about *feel* in the air.

The doctor stopped at a small table in the corner, by a window that looked out on the sidewalk along Chicago Avenue. 'We can talk here undisturbed.'

Father Watson jumped right in. 'First, Doctor Castle, thanks for seeing us on—'

'Excuse me, Father Watson,' she said, 'but I have class in half an hour. So what can I do for you? And please, both of you, call me "Nora".'

'Good,' Kirsten said. 'And you can call him "Wayne", like I do. Right, Wayne?'

'Um . . . absolutely . . . Kirsten.' He smiled. Still a little stiff, but she was getting to like him.

'Anyway, Nora,' she said, 'since your time is short, let me get to the point. All of us . . . including you, I'm sure . . . are disappointed that Fair Hope Clinic is closed.'

'Absolutely.' The doctor nodded. 'I loved Guyana, and Fair Hope. I'd been planning to recommend to my students that they volunteer there.'

'So,' Kirsten said, 'Wayne has asked me to assist in a sort of audit of the clinic, with a view toward possibly reopening.'

The doctor's eyes narrowed into a frown. 'Audit?' she asked. 'I'm not sure—'

Kirsten raised her hand, palm out. 'Not what you're thinking, Doctor . . . I mean . . . Nora. Medicine's not my expertise, and there's never been any concern about the quality of care . . . given the limited facilities.' She was on thin ice, now, not even knowing what facilities there were, but Nora seemed to be satisfied as long as no one was coming after *her*. 'No,' Kirsten went on, 'we're looking into the best use of the premises, what's economically most feasible, without compromising the quality of care.'

'I'm not sure how I can help with this.' The doctor was frowning again.

'For example,' Kirsten said, with what she hoped was an encouraging smile, 'from time to time, the clinic premises were also used by various other organizations, or companies. We're wondering whether this is an idea worth expanding. Could we lease them more often to create an income flow? Things like that.'

'Look, I'd like to help, but . . .' The doctor seemed to be getting bored.

'But *you* . . . the medical personnel . . . you're the heart of the clinic's mission, and we need to know, was the presence of any other entity on the premises ever a distraction? Did it hamper the care you were able to provide?'

'*Nobody* hampered us, or interfered. The only other "entity" when I was there was that mining company . . . Aurminex . . . but they stayed way down at a barn they fixed up. Far from us. We hardly even *saw* them. They came and went with trucks, and Jeeps, even helicopters. But that was usually at night and, apart from the occasional emergency surgery, we spent our nights a mile away, in town.'

As the doctor talked, Kirsten opened her shoulder bag, and took out a pen and a notebook. 'Wayne caught me in the car this afternoon, and I don't have my Fair Hope notes. What was the name of that company again?'

'Aurminex.' The doctor spelled it out. 'They weren't really mining, but exploring. Gold, I think. They were there . . . I don't know . . . two months? You must have a record of that.' She turned to Father Watson. 'Am I right, Fa . . . ah . . . Wayne?'

'Yes, we'll have to . . .' The priest hesitated. 'You see, if we *are* to reopen the clinic . . . and by "we", I mean the archdiocese, because I'll be leaving soon . . . but if—'

'That's right,' Kirsten said. 'Wayne's being made a bishop, and going to Spokane.' The doctor looked impressed, and Kirsten went on. 'Someone else was handling clinic affairs from this end when you were there, and we can look at the records. But anyway, you say Aurminex was there more than a month?'

'Oh yes. And then one morning they were gone.' She spread out her hands. '*Poof*. Vanished. I've since read that there are fly-by-night companies like that all over Guyana, poking around in remote areas for various metals and minerals, some with little regard to laws and regulations. But believe me, if they'd created a problem,' tapping her finger on the table for emphasis, 'I would have complained.'

'And rightly so.' Kirsten leaned forward. 'Any other complaints? About Aurminex, or anything else?'

'How could I have "other" complaints, when I haven't expressed any complaints in the first place?'

'*Touché*,' Kirsten said. 'Anyway, Nora, you've been a great help, and— Oh, one more thing. Father Landrew. Do you remember him?'

'Of course. He was a volunteer at Fair Hope for a week, then came back to Chicago and was murdered. I didn't hear about it until I got back to the States. Terrible. He wasn't medically trained, but he was very helpful. And very . . . intense. He didn't live in town with the rest of us, but spent his nights right out there at the clinic. He said he liked the solitude, considered his time there a sort of retreat.' She looked at her watch. 'So . . . if that's all, I have a class.'

'Of course,' Kirsten said, 'and thanks so much for your help.' She and Father Watson stood.

The doctor stood, too. 'I don't see how I've been much help, but working at Fair Hope was quite a satisfying experience for me, and I hope you can get it open again.'

'There's always hope,' Father Watson said, 'but the church has to follow the laws of economics, like any other business enterprise.'

'See, Nora?' Kirsten gestured at the priest with her thumb. 'He even *sounds* like a bishop.' The doctor seemed to enjoy that remark, and Kirsten reached out and shook her hand. 'We'll do our best,' she said.

As they walked back down Chicago Avenue toward the cathedral, Kirsten said, 'What's your take on all this?'

'It's very disturbing,' Father Watson said. 'That's a large piece of property down there, an abandoned sugar plantation. But I couldn't find one single record about anyone using any part of it, other than the clinic, in just the one building.'

'So . . . a chunk of remote wilderness a mile from town, close to the Venezuelan border. A so-called mining company . . . for whose presence there's no record . . . moves in and runs trucks, Jeeps and helicopters in and out, mostly at night. Then the "mining company" disappears. "*Poof!*" the doctor said. It's looking more and more like this confidential informant of yours, the guy who said the CIA was operating down there, had some basis for his belief.'

'I didn't say it was a man, and I thought you always guessed female.'

'I said "almost always". You gonna tell me it was a woman?'

'I'm not telling you anything.'

'What's really bizarre, though, is that this radical priest who loves to criticize both church and government leaders, comes home from working at the clinic . . . and gets murdered. "Disturbing", indeed.'

'But surely not a sufficient basis to run around making wild accusations.'

'No, not even close.' *She* sure wasn't going to start throwing that stuff around, and she didn't want him to, either.

By then they were at Rush Street and he turned to go back to his office, while she kept going on Chicago Avenue to get her car. Like all conspiracy scenarios, one could arrange the facts and string them together in a way that was, indeed, 'disturbing'. But her job was to get Dugan out from under a homicide charge, and tying any of this slippery international intrigue crap to the shooting of Johnny O'Hern would be quite a stretch.

It was only mid-afternoon, but it suddenly seemed much later. Waiting to cross State Street, she stopped walking and looked up. To the east, out over the lake, the sky was still bright and blue; but directly above, and as far as she could see to the west, the clouds were low and dark. The wind was from the west, too, not with a cold bite like a winter storm, but more ominous, a hint of worse to come, maybe even a tornado.

The light changed and she started across the street. There weren't many pedestrians now, and the few who crossed with her kept their heads down and moved swiftly. So did she. As she stepped up on to the curb on the other side, though, this big guy in front of her abruptly slowed and she almost ran into him. She sidestepped to go around him . . . and felt someone's hand on her right elbow.

He was behind her, and he held her elbow in a grip like a set of pliers. 'Jus' keep goin', honey,' he said. 'You be sensible and everything'll be fine.'

A black man, by the sound of it, and obviously as big as the white guy she'd almost collided with. And he'd dropped back now, to walk at her left side.

FORTY-FOUR

These two weren't cops, Kirsten thought, and they damn sure weren't FBI. Without another word, and with the black man never releasing his grip on her elbow, they hustled her into the cathedral parking lot. They quite obviously knew where her Camry was, and took her straight to it.

They steered her to the front passenger door and the white guy – actually, his copper skin and high cheek bones showed Native American blood – opened it and stood beside it. The black guy slipped her bag over his own shoulder, then searched the pockets of her jacket without actually touching her body at all. 'Get in,' he said. She did, and he added, 'Now hold out your hands.'

She did that, too, and he slipped a set of braided nylon wrist restraints over her hands and slid the locking block down toward her wrists, tight enough so she couldn't slip free, and no farther. The grace he moved with, and the care he took not to harm his opponent – and she *was* that, for sure – reminded her of an Aikido teacher, a *sensei*, she'd once studied with. He closed her door and got into the back seat behind her. The white guy went around and opened the driver's door and slid in behind the wheel.

She noticed a couple of wires hanging down below the steering column and thought about the expensive alarm and automatic ignition disabling mechanism she'd paid for. She'd have to complain to the dealer . . . if she ever got the chance.

'You didn't have to do that,' she said. 'I have the key.'

If the driver heard her, he gave no sign of it. He touched something thin and metal to the hanging wires and started the car. 'Fasten your seat belt.' His voice had a southern twang, or was it western?

'Who the hell are you to—'

'Listen up.' The man behind her, the *sensei*, spoke softly, his mouth close beside her ear, his hand resting on her shoulder. 'Let me show you something.' His hand tightened, squeezing her shoulder, and an electric shock of pain shot up into her neck. He loosened his grip and the stabbing pain stopped. He'd hit a nerve. 'Your cooperation,' he said, 'will make everything easier.'

She fastened her seat belt. Not so simple with her hands bound together in front of her, and when she'd managed it she sat back . . . and felt a thin cord drop around her neck from behind. She gasped and frantically grabbed at the loop with both hands, but he didn't pull it tight.

'Just a precaution,' he said, 'case someone's thinking of going somewhere.'

When they got to the exit gate they didn't need the key card Father Watson had given her. They had a card of their own.

They pulled out on to the street, Chicago Avenue again, and headed west.

A mile later they crossed Halsted, and were soon approaching

Ogden, where the agents in the SUV had led her and Dugan south-west the night before last. She wondered if she'd been wrong, if these two were FBI after all. But no, they kept going straight for another half-mile or so and then turned south on Ashland Avenue.

Nobody said anything. Whoever these guys were, they seemed to have no emotional investment in the job they were doing, which only added to their menace. Her mind raced in a dozen different directions, but escape seemed out of the question.

Ashland was a wide four-lane with lots of traffic, and moved well even though rush hour was under way. 'Mind telling me where we're going?' she finally asked.

'We're going south on Ashland Avenue,' the driver replied.

By that time they were passing through Little Village, an overcrowded Mexican neighborhood full of small shops and currency exchanges and taquerias, and possibly the dirtiest air in the city, thanks to two huge coal-fired generating plants nearby.

Approaching the bridge over the South Branch of the Chicago River, they passed a boat storage facility, maybe the one Dea Hannson and her friend had been headed for when they picked up Hecky Pasco after Dugan threw him in the river. This section of Ashland was still a broad, four-lane street, but traffic was lighter, more trucks than passenger vehicles. They went over the bridge and on their right, about where Twenty-eighth Street would have crossed Ashland if it hadn't dead-ended a mile to the east, was a large complex of buildings and truck docks, surrounded by acres of asphalt. The sign read: *Chicago Sun-Times, Printing and Distribution.*

'There,' the *sensei* behind her said.

'Got it,' the driver answered. But he didn't stop.

Instead, he went another block or so, threw a sudden U-turn just short of I-55, and then backtracked the same block. He stopped at the curb behind a blue Ford Taurus, in a section where the wide street had been made even wider to provide parking spaces.

The *sensei* lifted the loop from around her neck and got out of the car and opened her door, and she got out . . . also a little tricky with her hands bound. Once on the sidewalk, she glanced at the Taurus and from its license plate guessed it to be a rental car. She decided that what the men had spotted was the Taurus, not the *Sun-Times* plant, which was way over on the far side of the wide street.

The driver came around and the three of them – she in the middle, of course – left the sidewalk and went through a break in a low brick fence into a park-like open area. She noticed then, for the first time, that the sky was brightening in the west. The same wind was blowing, but it was driving the dark clouds and the threatened storm right on past the city and out over the lake.

They set out on a curving paved path, headed east toward a thin cluster of trees, fifty to seventy-five yards away. The trees had to be on the bank of a finger of the river which once bordered the Chicago Stockyards and was known as Bubbly Creek. The whole river-canal system was complicated, and she never quite got it all straight, but she knew the bubbles of Bubbly Creek used to rise up from decomposing blood and animal matter that even the creative stockyards people couldn't find a use for. At any rate, the water itself – which she'd heard didn't bubble up any more – couldn't be seen yet.

She'd never been here before, but she knew this was Canal Origins Park, sometimes known as the Canalport Riverwalk. Back in the mid-nineties the city had torn down a Sears warehouse and some other abandoned buildings along the water's edge, and created this small oasis in a gray urban desert. It was mostly native grasses, along with a few trees, some benches, and some bas relief sculpture tracing the canal system's history. It was pretty to look at, and maybe the air here was a little cleaner, too, but this was a noisy oasis. Trucks rumbled and clattered along Ashland behind them, while a persistent clanging and crashing of metal against metal rang out from across Bubbly Creek.

The noise wasn't as disturbing, though, as was Kirsten's recollection of something she'd read recently about the place. It was described as virtually unknown, so that on a weekday afternoon you could spend hours there, relaxing and watching a wide variety of birds . . . and not see a single other human being.

They came to a bench near the little group of trees on the river bank, and she sat down when they told her to. From there she could look out across the river and see that what had sounded like a facility for tearing cars into pieces and dropping them into piles, was in fact a yard full of scrap metal being loaded into barges. Within a year, she suspected, there'd be housing over there.

'Now what?' she asked.

'Now you wait.'

So she did. In a moment she heard footsteps on the path behind. She twisted around and saw the men walking away from her, while another person approached. The newcomer was a woman.

It was Janice Robinson . . . or whatever her real name was.

FORTY-FIVE

Dugan called the insurance adjuster, got put on hold, and then hung up before the guy came on the line.

It was only four o'clock and he seldom left the office before seven, but he was tired. Or . . . not tired. Bored? Not exactly. What it *was*, was that whatever he'd tried to do all day – reviewing law clerks' drafts of motions and memos, calling clients to discuss their cases, even arguing with adjusters, which could usually get him fired up – it all seemed . . . well . . . inconsequential.

The part about the adjusters was especially bad. He could be sick of the bullshit paperwork side of things and still get it done, and he could be worn down and still keep his game face on for the clients. But he couldn't tolerate not having his heart in a fight to get an insurance adjuster to give a fair shake to a single mom whose kid severed a tendon *and* an artery, because the hotel didn't get the glass off the bottom of the pool. Go into a negotiation like that without feeling the buzz? That wasn't fair to his client.

So he hung up, and when the adjuster called right back – generally a good sign – he told Mollie to take a message.

Funny how waiting for the sword of a homicide indictment to fall made everything else in your day seem . . . well . . . the word was 'inconsequential'.

* * *

Renata Carroway had called earlier that day, a little before noon. 'I just talked to the state's attorney,' she said.

'Lucky you.'

'She says they're about ready to indict.'

'I guess you're talking about *my* case, huh?'

'That would be your case, yes.'

'What does "about ready" mean, exactly?'

'They're offering a deal, and my feeling is they hope you take it before they have to indict.'

'I made a vow as a young boy never to plead to anything more serious than a traffic violation.'

'Good for you. You wanna hear the deal?'

'No.'

'I'll put it in an email. You can read it. Then you can email me back and tell me whether you accept the offer, and I'll relay your position.'

'I'm telling you right now.'

'Read my email and send a reply,' she said, and hung up.

Whatever 'about ready to indict' meant, it wasn't good. He'd called Kirsten and gotten her voice mail. Now he was sitting at his desk, not opening his email, not accomplishing anything. He needed . . . what? Damn, he needed a total retreat from reality and—

'Hey!' Larry Candle stood in the open doorway. 'How they hangin', Doogie pal?'

'Damn,' Dugan said. 'Did you just get a message from somewhere . . . that I needed you?'

'Message? I don't *think* so. I was on my way to take a leak. But hey, lemme grab a couple of beers on my way back and we can chat.'

Dugan looked at his watch. 'It's . . . a little early.'

'Doogs, m'boy,' Larry said, in a terrible attempt at an Irish brogue, 'sure an' don't go bein' a slave ta convention. Besides, I been thinkin' about your problem . . . and you look like you could *use* a bit of an idea. Back in five.' He disappeared.

Dugan buzzed Mollie and told her he'd be in his office, but if anyone called – unless it was Kirsten – he was out for the day. Mollie sputtered a little and he hung up and waited. Larry's ideas were usually less than helpful. But a beer would do just fine.

Larry came back with two bottles of Dos Equis, the caps already popped, and set one in front of Dugan.

'What,' Dugan said, 'you're not tossing loaded beer bottles today?'

'I tole ya, that's for when I think you're up to it. But today? I don't think so. Bad news?'

Dugan took a long pull on his Dos Equis. 'My lawyer says the state's "about ready to indict", whatever that means.'

'Hey, not to worry. Kirsten'll come up with the real killer.' He paused. 'Um . . . she got any possibilities yet?'

'She's . . . eliminated one or two.'

'So that's a start. Keep the faith, Bucko.'

Dugan tilted his bottle again and was surprised to find it empty already. He set it down and stared at Larry. 'I thought you had a couple of ideas.'

Larry popped up from his chair. 'First . . . more beer.'

Dugan waited and wondered if Larry really had any suggestions, or if he just wanted to pump Dugan for information. Larry was a bundle of curiosity. Still, more beer was itself a good suggestion.

But Jesus, *Bucko*?

'I'm back,' Larry said. This time he had four bottles, and when they were evenly distributed, he said, 'Here's what I'm thinking.' No brogue now. 'This thing's got the mob hit look. First, the style. Then, because O'Hern, known to be mixed up with a guy who was mixed up with the big bambinos, was also known to be talking to the feds. So the first thing you gotta think of is Outfit, right?'

'Unless you think of me.'

'Which we don't. But I'm not thinking Outfit, either.'

'Why not?'

'Because,' Larry said, 'Polly Morelli runs that particular show around here, and Polly would never order a cop killed. Period. Not even a crooked cop. He knows there'd be no let up. He'd be finished.'

'Could be somebody lower echelon.'

'Such as the recently deceased Vincent Rondo?' Larry downed some of his beer. 'Believe me, it wasn't Rondo. He was a mean, nasty weasel. He could beat a guy into a vegetable in a five to one fight, but word is, he didn't have the balls to kill a cop. Plus, there's talk the feds had him in their pocket already. So why would he need to shut O'Hern up?'

'I don't know.' Dugan finished his beer and decided to hold off on number three. 'So if it wasn't me, and it wasn't Morelli or Rondo, who was it? That real estate guy? Barry Zelander?'

'Zelander?' Larry waved his hand dismissively. 'No way. He's got money; he's got political clout; and he's got the feds all over him. Guy like that works a deal. He doesn't murder witnesses. Makes him too obvious a suspect.'

'It's not unheard of that people in trouble kill witnesses.'

'Yeah,' Larry said, 'but those are low-lifers, like gang-bangers or mob guys.'

'So mob guys *do* kill witnesses.'

'Witnesses, yes. *Cop*-witnesses, no.' Arguing was Larry's favorite sport, and the little guy was having a great time. 'Ya gotta remember,' he went on, 'just 'cause a guy's singin' to the feds doesn't mean that's the only possible motive for killing him.'

'Can't argue with that,' Dugan said. 'But damn, everyone who knew him hated his guts. So, what's your theory?'

'Simple.' Larry picked up his third beer and took a slow sip . . . obviously trying to build suspense. 'Most murders are committed by family members or close friends of the victim . . . if he has any friends.'

'That's it?' That bit of non-news called for a third beer, and Dugan grabbed his. 'That's your *theory*?'

'Actually, more a fact than a theory. Go with the statistics. Start with O'Hern's family. Wife? Divorced for years . . . no motive. Kids? Just one, and he's dead. So you move on to his birth family. Sister? Estranged and gone for years, no hope of inheritance . . . no motive. But the others . . . brother, father, mother . . . they're around, rubbing up against this "everyone-who-knew-him-hated-his-guts" guy all the time.' He tilted his Dos Equis toward Dugan. 'Like I said, kiddo, Kirsten's a genius. If she looks at those three, I bet she finds something that takes that general gut-hating thing and ramps it up into a bona fide motive for murder.'

'Yeah, well, I'll be sure to pass that along to the genius.'

'Good. And tell her if she needs any help I— Jesus.' Larry looked at his watch and jumped to his feet. 'Gotta pick up my baby at ballet and get her to her mom's in time for the math tutor.' He set his bottle on Dugan's desk and stared down at it. 'Jesus,' he said, 'helping you think through your problem just cost me a bundle.'

'A bundle of *what*?' Dugan added his empty to the collection. 'I buy the beer around here.'

'Yeah, and the two of us just knocked down a six-pack in less than a half-hour. I don't need a DUI, so now I gotta take a *cab* to pick up my daughter.' He was looking in his wallet. 'That'll be fifty bucks, easy, by the time I . . .' He shrugged and looked up. 'Say, Doogie pal, I was wondering . . .'

'Yeah, I know,' Dugan said. He was on his feet now, too. He leaned across the desk and handed Larry a fifty. 'Thanks for the insight.'

FORTY-SIX

Kirsten stood and watched Janice Robinson approach. She'd only seen the woman that one time, the day of her brother Johnny's funeral, and it struck her now how much Janice resembled the little girl in the first communion photo on the O'Hern mantle. Now, though, she was tall and slender, her coal black hair cut short. With her darker complexion she resembled her father and Richard, more than her mother and Johnny, who were fair-skinned.

She wore a tan raincoat that was belted at the waist and came to her knees, and calf-length leather boots. Her hands were stuck in her coat pockets, and she wasn't carrying a purse. She walked smoothly, with the erect posture and casual grace of an athlete. Very composed, very sure of herself.

But if things were all going the way you'd like them to, Janice honey, you wouldn't have gone to so much trouble to meet with li'l ol' me.

Janice stopped about six feet away, and Kirsten silently stretched out her hands, still bound by the restraints.

Janice nodded, smiling slightly. 'You may be thinking,' she said, 'that with your hands free you'd be able to run faster, and I'm sure that's true.' Her voice was as strong and self-confident as her appearance, and could be heard easily, despite the incessant clanging from across the river. 'But not fast enough. Those two would bring you back, and you'd only have wasted time and energy. Are we clear on that?'

'What *you* need to be clear on is that, restraints or not, I could do you serious damage before your stooges can get here.'

'My, my,' Janice said, 'I suppose that comes from dealing mostly with men. Posturing, blustering, boasting about who's got the bigger this or that. But assuming you did "damage" to me, which I *don't* assume, what would you have accomplished?'

'What do you want from me?'

'Your attention. I have something to say.'

Kirsten raised her arms again. 'I'm having trouble hearing.'

Janice took her hands from her pockets, and in one of them she held a flat plastic implement, about the size and shape of a large match book, with a sort of finger, or hook, along one side. She stepped forward and, sliding the finger under the cord around each wrist, easily cut Kirsten's hands free. 'Is that better?'

'A little.'

'Then let's sit down.'

They sat at opposite ends of the park bench, each twisting to face the other, and Kirsten, anxious to grab the lead, asked, 'Who are you?'

'I'm Johnny O'Hern's sister.'

'That much seems true. But on the faculty of Mount Saint Joseph College in Maryland? That's bullshit.'

Janice shrugged. 'That's up to Mount Saint Joe's, not you. I'm on sabbatical.'

'They carry you on sabbatical for *four years*?'

'Maybe they value me, want to hold on to me.'

'So who *do* you work for?'

'Does that really matter?' Janice lifted one flap of her raincoat and folded it more tightly across her knees. 'I mean, you're a self-employed private investigator. But . . .' She leaned toward Kirsten. 'If you ever *finally* get pregnant . . . and maybe Doctor DeMarco can help . . . you'll be a mom, and your *work* situation will change, and—'

'Stop!' Kirsten fought to keep the tremor out of her voice. She felt a touch of fear, of course, and shock at how much this woman knew. But mostly she was angry. 'You have no damn business poking around in my life.'

'Oh, don't be silly.' Janice was smiling again, clearly pleased with the effect she'd had. 'You spend most of your waking hours "poking around" in other people's lives. But right now,' the smile disappeared, 'what I have to say is more important than who I *work* for.'

'You're with the CIA. You *must* be.'

Janice didn't seem bothered. 'You know the stock answer,' she said. '"If I *were*, would I *tell* you?" But that's such a cliché, so I'll answer directly: No, I'm not.'

She certainly *looked* believable, but Kirsten said, 'I think you're a skilled liar.'

'Think whatever you like. But even if I *were* a CIA agent, I'd put your chance of proving it at a little below zero percent. So what's the point?'

Kirsten stared at her. 'The point is that my husband may be going on trial soon, for a murder he didn't commit.'

'So you want to prove that someone else did it,' Janice said. 'And do you actually think you could prove that the CIA was involved?'

'I have information to support the suggestion that the CIA was using a Catholic Church facility in Guyana a year ago, and may have been involved with the murder of a priest who'd been working there, a murder your brother was personally selected to investigate.'

'Jesus, listen to yourself.' Janice shook her head. 'You have "*information* to support the *suggestion*"? You're hallucinating if you think that will save your husband.'

'Really? So then, why pick me up and drag me down here?'

'Because,' Janice said, 'I don't want you needlessly harming innocent people.' She stood up suddenly, and walked toward the edge of the river bank. She seemed to be staring down at the water, but then she came back and sat down. 'I really don't care whether you prove that someone other than your husband killed my brother. But I *do* care that there are others you may harm, people who don't deserve it.' She paused, then added, 'You know, of course, that people have *already* died because of your actions.'

'What are—' Kirsten was stunned. 'What do you know about my "actions"?'

'I know you're in touch with Polly Morelli. My guess is he wants to know what you're finding out about Johnny's death, and whether any of his people were involved. I know someone tried to scare you off, and I know about your visit to Vincent Rondo's boat. I'm guessing you told Morelli the person behind the threat was Rondo.'

'I didn't—' Kirsten caught herself. 'Get on with your story.'

'Whatever you did or didn't tell Morelli, you led him to believe Rondo was a liability. The next thing Rondo knows, he's being gunned down in a sandwich shop, along with that Stolecky guy. Do you really think you had nothing to do with that?'

'And those two,' Kirsten said, 'they're the kind of "innocent people" you want to protect?'

'Vincent Rondo was as rotten as they come. And Stump Stolecky, and that other guy, Hecky Pasco? Thugs for hire, to do whatever they're told. No, it's not them I'm concerned about. My point is, there's no sign Rondo had any part in my brother's murder, and now he's dead. That's what happens when people . . . *you*, in this case . . . go flailing around, setting things in motion they don't understand, and can't control.'

'Thanks for the advice.' Kirsten stood up. 'But there's one thing *you* can't control . . . and that's *me*. I intend to keep "flailing around" until I get to the truth. I'll drive myself home, thank you.' She turned to leave.

'What you'll do,' Janice said, her voice with a new hard edge, 'is hear me out.'

Kirsten started toward her car. The sun was low in the west now and directly in her eyes, making her squint, and at first she didn't even see the two men. They had come back, and were about thirty yards away, spreading apart from each other and coming toward her. She knew she could run faster than most people, and could keep running longer. But these two weren't *most people*. She turned back to Janice, who was standing now, too.

'Come back and sit down,' Janice said. 'No one here wants you hurt.'

They both sat on the bench again and Kirsten said, 'I intend to get my husband out from under this murder charge, which means finding out who killed your brother.'

'Fine, but dragging in some supposed year-old CIA

operation? And trying to tie that to the murder of a priest? That might get you some tabloid coverage, but you'll be considered a headcase by most people. Which is not my problem. The fact, though, that you may do real harm to people who don't deserve it . . . that's my concern.'

Kirsten shook her head. 'What people?'

'Look.' Janice sighed. 'To help your husband you don't need "information to support suggestions". You need proof, and you won't prove *anything* about the CIA.'

'What *people*?' Kirsten asked again. 'Besides yourself, I mean.'

'Leave me out of it. I can't be touched on this. But your question proves my point: *you don't know* who will be dragged in by your claims, ruined by the implication that they've been part of, or complicit with, a clandestine CIA operation. It won't matter whether they knew about any operation, or whether there'd ever *been* one. And you will have accomplished nothing for your husband.'

'What the hell? The *church* sent you to snatch me, threaten me, scare me off?'

'I don't care about "the church", and no one "sent" me. You're here because I want you to see how useless, and potentially harmful, it is to go down the CIA route.' She paused, then added, 'I'm not "threatening" anyone. I'm not in the "threat" business.'

'So . . . if I stay away from the CIA angle, what will *you* do for *me*?'

'Nothing. I'm saying you can avoid causing harm, and you can save yourself trouble and time. But we're not making a deal here.'

'You're worried about someone, but you don't care who killed your brother?'

'My brother, alive or dead,' Janice said, her voice dropping to a cold monotone, 'meant nothing to me.'

'That's obviously not true. He *did* mean something to you. You hated him. You may even have killed him yourself.'

That seemed to catch Janice by surprise, and she laughed. 'Go where you can with *that*,' she said. 'But at least you're on better footing. We both know that reasons for killing are seldom as complicated as what conspiracy theorists like to conjure up. Look for hatred, anger, revenge . . . and, of course, money . . . that's why people kill.'

'Fair enough. And like I said, you hated him.'

'Yes, as a teenager I thought no one could hate anyone as much as I hated Johnny. And with good reason. But I was mistaken. Patrick hated him just as much.' She paused. 'I say "Patrick", because he doesn't deserve the name "father".' She shook her head. 'Anyway, the difference is that Patrick never gave it up. I did.'

'What about Richard?'

'Richard was very young when I left. But he never liked Johnny, and it's clear now that he still resents the fact that our mother so clearly favored Johnny. She even . . .' Janice didn't finish. She looked at her watch and shook her head. 'You don't think Vincent Rondo had my brother killed, do you?'

'I . . . no I don't.'

'And if you'd done things differently, would he and Stolecky still be walking around?'

'I don't know that.' But she *did* know. 'Yes, they probably would be. But I never—'

'What about Hecky Pasco? Did he kill Johnny?'

'I don't know.'

'And you still don't know who hired him and Stolecky to talk to your husband.'

'I thought it was Rondo. That seemed the most probable.'

'So you acted on what seemed "probable", and as a result Rondo and Stolecky are dead.'

'I didn't intend for that to happen.'

'But it *did* happen. And I'm saying you can avoid causing further unintended results, by doing things a little differently.' Janice stood. 'Let me show you something.'

'Where?'

'This way.' She went toward the river. 'Before it's too dark.'

Kirsten stood up, and noticed then that at some time during their conversation the banging and clanging from the barge loading had stopped. She followed Janice to where the ground dropped off sharply, a sort of cliff, down maybe six feet to a narrow, rocky shelf along the water's edge. The sun was too low in the sky to reach down there, and the rocks and the water were in shadows.

'Over here,' Janice said, and took Kirsten's arm and pulled her to the left.

Kirsten yanked her arm away. 'What is it? What are you talking about?'

'Down there.' Janice pointed. 'I'm wondering when you were going to tell your friend Morelli you made a mistake.'

The body lay on its back on the rocks, the gaping hole in its chest probably a shotgun wound. But the face was untouched, and although Kirsten had never seen the man in person, she'd heard him described. And she'd seen the sketches. No question. It was Hecky Pasco.

FORTY-SEVEN

Janice walked Kirsten back to her car, trailed by the two men. 'The wiring's fine and you won't have any problem starting it,' Janice said.

'Where's my purse? My keys are in it.'

'Yes, along with your cell phone, and your gun. You'll find your purse under the car. Sorry for the inconvenience.'

'Yeah, well, you never know. Maybe I can return the favor some day.'

'I *do* know. We won't be meeting again. There'll be no need. Even if you don't follow my advice, I'm not the one who'll get hurt. And I can't speak for the CIA, but I'm sure they can live with one more unpatriotic kook, claiming a federal agency conspired against a government hostile to the United States.'

When they reached Ashland Avenue, the man who'd driven her Camry slid under the wheel of the Taurus – which was now behind Kirsten's car and facing the opposite direction. He started the engine while Janice went around and got into the front passenger seat. The other man, the *sensei*, stayed with Kirsten, holding her arm just tightly enough to keep her from running over and diving under the Camry for her purse – if she'd been so inclined.

They stood there waiting, and when there was a break in the traffic he looked down and gave her a surprisingly pleasant smile. 'Stay well, sugar,' he said, and let go of her arm. He ran and got into the Taurus and it sped off, crossing over to the southbound lanes, and was gone.

Although it was getting dark, she had no trouble spotting her purse. But she had to lie flat on her belly on the pavement to reach it, and by the time she was back up on her feet she couldn't see the Taurus and it had too big a start for her to follow it.

She got out her phone and called Dugan.

The cold gin made the entire inside of Kirsten's head tingle, in a most delightful way, so she took another sip. 'All in all,' she said, 'it was a very strange conversation.'

'Damn,' Dugan said, 'and I thought my talk with Larry was strange.'

'Nope. Conversations with Larry Candle don't count. They're *always* weird.'

They'd been sharing the events of their afternoons with each other in the lounge at the Four Seasons Hotel. The plan was to have cocktails there – which meant a martini for Kirsten, who figured the hell with it, there was no baby yet – and then head out for some sloppy Italian beef sandwiches at Al's #1.

'Anyway,' she said, 'what's *really* strange is that we each got pretty much the same advice, from two wildly different sources. Janice said I should focus on the family, and—'

'"Focus on the Family." That sounds familiar.' Dugan was drinking scotch, straight up. 'Isn't that a radio pro—'

'Yes, but let's not go there. You're distracting me.'

'Sorry,' he said.

'Accepted. So both Janice and Larry say we should look at the family and close associates, and stick with the tried and true murder motives: like hate, and greed.'

'Right,' Dugan said, 'not to mention lust and anger and . . . whatever the rest of those seven deadly sins are. But first, do you think this Janice person *is* with the CIA?'

'I really don't know.' Kirsten speared an olive and slid it off the toothpick into her mouth. 'Whoever told Father Watson about her must have seemed credible to him. And she's with *someone*. It takes resources to gather all the information she has, but there's no proof that either she or the CIA was in that clinic in Guyana.'

'No proof maybe, but isn't that why they get all those tax dollars? To run around the world conjuring up regime change schemes? I move that we assume they were down there.'

'That motion passes,' Kirsten said. 'But if we add the rest of it, it gets to be quite a conspiracy theory: the church lets the CIA run an operation, headed by Janice, out of its clinic; a visiting priest catches on and comes home, ready to blow the whistle; the CIA kills him to shut him up, then gets the cops to reassign the case to Johnny O'Hern and he shuts down the murder investigation; a year later Johnny himself's in a talkative mood, so the CIA kills *him*, too, and then gets the cops to shut down *that* investigation; but this time it's a cop that's been killed, so they gotta charge *someone*, and they're left with you.'

'Man,' Dugan said, 'that's a lot to swallow.'

'Anything's possible,' Kirsten said, 'but I agree, it's a mouthful. And I also agree with Janice that we could spend a lot of precious time on it and, even if it was the right theory, we'd never actually *prove* it.'

'So,' Dugan said, 'we set aside the CIA theory. First, because it's unlikely; and second, because we can't win that battle anyway. Instead, we go down the hatred, greed, *et cetera* road . . . the good old seven deadlies . . . because that's a battle we *can* win . . . *if* it's the right road.' He was starting on his second scotch. 'Life is complicated.'

'That it is.' Still nursing her first martini, she took two more sips. Delicious.

'Did it occur to you,' he asked, 'that maybe Janice . . . or the CIA or whoever . . . killed Hecky Pasco? I mean, how did she know where his body was?'

'I don't know how she knows half of what she knows, and yes, I thought of that. But my money's on Polly Morelli for that one. I think she took me there, and showed me the body, to help make her point.'

'That's a hell of a lot of trouble to make a point.'

'I think she truly wants to protect someone from harm. And really, that's *all* she did, tried to talk me out of going the CIA route. I mean, they could have killed me and dumped me next to Pasco. But she didn't even threaten me.'

'Yeah, well, she saw what happened to the *last* guy you thought threatened you, and—'

'Uh-uh, Dugan, that's not funny. I should never even have mentioned that threat to Morelli, not before I was sure who was behind it.' She lifted her martini and finished it off in one gulp, still surprisingly upset about the deaths of three men who, when they were alive, made sewer rats look good. She'd barely set her glass down before the waiter was there. She ordered another and he hustled off to get it. 'My point,' she said, 'is that Janice didn't say I should stop looking for O'Hern's killer. She said if I pursued the CIA and the Guyana stuff, I could do serious harm to someone – meaning some church person, I think – and still not help *you*.'

'So who's the church person? The cardinal?'

'Possibly. But unless Father Watson's wrong, if the CIA was down there the cardinal never knew about it. There was a priest, though, who was sort of the liaison between the archdiocese and the clinic. I thought he might be the one Janice wants to protect.'

'From what?'

'From being fingered as the priest who secretly got the Catholic Church involved in a CIA operation. Not a great career move.'

'Well, then, we have to talk to that *priest*.'

'We can't. I mean *I* can't. *You* don't talk to *anybody* about anything concerning your case, remember? Anyway, the priest is gone.'

'Gone where? You mean . . . *dead*? Jesus.'

'I don't know if he's alive or dead. And if he's alive I don't know if he's the one Janice wants to protect. We're in total guesswork territory here.'

The waiter was back with her new martini. She took a sip and it tasted as good as the last one, maybe better. Pointing at Dugan's scotch, she said to the waiter, 'Bring him a refill, too.'

'Of course.' He gave her a slight smile, and a nod, and left.

'That'll be my third,' Dugan said.

'Good.' She looked around the elegant room, with its indirect lighting and its genteel, soft-spoken clientele. 'It's nice here.' In one corner a jazz trio was just launching into 'Night and Day', and she realized they'd probably been playing all evening and this was the first time she'd heard them. 'Let's skip the beef sandwiches,' she said, and lifted her glass. 'Hang out here awhile, get a nice warm glow on, then go home and . . . I don't know . . . have a bowl of oatmeal.'

'Sounds like a plan. But we'll have to mind our manners. Remember . . . the CIA may have the place wired.'

'I'd rather forget the CIA. For now, anyway. On the way here I got a call from Richard O'Hern. He's meeting me in the morning with the keys to his brother's house, so I can search it. I doubt I'll find anything helpful, but it's possible. Also, it's a chance to talk to Richard again about the family. I'm getting back on the "seven deadlies" road.'

FORTY-EIGHT

Johnny O'Hern's house was out on the north-west edge of the city. It was a so-called 'typical Chicago bungalow', a brick, one-and-a-half-story home with a low-pitched roof, horizontal sight-lines, and lots of leaded windows. But untypically, it wasn't set on a north-south street along one side of a rectangular block. Instead, the street was a self-contained circle, dropped by some misguided early-twentieth century real estate developer into the middle of a group of angled streets that mostly went nowhere. She might as well have been in Boston.

It didn't help, either, that it was only seven fifteen in the morning and she was a little hung-over. But she found the place . . . mostly because there was a yellow cab sitting at the curb and Richard O'Hern was pacing up and down on the sidewalk. They'd agreed to meet at seven because he had to be in court at eight thirty and would be tied up all day.

She parked behind the cab and got out and walked over to Richard. 'Sorry I'm late.'

'I'll just leave the key with you,' he said. 'You don't need me, right?'

'Stick around for a few minutes. I'm sure I'll have things to ask when I see the inside.' She already knew some of the things she wanted to ask.

'The cab will cost me a fortune, but . . . I'll stay as long as I can.'

They went up a set of concrete steps to a covered porch, and went inside. 'This is only the third time I've been in here myself,' he said, and handed her the keys. 'There's the living room here, which opens into that small sun room. The dining room is through there,' he said, pointing, 'and beyond that the kitchen, and two bedrooms and a bathroom. There's a basement, of course, and an attic that someone made into a couple of small bedrooms, probably fifty years ago. But I doubt Johnny ever used the upstairs.'

She looked around. The living room had obviously been assembled – carpeting, furniture, even the pictures on the walls – with loving care, a long, long time ago. 'All this furniture, Johnny didn't bring it when he moved in, did he?'

'No, the place was fully furnished when he bought it. An older couple lived here. I don't know the details, but that's what my mother said. She loves the place.'

'I bet she does. It's all so neat and clean. Sure doesn't look like a single guy lived here.' Especially not a *cop*, she thought.

'Like I told you, my mother cleaned for him. She said Johnny *deserved* a clean place. The old man would complain about the time she spent here, but their own place is just as well taken care of . . . no thanks to him . . . so he can't rant on too much.'

'Your father hated Johnny, didn't he?'

'My father hates ev— Yeah, he did. I think he only went to the funeral to make sure Johnny got put underground.'

'So . . . is it possible he hated him enough to . . . you know . . .'

'Hell, his opinion hasn't changed since Johnny was a kid. Why would he suddenly do something now? Especially when for all these years he hardly even had to *see* Johnny. It's not like any of us even spent holidays together. I have to say I hated Johnny myself . . . back when we were kids. My big brother the bully. Then the super macho cop, y'know? But we went our separate ways, and the bad feeling sort of dulled down. For me anyway.'

She walked into the dining room, then into the hall to the bedrooms, and he followed. 'Just one bathroom?' she asked.

'And a little half-bath by the back door.'

'What about Janice?'

'What, you mean did *Janice* hate him enough to kill him?

Jesus, she hasn't been back since she went to college. She doesn't *visit*. Why the hell would—'

'She hated him, though. I mean . . . didn't she?'

'I was still pretty young when she went away. But yeah, I'd say she hated him. I think she . . . well . . . she had a special reason.'

'What was that?'

'Well, he'd always picked on her . . . and me, too . . . but about the time Janice went into high school it got worse for her. She started complaining to our mother that Johnny was . . . *bothering* her. I didn't really get it at the time, but she'd say he . . . *touched* her, brushed against her, wouldn't leave her alone, things like that.'

'What'd your mother do?'

'Are you kidding? Nothing. Said Johnny was a good boy and he was just teasing.'

'So . . . you think he ever . . . *molested* her?'

'Like I say, I was a kid. But thinking back, I'm not sure. Anyway, it didn't last long.'

'What do you mean?'

'Well, this went on for awhile, and then . . . things changed. And her complaints? About the touching, brushing up against her, all that? They stopped. Like turning off a switch. Like one day she's complaining, and the next day . . . no more. Thing is, he stopped teasing her, too. Period.'

'What, like they were suddenly . . . *friendly*?'

'Oh no, not that. I remember I was in fifth grade and he'd just started his senior year in high school when things changed. He still picked on *me*, but I don't think he ever said two words to her that whole year. But not like they were friends. More like he was *afraid* of her.'

'Sounds to me like she *broke* him, scared the living crap out of him.'

'Maybe. I never really thought about it much. It just stopped. Then he graduated and went right into the army, I guess to get away from the old man. And Janice left while he was still gone. Far as I know, they never saw each other again.' He looked at his watch. 'I better be going. You can—'

'Wait. Just a couple of things.' They were in the dining room again, and she swept her arm around. 'Look at all this. Exposed woodwork. Built-in cabinetry. This is a *very* nice house.'

'He said he got a deal on it. The couple who owned it died within a few months of each other, and their only son lived in . . . I don't know . . . Shanghai or Hong Kong or something, and just wanted it sold. But yeah, it wasn't cheap. I couldn't believe it myself when he bought it. It was right after his divorce and I was sure he was broke.'

'So how'd he do it?'

'My mother.' His face went suddenly red, and she realized it was flushed with anger. 'She gave him the whole goddamn down payment. Not a word to anyone. I only found out about it when I made Johnny produce all his financials when he claimed he couldn't afford a lawyer.'

'You mean . . . she had money no one knew about?'

'Yeah. Apparently she inherited money from her brother when he died, and never told anyone. I mean, she's living in *my* two-flat, paying just taxes and utilities, and no rent, and she helps Johnny buy a house. When I found out I was furious. I yelled at her and she told me Johnny promised to sell the house in a few years and pay her back with interest and she'd move into a retirement home. She's fucking crazy when it comes to Johnny, but at least she knew enough to have both their names put on the deed.'

'Really. So it's her house now?'

'Yeah. And you know what? I think she'd leave my father in a second and move in here. I don't know what's owed on the place by now, though, or what the payments are, or what it's worth with the market down so much.'

'OK, but—'

'Look, I'm sorry.' He lifted his arms, as though in surrender. 'But I *gotta* get to court.' He turned and hurried into the living room.

'Wait.' She called, following him. 'Did your father know all this, her helping Johnny buy the house and all?'

Richard was already at the front door. He pulled it open and turned back. 'No way, not until a few weeks ago, when I told him. Which I knew I shouldn't do, but I was so pissed off I couldn't help myself. Just gave him something else to yell and scream at her about.'

With Richard gone, Kirsten finished the tedious business of searching. The cops had already been through the place and she found about what she'd expected . . . nothing. But it's what you do. A guy gets murdered, you search his house.

Or, in this case, his mother's house. Betty's house, now that her beloved Johnny was dead. And even though it was in her name only, that would surely be of benefit somehow to her husband. Wouldn't it?

FORTY-NINE

'I need to talk to your husband,' Kirsten said. 'It's important.' It was three thirty and she'd been trying to reach Betty O'Hern since ten that morning, and when the woman finally answered her phone her voice had a different sound to it. A deep weariness.

'He doesn't . . . he's not here right now. And he won't . . . oh, I don't know.'

'Is there something wrong, Betty?'

'Wrong? My son is dead. Could anything be more wrong?' So not weary, really, but sad. Terribly sad.

'I understand, and I promise, I'm going to find his killer. And whatever the police say, it *wasn't* my husband. Do you still—'

'I already told you, I know those detectives are wrong. Anyone who says my John was mixed up in something crooked with your husband . . . is ignorant, didn't know John. He was a good son, a good police officer, a good man.'

'Of course he was.' Kirsten almost gagged. 'But I need to talk to Patrick. He might have information for me. He might be able to help.'

'He won't help you. Anyway, he went out. We don't have a car any more since he's been sick, but his friends pick him up. They usually go to one of those off-track places.'

'An off-track betting parlor?'

'I guess so. What do I know?' She sounded like a woman being sucked down into quicksand. 'He might be home around six.'

'He *might* be?'

'He usually is. Sometimes it's real late, or once in awhile all night, even. But usually six or a little after. I don't know. I . . . I don't care any more if he ever comes home.'

That was certainly new. She'd been making excuses for Patrick the last time Kirsten talked to her. Pretending he wasn't the worthless piece of shit she certainly knew he was. 'Quarter to six, Betty. I'll be there. If he calls, don't tell him I'm coming. OK?'

'He won't call. And if he sees you he'll be really mad.'

'I'll tell him I forced my way in. He'll be mad at *me*, not you.'

'I don't care any more if he's mad at me. What more can he do to me? What more can anyone do? But he'll be mad. He won't talk to you.'

'We'll see. I'll be there, and we'll sit together and wait for him.' *And won't that be fun?*

When Dugan answered his phone he didn't sound a whole lot better than Betty O'Hern. So Kirsten tried to be upbeat, even chipper. 'I got some very interesting info from Richard O'Hern. I'll fill you in when I get home tonight. But you go ahead and eat. Don't wait for me. I might be—'

'Hold on,' he said. 'I'm going *with* you. Remember?'

'What?'

'Doctor DeMarco's office. Five o'clock. I'm going with you.'

'Oh. Jesus, I forgot. I'll have to call and cancel.'

'Cancel? You sure? Doesn't that mean the next appointment has to be . . . like . . . another month out?'

'Yes, Dugan, I *understand* that. It's *my* body, y'know?' So much for *upbeat*. She didn't know why she suddenly felt so pissed off. 'I'm meeting with Betty O'Hern, and waiting with her for Patrick to come home. He should be there at six or so. After I talk to him, I—'

'You mean if he doesn't throw you out on your ass. I think you should keep the doctor's appointment. We specifically picked Tuesday because she has late hours on Tuesday. It's important.'

'Maybe you should let *me* decide what's important with my own health, OK?'

'Hey, it's not *about* your health, kiddo. It's about having a baby. *Us* having a baby.'

'Oh? And am I going to raise this baby alone, while you're playing fucking gin rummy with your cellmates in some godforsaken shithouse?' Her voice was too loud, too high-pitched. 'Pontiac, maybe? How'd that be? Or would you prefer Menard, or some—'

'*Yoo-hoo!* Kirsten? It's me, your favorite client. Remember?'

'Yeah, yeah, I know. Sorry.' *Damn, is this baby stuff driving me crazy, or what?* 'I'm just . . . I'm upset . . . about forgetting the doctor's appointment. But still, I talked Betty into letting me come and ambush Patrick, and I *have* to be there. I might be on to something.'

'OK, great. So instead of meeting you at the doctor's, I'll meet you at the O'Herns' place. I'll scare the shit out of the bullying bastard, and you can interview him without getting tossed out a window.'

'Dammit, you *know* you can't—' She stopped, suddenly realizing this was *Dugan*, and he was kidding. 'I'm not entirely certain a defendant should sit in on a witness interview in his own case, and intimidate the witness while he's at it.'

'Yeah, maybe you're right. Imagine how pissed off the defendant's *lawyer* would be.'

She had to laugh. 'Tell you what, if he's there at six I should be done by about six thirty, and I'll call you. Or even if he's *not* there by about six thirty, I'll call you anyway. We'll meet somewhere for dinner.'

'Great. Call me on my cell. You won't forget, right? Six thirty or so?'

'I won't forget. I promise.' She wouldn't be able to stomach sitting alone for very long with Betty O'Hern, anyway.

'And we'll drink ginger ale this time,' he said, 'and you can whisper in my ear and tell me all the reasons why I'm *not* going to the shithouse, after all.'

FIFTY

At five forty-five Betty O'Hern buzzed open the gate in the wrought-iron fence, and appeared at the front door of the two-flat to let Kirsten in. Even though Betty's voice over the phone had given warning that she wasn't doing well, the change in her appearance in just a week took Kirsten's breath away. The stout woman's face looked strangely gaunt, her skin sallow except for the darkness around her eyes, which appeared to be shrinking back into their sockets. Her white hair was frizzy and uncombed, and her thin pink bathrobe, unbelted and stained down the front, had been lived in for too many days.

'He's not here,' Betty said, and let Kirsten into the foyer. To the left of the stairway to the second floor was the door to the first-floor apartment. Betty unlocked it, and they went inside and down the hall a few steps, and into the front parlor, where they sat on opposite ends of the sofa, as they had on Kirsten's previous visit.

The room, too, was much as Kirsten remembered it. The worn furniture, the old telephone, the garish painting of parrots on black velvet, the family snapshots flanking the rosy-cheeked Virgin Mary on the mantle, even the shopping channel ladies pitching jewelry to stay-at-homes on the flat screen TV, muted. The same as before, yet very different . . . very wrong.

What hit her first was the smell of stale cigarette smoke, even thicker in the air than before, and no window open to let in fresh air. Beyond that, the room, neat and spotless last week, was a mess now, as though nobody cared. A thin layer of dust covered every flat surface, newspapers lay open and scattered around, and unsorted laundry overflowed the clothes basket which sat, ignored and forlorn, on the floor beside Betty's place on the sofa.

Understandably saddened and frustrated a week ago, Betty seemed now to have fallen into a serious depression. No apologies for the mess, no gathering papers into piles, no offer of tea. Nothing.

'I don't suppose your husband called,' Kirsten said, 'to say when he'll be home?'

'He doesn't do that.'

'No, of course not.'

'And that wouldn't bring back my son.'

'No.'

'He didn't deserve to die, you know. He was a good son, a good policeman. Everyone who *knew* Johnny, knew that about him.'

'Yes.'

That's how it went: Betty describing in monotone how she'd lost a son with the courage of Eliot Ness and the moral fiber of Sergeant Preston of the Yukon; Kirsten agreeing in single syllables and checking her watch way too often.

She tried once to change the subject. 'Richard says you helped Johnny buy his house, Betty, and now it's yours. What will you do with it?'

'Oh, that *wife* of his. She took all of his money in the divorce. When he got on his feet he was going to sell the house and give me my share, and I could go to one of those retirement places. But now? It's just . . . what does it matter? With John dead, nothing matters.'

At six twenty-five Kirsten couldn't take it any longer. She stood up and reached into her coat pocket. 'I have to call my husband,' she said. 'He'll be—'

A door opened, then slammed shut, at the rear of the apartment.

'*Betty Clare?*' It was Patrick, the same harsh and angry voice. 'Goddammit, where are you?' A slight pause. 'Jesus, where the *fuck* is my supper?'

Betty didn't answer, didn't stand up. If she moved at all, it was to sag a little more deeply into despair.

Kirsten stood there, suddenly aware that she'd reached instinctively into her shoulder bag, and had her hand on the Colt 380. Every cop on patrol knew that a domestic violence call could be as nerve-wracking, and often as dangerous, as an armed robbery in progress. The information she had in this case, which came from Richard, was that Betty had never fought back, and that Patrick, the archetype of the verbally abusive coward, had never actually hurt anyone in the family, not physically.

Except Johnny.

She listened as Patrick stomped around the kitchen, opened the refrigerator door, slammed it shut. The can he popped open wasn't a soft drink, she'd have bet her wedding ring on that. If he'd spent the day at the betting parlor, he hadn't been winning. Not from the sound of things. And maybe he'd 'overcome' his alcoholism, like Betty said, but that hadn't lasted.

She kept her hand on her gun. Patrick – besides being a mean bastard who'd done terrible damage to his family – was a homicide suspect. Had been since she'd talked to Richard that morning, and to a lawyer about Johnny's house after that. She didn't have enough to go to the cops with, but to her mind he was a suspect, or the closest she had to one. Not to mention that he was a mean, angry drunk, and he was coming her way.

'Betty Clare!' As he got closer Kirsten could hear his labored breathing. 'Where the hell are—' He appeared in the doorway and stopped, staring at Kirsten. 'What the fuck?' He wore a plaid shirt and light tan chinos. He came a few steps into the room, one hand using his cane, the other gripping a can of Bud Light. He turned to Betty, his thin shoulders heaving with the effort to breathe. 'You stupid cow. What did I tell you about this bitch?'

'Hold on,' Kirsten said. 'She couldn't help it. I forced my way in, and—'

'No, Patrick.' Betty slowly got to her feet. 'That's not really true.' She was shaking visibly, and her voice could barely be heard. 'I let her in. I opened the door.'

'Don't you think I *know* you did?' Patrick's face was red with rage. 'This bitch,' nodding toward Kirsten, 'lies for a fucking living.' He moved to his left and set his beer on the table beside the TV, then looked at Betty and pointed at Kirsten. 'She's just *using* you, and you're too stupid to even *care*.'

'Mr O'Hern,' Kirsten said, 'I'm trying to find out who killed your son.'

He acted as though she wasn't even there, and she suddenly *got* it. He *couldn't* talk to her, wasn't able to deal with her at all. He stayed focused on Betty, the one he had power over. 'You see?' he said. 'Lying again. I don't want her in my house.' His breath came in great, heaving gasps. 'Those are one syllable words. Are you too dumb to understand them?'

'You don't . . .' Still shaking, Betty took a tiny step forward. 'You don't . . . *have* a house. You live in an apartment in *Richard's* building.' She drew herself up and lifted her chin, her fists clenched at her sides. 'I'm the only one here who has a house.' She broke then, and turned and ran from the room. A door slammed down the hall.

'Look, Mr O'Hern, I—'

But he still ignored her. Leaning on his cane, and with his other hand sliding along the wall for additional support, he went through the door and into the hall, wheezing now, like a man suffering an asthma attack.

She followed him to the doorway and called after him. 'You aren't well, Mr O'Hern. You better calm down.'

No response.

He went to a closed door halfway down the hall and tried to open it, but it was locked. He paused, catching his breath, then called through the door. 'Yeah, lie on your bed and cry, dummy, like you always do. But here's something *real* you can cry about. That house you think is all yours? Shows how dumb you are. Johnny's dead, in case you forgot, and that means you're gonna have to split that house with me. The lawyer for the police union says I got a good case on that. And he got me the name of a downtown lawyer who does that kinda shit.' He paused. 'You understand that, heifer? Or do I have to write it down and—'

The click of the lock cut him off, and the door was pulled open from inside. Patrick stood frozen for an instant, eyes wide. He took a step back, tried to spin around, and lost his balance. His hand flew out and banged into the wall and he dropped his cane. Not stopping to pick it up, he limped frantically toward Kirsten.

And behind him Betty stepped out of the bedroom, holding a semi-automatic pistol in two hands.

Kirsten moved out of the doorway back into the parlor, and stepped quickly off to the side, by the sofa. Patrick came in after her. Wheezing, gasping, fighting for breath, he looked around wildly, as though there might be another way out. But with no other doors and nowhere to hide, he turned back to face the doorway and then, keeping one hand on the wall beside him, he eased backwards, until he bumped into the table holding the TV, across the room from Kirsten.

And then Betty came in, her mouth a tight, grim line, her thin white hair sticking out from her head, her eyes wide and glassy. Walking slowly and carefully, with her arms stretched out in front of her, keeping the gun aimed in Patrick's direction, but waving it unsteadily from side to side.

She took no notice of Kirsten, standing off to the side. Unlike Betty, though, Kirsten's hands and stance were rock steady as she held her own gun, aimed at Betty's legs. Her mind, though, was racing. *Would a leg shot even stop her? And just where* are *her legs under that robe?* She raised the barrel toward the stout woman's torso. *God, I can't* do *this.*

She had reliable information that Patrick had never been physically abusive to Betty, and just now he was unarmed and backing away. Mumbling incoherently, tears streaming down his cheeks, the front of his chinos turning dark as his bladder let go. Betty, the lifelong victim, was completely unhinged. Would she actually fire that weapon? *Could* she? And if she did, would she even manage to hit Patrick?

'Put the gun down, Betty.' Kirsten kept her voice low and soothing. 'Just relax, and put it down.'

FIFTY-ONE

Dugan had left his office at six ten, a little later than he'd planned, but had found a cab easily.

He planned to surprise Kirsten and already be out in front of the O'Hern house when she called. These days they needed every pleasant night out together they could get, but she hadn't been getting much sleep, and he didn't want to keep her out too late. Between trying to beat back this damn murder charge against him – not as easy to laugh off as both of them pretended – and trying to get pregnant, she was way too strung out. She'd given up alcohol months ago, getting a start on what they were sure would be a quick pregnancy, and he'd been surprised as hell last night when she ordered a martini . . . and then another.

He hoped she wasn't giving up on the baby. For *her* sake more than his. He'd never felt an overwhelming *need* to be a father. He just always figured it would happen some day, and he'd deal with it. Expensive, sure. A bigger condo and all that. A lot of work, certainly. But it might even be fun. The problem was, time had a way of sneaking by without keeping you up to speed on its progress, and Kirsten had woken up one day and suddenly made up her mind. 'Hey!' she said. 'We better hop to it.' So they'd hopped . . . and hopped . . . and nothing happened.

So here they were, and—

'Here we are,' the driver said, slowing to a stop on a street lined with two- and three-flats, and cars parked along both sides.

Dugan paid the guy and got out, and discovered he was standing next to Kirsten's Camry, a ticket stuck to its windshield. Parking was for residents only.

He could have rung the bell on the wrought-iron gate, but there was no sense breaking in on Kirsten's interview of Patrick – if Patrick had shown up. And if he hadn't, it was barely past six thirty. She'd be giving up on waiting pretty soon, and call. Meanwhile, the sun wasn't quite down yet, and he'd just enjoy the crisp fall evening. He walked to the end of the block, turned and started back . . . which is when he saw a man coming out the front door of the O'Hern place.

The man was carrying something, and wasn't limping or hunching his shoulders, which is how Kirsten described Patrick. And since Johnny's brother, Richard, owned the place and lived on the second floor, that's who it probably was. Dugan wanted to see what he was like. After all, they were co-clients of Kirsten's. Also, the guy was Johnny's brother, which – statistically speaking, as Larry Candle had reminded him – made him at least a possible suspect. As was, Dugan remembered, Johnny's father.

He hustled down the street and got there just as the guy was coming out the gate. 'Hi,' he said. 'You're Richard O'Hern, right?'

'That's me,' the man said. It was a tennis racquet he was carrying, and he looked like he was in a hurry. 'What can I do for you?'

'Did you see Kirsten in there? My wife?'

'Um . . . your wife? And you are . . . ?'

Dugan introduced himself and gave Richard a business

card. 'Kirsten's car's right here. She's inside, talking to Patrick . . . if Patrick's there.'

'I wouldn't have seen her,' Richard said, pulling the gate closed behind him. 'I live upstairs. But my father's there, all right. I could hear him screaming and hollering at my . . .' He stopped, apparently deciding not to hang out the family laundry. 'Anyway, he's home.'

'Let's go inside.' Dugan checked his watch, feeling suddenly – and unaccountably – very nervous.

'What?'

'He might be "screaming and hollering" at Kirsten.'

'Look, I'm on my way to play—'

'She should have called me by now.' He stepped right into Richard and, grabbing his arm, turned him back toward the gate. 'Unlock it.'

'Listen here, you can't—'

Dugan put his face an inch from Richard's. 'Unlock . . . the fucking . . . gate.'

FIFTY-TWO

'Put the gun down, Betty,' Kirsten repeated, 'please.' But her soft, soothing voice got no response, and she switched to command mode. 'Drop the gun! *Now!*'

Betty jumped, as though startled awake. She shook her head slightly . . . and then fired three times in rapid succession, the sound deafening. The first two shots hit Patrick in the chest. The third hit the flat screen TV and caused one more explosion, not as loud, but with a great shattering of glass.

Kirsten held fire.

If Patrick made any sound at all, she couldn't hear it over the ringing in her ears. She saw him cough, and spew out spittle and blood. He dropped first to his knees, then tipped over on to his left side like a top-heavy bag of groceries. He lay there, still breathing in great heaving gasps, and blood oozed from under him out on to the floor.

Betty had lowered the gun, holding it in just her right hand now, pointed at the floor by her feet.

'Drop it, Betty.' As she spoke, Kirsten punched out 911 on the phone beside the sofa.

Betty turned her head. 'It's all Richard's fault, you know.'

'*Richard?*' Kirsten's ears were clearing and she heard the 911 operator answer. She didn't respond, though, just set the receiver on the table. It was a land line, and they'd have the address. 'Why *Richard*?'

'He told Patrick about the house. I begged him not to, but he did. And Patrick wouldn't let up about it. Ranting, day and night. Finally I couldn't take it and . . . after all these years . . . I told Patrick the truth.'

'Told him *what* truth?'

'How Johnny wasn't even his son. How I tricked him, and he married me.' Betty paused. 'That shut him up *good*, and I was *glad* I told him. For days he never said a word to me. Just sat in the kitchen, cleaning his gun.' She stared down beside her. '*This* gun. At first I thought maybe he'd kill me, and . . . and I didn't even care. I *never* thought he'd kill Johnny. But he did.'

Kirsten continued to ignore the 911 operator. '*Patrick* killed Johnny? How do you *know*?'

'He *told* me. Yesterday. He was screaming again, about how I was useless, not keeping the house up. He said he should have known from the start that Johnny wasn't his son. He said, "I *should* have killed that bastard son of yours a long *time* ago." Then he said, "I ought to kill you, *too*, but I don't need—"'

A crash came from the building foyer, like a door slamming against a wall. And voices. Coming inside, in a hurry. There'd been no sirens, but whoever it was wanted in. The apartment door was locked, and they were banging on it.

'*Mother?*' a man called. 'Open up!'

'It's Richard,' Betty said, turning toward the parlor doorway.

'*Kirsten?*' Dugan this time. What was *he* doing here? 'Kirsten? Are you in there? Are you OK?'

'I'm fine,' she yelled back. 'Everything's under control. The police are on their way. But please, don't come in here.' *Oh dear God, I don't want to hurt this poor creature.*

Betty was shaking her head again, as though confused. 'It's Richard's fault. He should never have told Patrick.'

'Dugan! Richard!' Kirsten yelled. 'Do *not* come inside.'

But Richard must have had a key, because she heard the apartment door open and them coming in, both of them calling. Betty went into the apartment hallway.

'Betty, wait!' Kirsten called, and ran after her.

She found Betty standing in the hallway, facing Richard and Dugan. Both men seemed frozen in place. Betty still had the gun in her hand, pointed at the floor.

'Mother?' Richard said. 'Are you . . . OK?'

'Patrick killed my Johnny. He told me.'

'What? But how—' Richard stared. 'He *said* that?'

'My Johnny's dead,' she said, 'and it's your fault.' She started to raise the gun.

Kirsten finally fired, but into the ceiling. Betty jumped at the sound, and spun around, wild-eyed, and Kirsten charged her, knocking her backwards. Betty's arm slammed back against the wall and she screamed . . . and her gun went off. But she didn't drop it.

Kirsten grabbed Betty's wrist, but then heard Dugan's voice. 'Oh, no,' he said, his voice a low moan. 'Oh God, no.' She turned, and he was on his back on the floor, with Richard kneeling over him.

'*Dugan!*' she screamed, and in that instant Betty wrenched her arm free and ran the other way, down the hall toward the rear of the apartment.

Kirsten backed up toward Dugan, keeping her eyes on Betty, and when Betty turned and went through a door, into the kitchen probably, Kirsten turned to Dugan. He was still on his back, twisting and writhing now under Richard, who was sprawled across him.

'*Where*, Dugan?' she yelled. 'Where are you hit?'

'Not *me*, goddammit. Richard!'

'OK, OK. Don't move. Just let him lie there. The cops are—'

'*Police!*' a man yelled from the foyer. 'Whoever's in there, step outside the apartment. Nice and slow. Hands in the air.'

'I'm coming out, officer,' Kirsten called. She slipped the Colt into her pocket. 'Relax, Dugan. Don't move him. Let the paramedics do that.' She went to the apartment door. 'I'm coming out,' she called again, and then went through the door, holding her hands spread wide, palms forward.

There were two uniformed cops, with more on their heels.

'What's going on?' one of them said. He had his weapon aimed at her, but lowered it and held it, elbow bent, down by his waist.

'You got a wounded man in the hall and another in the front room,' Kirsten said. 'Front room's probably dead already. Multiple gunshots. Shooter's a heavy-set white woman. She's in the rear of the apartment. She's still got the gun, but I don't think she—'

A shot rang out and echoed down the long hallway.

'Who's back there with her?' the cop asked.

'No one,' Kirsten said. 'And I don't think she'll be a problem now.'

FIFTY-THREE

Dugan was late, and was glad to see Kirsten still sitting there when he entered the room. It was a little past five o'clock and they were the only people in the waiting room. They were there for the appointment with Doctor DeMarco they'd missed a month earlier, on the day Betty O'Hern shot and killed her husband and herself, and shot her son in the shoulder, putting his tennis game on hold for awhile.

Kirsten tilted her head and he kissed her on the cheek, then dropped down into the chair beside her. She went back to paging through some woman's magazine.

'Renata Carroway called this afternoon,' he said.

'Did she?' She didn't look up from the magazine.

'Yeah. I don't know why it took a month, but the cops have closed the O'Hern case . . . officially . . . as of today. Principal suspect: Patrick O'Hern, deceased. Said to have made self-incriminating statements to his wife, Elizabeth O'Hern, also deceased.'

'That's good,' Kirsten said, but her mind was obviously elsewhere.

'Yep. Renata thinks the cops knew that Zelander and Rondo were both already close to agreements with the feds, which meant neither had any reason to kill Johnny. But they were anxious for a suspect, and I was handy.'

'Uh-huh.'

'She also said she filed her appearance on my behalf at the Disciplinary Commission. Remember that cute little lawyer there? Peter Pan? She wants to take my sworn statement.'

'Her name's Gina Chan,' Kirsten said, proving she *was* listening, after all.

'Anyway, I guess Renata got along with her pretty well. Turns out Harvey Starr's testimony showed he has no actual knowledge that I ever paid O'Hern, or anyone, to solicit clients. So, with Johnny O'Hern dead, they have no witnesses.'

'That's nice.'

'And there's no paper trail to support the charge.'

'Uh-huh.' She paused and looked up from her magazine. 'So they have no case against you?'

'What they'll do, Renata says, is put me under oath and ask me if I ever paid anyone to steer me a client. And guess what? I'm not gonna lie.'

'I didn't think you would.'

'If I tell the truth . . . how many times, how much, how long ago . . . it's pretty small potatoes. Renata says I won't be disbarred, but they'll suspend my license. Anyway, I'm not going to—'

The door opened and a woman in a white lab coat looked in. 'Doctor DeMarco's running a little behind. Won't be *too* much longer.'

'That's fine,' Kirsten said. 'Thanks.'

The woman disappeared and Dugan went on. 'I'm not going to answer any questions. I'll invoke the fifth amendment.'

'And then what?' She put her magazine on the table and picked out another one. He knew she wasn't reading any of them.

'Then I'll be suspended anyway. For failing to cooperate with an ARDC investigation. And you know what? That's probably a good thing.'

That got her attention. She turned toward him. 'What are you saying?'

'I'm saying a suspension might be just what I need. It's a chance to take my life in a new direction, a chance I might otherwise never take.'

'Damn,' she said. 'What is *happening* with you guys? This "new direction" stuff.'

'What "guys"? I mean . . . who besides me?'

'Father Watson. I thought by now he'd be out in Spokane, but he called me this morning. He had some sort of "heart scare", not long after he and I met with that doctor at Northwestern. Not really a heart *attack*, but *something*. Anyway, it shook him up, and . . . well . . . he turned down the bishop thing. He said he wants to go a different direction, try to get Fair Hope Clinic open again. Or, he says, something like it, somewhere.'

'Did he bring up the CIA business?'

'Yeah, that's why he called. I told him the truth, that I found no real evidence linking either Johnny O'Hern or the CIA to Father Landrew's murder. He seemed relieved to hear that.'

'So, like Renata said, the O'Hern case is closed . . . officially.'

'Yes.' She picked up yet another magazine, then put it down. He knew she wanted to say something, and he was sure he knew what it was about. They hadn't really talked about it in weeks.

'It's this baby thing, isn't it?'

'What?'

'This fertility stuff,' he said. 'It's getting to you.'

'Yeah . . . well . . . I'd be lying if I said it wasn't.'

'I know, and—'

'But there's something else. I wasn't going to tell you, but . . . well . . .'

'You can't *not* tell me. It's just not allowed.'

'OK then . . . it's Patrick . . . you never saw him. Not alive anyway. But I told you about him. The emphysema, and the cane and all. It's just so damn hard to see him having enough stamina to go clear up to Johnny's house . . . in what? a cab? a rental? they didn't have a car . . . and wait around half the night, and then shoot him and get back home. I mean, I suppose it's *possible*. But the guy could hardly walk.'

'You sure he wasn't faking it?'

'Not a chance. Plus the shooter must have used a silencer. Middle of the night? Three shots in a quiet neighborhood full of cops and fire fighters? But no silencer was found in the O'Hern place. I verified that.'

'You don't *know* a silencer was used. And maybe he got rid of it.'

'There are just too many problems. But maybe most important of all . . . Patrick O'Hern was a total coward. He could demean and destroy a weak-minded wife, and he could beat up a child. But he couldn't even look *me* in the eye. And Johnny, by all accounts, was one tough critter. Patrick wasn't up to facing him.'

'Damn, Kirsten, you're not kidding, are you?'

'No. It wasn't Patrick.'

'So why'd he tell his wife he did it? Or did she make that up? Jesus, you don't think *she*—'

'No. I think she *thought* Patrick was saying he'd killed Johnny, when he said he *should* have killed him a long time ago. And I'm sure he wished he had. But no matter what he wished, Patrick had nothing to do with Johnny's murder. Can you imagine trying to convict anyone on what Betty said, even if she was alive and it was admissible?'

'It was good enough for the cops, and the state's attorney.'

'Yeah, because the accused was dead and couldn't put up a fight. And they could close their case.'

'Well, it wasn't *me* who shot Johnny, I swear. Jesus. Maybe it was one of your other clients. Polly Morelli. Or Richard O'Hern.'

'Polly? He's a killer, no doubt. He took out Vincent Rondo and those two mopes, or at least ordered it done. But kill a cop? Not Polly.'

'And Richard?'

'Not a chance. Richard somehow survived his childhood and came away a decent guy.'

'So . . . Kirsten . . . where you going with this?'

'Remember that bar where Johnny was drinking the night he was killed?'

'Flight Plan II,' Dugan said, 'where we did the safety inspection. We spoke to a woman bartender. Her name was Teddy, but otherwise I don't remember a thing about her.'

'Right. Except for her ass, and a few other pertinent parts. Anyway, you remember what she said about that "part-Asian" woman . . . the hooker Johnny left the bar with? How she'd been talking to some other people before Johnny got there?'

'Right. Wasn't there a dog show in town?'

'And some of them had pictures of their dogs,' Kirsten said, 'and were showing them around. Teddy said the Asian woman talked to a man and a woman, and looked at some photos they showed her.'

'Damn,' he said, 'I'm thinking maybe you *shouldn't* tell me, after all.'

'The thing is, I wanted to let it go, but the case was driving me crazy, and I suddenly had an idea. This afternoon I drove out to Flight Plan II, and showed Teddy a photo *I'd* taken. A picture of a woman. And Teddy, being no dummy and not wanting to get involved, was careful to say that she could "obviously never swear to it", but she was "pretty positive" the woman whose photograph I showed her was the woman she'd seen showing pictures to the Asian woman. She *assumed* they were pictures of dogs.'

'And the photo *you* showed her? Please don't tell me it was a picture you took on the day of Johnny's funeral.'

'Sorry,' she said, 'but CIA or not, it was Janice Robinson that Teddy saw talking to that hooker, showing pictures to her. And I'm sure they included a photograph of Johnny, the guy the hooker was being paid to pick up when he came in.'

'So he'd be sure to go straight home, and sure to be a little distracted.'

'I can't prove a thing, though. And I see no reason to try.'

'Right,' he said. 'Sleeping dogs and all that. After all, you satisfied your three clients. And by the way, I hope the other two paid you.'

'Richard paid the little I charged him, and Polly paid a *lot*. Polly's money, though, it was cash and it's all going to Father Watson . . . for the clinic.'

'Good.' He nodded. 'And about this fer—'

The door opened and the woman in the lab coat looked in. 'Doctor DeMarco will see you now.'

Kirsten stood, and Dugan did, too. 'Listen,' he said, 'a few minutes ago you said this . . . this fertility business is getting to you. And you know? It's your call. Whatever you decide? It's OK. Really.'

'I love you,' she said. She kissed the tip of her finger and touched it to his lips.

'So . . . what're you gonna tell the doctor?'

'I don't know,' she said. 'I'm still thinking about it.'